D0630686

The
Redemption
of Time

THE
REDEMPTION
OF TIME

A THREE-BODY PROBLEM NOVEL

Baoshu

TRANSLATED BY
Ken Liu

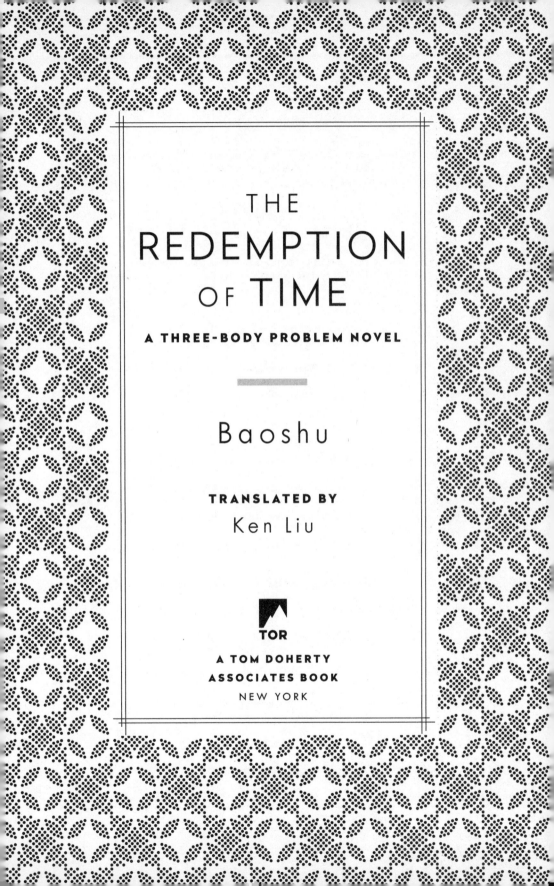

TOR

A TOM DOHERTY
ASSOCIATES BOOK
NEW YORK

THE REDEMPTION OF TIME

Copyright © 2011 by Baoshu (宝树)

English translation copyright © 2016 by China Educational Publications Import & Export Corp., Ltd.

Translation by Ken Liu

Originally published as 三体X：观想之宙 in 2011 by 重庆出版社 (Chongqing Publishing House) in 重庆 (Chongqing, China).

All rights reserved.

A Tor Book
Published by Tom Doherty Associates
120 Broadway
New York, NY 10271

www.tor-forge.com

Tor® is a registered trademark of Macmillan Publishing Group, LLC.

Library of Congress Cataloging-in-Publication Data

Names: Baoshu, 1980– author. | Liu, Ken, 1976– translator.
Title: The redemption of time / Baoshu ; translated by Ken Liu.
Other titles: San ti X. English
Description: First edition. | New York : Tor, 2019. | "A Tom Doherty
  Associates book."
Identifiers: LCCN 2018054860| ISBN 9781250306029 (hardcover) |
  ISBN 9781250306012 (ebook)
Classification: LCC PL2931.A67 S2613 2019 | DDC 895.13/6—dc23
LC record available at https://lccn.loc.gov/2018054860

Our books may be purchased in bulk for promotional, educational, or business use. Please contact your local bookseller or the Macmillan Corporate and Premium Sales Department at 1-800-221-7945, extension 5442, or by email at MacmillanSpecialMarkets@macmillan.com.

First U.S. Edition: July 2019

Printed in the United States of America

0 9 8 7 6 5 4 3 2 1

This book is dedicated to Mr. Liu Cixin.

CONTENTS

PREFACE TO THE ENGLISH EDITION

Writing *The Redemption of Time* is one of the most remarkable events of my life.

Like many others, I became a loyal fan of Liu Cixin at the beginning of the twenty-first century, when Liu was just starting to make his mark as a science fiction author. We called ourselves *cítiě* (meaning "magnets," which is a pun for the Chinese abbreviation of "die-hard fans of Liu Cixin") and passionately discussed his stories on internet forums. As each of his stories was published, the news spread among us like wildfire and we rushed out to buy the magazine issue. In 2006, when *Science Fiction World* serialized *The Three-Body Problem*, the first book in his magnificent Remembrance of Earth's Past trilogy (also known as the "Three-Body" trilogy), I devoured each installment and hungered for the next, utterly entranced.

The stand-alone edition of *The Three-Body Problem* was published at the beginning of 2008, and the first sequel, *The Dark Forest*, came out about six months later. Although the books hadn't yet penetrated mainstream literary conversation, science fiction fans enjoyed the rich imaginative feast presented by these two books. However, after those first two books, I and the other *cítiě* had to resign ourselves to a long wait for the next installment.

Two and a half years later, in November of 2010, the last volume of the trilogy, *Death's End*, finally went on sale in China. At the time, I was in graduate school in Belgium and could not get my hands on the book. I seriously considered flying back to China just to buy it. In the end, my friend Gao Xiang helped me out by photographing every page of the book and emailing the pictures to me.

I was deeply touched by my friend's gesture, but it wasn't until much later that I understood the full significance of the publication of this novel for me. After I finished *Death's End*, along with fans in China who had bought the book as soon as it came out, we debated and explored every detail in the book over the internet. But no matter how many posts we wrote, the magnificent, grand arc of the trilogy was at an end, and we felt ourselves drifting away from the story day by day. The melancholy that seized us made me decide to write separate stories for a few of the characters in the trilogy and extend the epic tale a little longer. Two days later, I wrote down a dialogue between Yun Tianming and 艾 AA on Planet Blue and posted it on the Web under the title *Three-Body X*. "X" didn't mean "ten"; rather, it stood for "uncertain."

This wasn't the first time I wrote Liu Cixin fanfiction, and I certainly wasn't the first to do so. But before my tale, most such efforts were written by fans for a small group of other hardcore fans. I had no idea that the context for *Three-Body X* was entirely different. What I wrote was exactly what tens of thousands of readers needed at that moment: more stories from the "Three-Body" universe. Its timely appearance (barely a week after the publication of *Death's End*) allowed it to receive far more attention than could be justified by its inherent quality, and the praise encouraged me to continue writing, developing, and growing the story line I had in mind until it gradually took on a shape of its own. Three weeks later, before Christmas 2010, I completed my novel.

By then, *Three-Body X* had spread to every corner of the Chinese Web, and received almost as much discussion and attention as *Death's End* itself. Mr. Yao Haijun, Liu Cixin's good friend, who is nicknamed "the Chinese Campbell" for his role in developing new writers as the executive editor of *Science Fiction World*, contacted me to ask if he could publish it as a stand-alone book. A few months later, as "Three-Body" fever continued to sweep Chinese SF fandom, more fanfiction appeared. But the brief window of opportunity was gone, and these new works did not receive nearly as much attention as mine. I knew that I was lucky.

When I first posted my story online, I wasn't thinking much about copyright; of course, once a formal offer of publication came from Mr. Yao, I was faced with a complicated set of issues. But Liu Cixin displayed incredible generosity and kindness toward new writers by giving me permission to publish, and I cannot express the full extent of my deep gratitude. As soon as the book came off the presses, I sent a copy to Liu Cixin. A few years later, after I'd published some original stories and become a regular member of the small circle of Chinese science fiction writers, Liu and I became friends and often met at fandom events. He told me that he enjoyed *Three-Body* X, and indeed, had even voted for it at Chinese science fiction awards. The book didn't win, but Liu's encouragement and approval were better than winning ten such awards.

The subtitle for the paraquel, "The Redemption of Time," and some other names in the novel have special meanings for fans, though few now probably remember the sources of the allusions. Between 2008 and 2010, while fans impatiently waited for the arrival of the last volume of the trilogy, many speculated on potential directions the plot could take and spread various rumors centered around supposed "leaks" from Liu Cixin's draft-in-progress. Of course, all of these rumors turned out to be hoaxes, and not a single one matched the published book. But even such rumors brought eager fans some joy in imagining the conclusion of Liu Cixin's masterpiece, and so I referenced some keywords from those rumors as a memorial to that innocent time when "Three-Body" was still a relatively obscure playground known to only the most dedicated fans.

To be sure, my paraquel did not receive and could not have received the sort of plaudits that accompanied the "Three-Body" series proper, but it was also true that many readers enjoyed it greatly. I certainly make no claim that *Three-Body X* constitutes a part of the "Three-Body" canon, though it was published by the same publisher as the original trilogy and sold together with Liu Cixin's books. I view it as a dedicated fan's attempt to explain and fill out some of the gaps in the original trilogy, one of countless possible developments of the "Three-Body" universe. Any fans of the trilogy proper could reject it as incompatible with their vision, or could enjoy it without treating it as part of the universe. I think these are all perfectly reasonable responses.

Four years after the publication of *Three-Body X*, China Educational Publications Import & Export Corporation, Ltd., decided to introduce this book to Anglophone readers after the publication of the English edition of the "Three-Body" trilogy. I feel both anxiety and trepidation at this prospect. There certainly have been some notable works of fanfiction in the history of English science fiction, such as the Second Foundation trilogy, by Gregory Benford, Greg Bear, and David Brin, as well as Stephen Baxter's epic *The Time Ships*, a continuation of H. G. Wells's *The Time Machine*. And I haven't even mentioned shared universes like *Doctor Who* and *Star Trek*, which have provided fertile ground for the creativity of many other authors. I don't pretend to claim that my novel is the equal of these successful classics, but there is something that unites all of them: Great works of uncommon genius will call for us to return to their worlds again and again, enticing us to pour our passion and enthusiasm into them so that time may continue to cycle and progress, beloved characters may return to life, and the universes may continue to evolve and develop, without cease.

—*Baoshu, August 30, 2015*

CALENDAR ERAS

Crisis Era   201X–2208

Deterrence Era   2208–2270

Post-Deterrence Era   2270–2272

Broadcast Era   2272–2332

Bunker Era   2333–2400

Galaxy Era   2273–unknown

Planet Blue Era   2687–2731

Timeline for Preparation of Universe 647
                                        2731–18906416

Timeline for Universe 647   18906416–11245632151

Terminal Era   11245632142–11245632207

New Universe Timeline   11245632207– . . .

The
Redemption
of Time

Prologue

A long, long time ago, in another galaxy . . .

The stars still shone brightly, the galaxy still swirled like a mighty river, and countless life-forms still hid behind each sun, divided by the vastness of space. They concealed themselves in the nooks and crannies of the galaxy, growing, developing, struggling, slaughtering; the rhythms of life and the laments of death filled this obscure galaxy just as they filled every other part of the universe.

However, this ancient and far-flung universe was nearing the end of its own life.

In a sphere with a radius of ten billion light-years, stars were dying at an unimaginable rate, one by one. Civilizations winked out; galaxies dimmed . . . and all were returning to the void, as though they had never existed.

The countless lives in this galaxy did not know yet that all their struggles and setbacks, their concealments and slaughters, had lost meaning. Against the greater background of the universe as a whole, a terrifying, unanticipated change was about to take place. Their very existence was about to be reduced to nothingness.

Faint photons from already dead galaxies billions of light-years away had traversed the endless darkness of space to illuminate this out-of-the-way galaxy, like letters without recipients silently recounting bygone legends of the vanished.

One of these beams had originated in a little-noticed nook of the universe once known as "the Milky Way." It was so faint that the eyes of the vast majority of living beings could not detect it, yet it contained innumerable legends that had once moved heaven and earth, shocked belief and understanding.

Ye Wenjie, Mike Evans, Ding Yi, Frederick Tyler, Zhang Beihai, Bill Hines, Luo Ji, Thomas Wade . . .

Red Coast Base, the Earth-Trisolaris Organization, the Wallfacer Project, the Staircase Program, the Swordholders, the Bunker Project . . .

The ancient stories remained as vivid as though they had taken place yesterday; the figures of heroes and saints continued to twinkle among the constellations. But knowledge of the tales had faded, and there was no one left to mark their passing. The curtain had fallen and the players had departed from the stage; the audience had scattered to the winds; even the theater had long since fallen into ruin.

Until—

In the endless darkness of space, in a forgotten corner a long way from any star, a ghost appeared out of the void.

Faint gleams of starlight limned a shape vaguely resembling a creature that had once been known as "human." The ghost knew that for billions of light-years around this spot there were no other beings who would have recognized a human shape. Its world and species had long ago disappeared, leaving no trace behind. That species, which had once created a civilization that had lit up a galaxy, conquered billions of worlds, destroyed countless foes, and enacted magnificent epics, had submerged in the river of history, which had, in turn, melded with the ocean that was time. Now even the ocean of time was about to dry up.

But at the end of the universe, at the moment when time was about to cease its flow, this ghost stubbornly wished to continue writing a story that was already concluded.

Floating in darkness, the ghost extended a limb—let's call it an arm—and spread out five fingers. A tiny silvery spot of light hung in the palm.

The eyes of the ghost reflected the countless stars as it stared at the silvery dot, as though lost in reminiscence. The bright spot of light drifted up and down like a delicate firefly, so small that it could wink out at any moment, but also, like the singularity before the birth of the universe, embodying all possibilities. The bright dot was a minuscule wormhole connected to the great black hole at the heart of a galaxy, capable of releasing a galaxy's worth of energy.

After some time—no one knew how long, as there was no one around who cared to measure the passage of time—the ghost issued its order. The bright dot dissolved into a silvery thread extending into the distance like an infinite timeline. In another moment, the thread unrolled into a white plane. A third dimension appeared as the plane undulated and gained thickness, but the thickness was insignificant compared with the width and breadth: The ghost had unfurled a giant sheet of blank drawing paper, and now floated above it.

The ghost spread its arms and glided. A light breeze followed its movements, and an atmosphere materialized out of nowhere. Beneath it, the sheet of paper seemed to react to the breeze, forming wrinkles and waves. The peaks and valleys soon solidified into mountains, hills, canyons, and plains.

Then came fire and water. As massive explosions erupted everywhere, oxygen and hydrogen, formed out of pure energy, combined into bright flames that coalesced into a sea of fire. New water molecules generated by the reaction fused into droplets, merged into clouds and mists, and then consolidated into torrential rain that fell against the newborn earth. The endless rain flooded the plains, converting them into vast oceans.

The ghost swept over the waters like a gigantic bird and landed on an empty beach. Stretching out its arms—one toward the waves and one toward the hills—it lifted both at once. Brontobytes of data stored inside its body came to life and, absorbing energy from the surroundings,

took form; life appeared in water and on land, as though deposited
there by a cyclone. Shoals of fish and pods of whales leapt out of the
tides to honor their creator; patches of grass and stands of trees erupted
from the soil, with beasts and creeping things wandering among them;
flocks of birds large and small swept across the sky. The noise and bus-
tle of life filled this new world, and as living things materialized, so did
forests, grasslands, lakes, and deserts.

Having completed these tasks, the ghost still felt that the world lacked
something important. It gazed thoughtfully into the dark sky until it
realized what was missing. With a single finger, it described a circle
against the dark velvet empyrean. Then, pulling the hand back, it
flicked that finger, and a bright dot shot into the circle in the sky, turning it into a fiery golden orb. The familiar Sun had reappeared, or so it
seemed. As sunlight refracted through the atmosphere, the whole
world lit up: azure sky, clear and smooth as a mirror; cerulean sea, sparkling and shimmering.

The ghost bathed in the new light, which had long been absent from
its existence. Intoxicated, it gently lifted its head.

This is just like that golden age long ago . . .

Sunshine gleamed against his skin and hair, filling in the outline of
a typical human. It was obvious now—or would have been, if anyone
had been around to observe it—that the ghost was no mere spirit, but
a person, a "he," a man from that long-ago world once known as "Earth."

And this new world, just like the mythical Earth, beckoned to him
with a sense of familiarity.

It was a shadow cast at the end of the universe by that ancient planet,
long after it had been destroyed along with the innumerable human
civilizations that had once inhabited it.

The ghost knew that, compared with the grand universe that had
once existed, compared with even just the real Earth, this artificial
world was tiny, inauthentic, and insignificant. He had created it anyway, so that the cosmic epic that had already concluded could go on

just a bit longer. Even if his addition would not be a true continuation, wasn't it a joy to be immersed in this virtual world for a few more moments, and to experience the dying embers of that imitation Sun, as the universe irresistibly wound down?

"Sunset for the universe," he muttered.

PART I

The Past
Within Time

The sky was a misty, dark gray. A familiar afternoon drizzle enveloped the lake in a gentle mist. The grass at the shore dipped and swayed in the breeze, thirstily drinking the sweet raindrops. A toy boat woven from blades of grass drifted over the water, riding farther and farther from the bank on ripples spawned by the rain.

As though it's heading for the world's end . . .

Yun Tianming sat on the shore and aimlessly tossed pebbles into the lake, watching the ripples crisscross each other. A woman sat next to him, gazing at him without speaking. The breeze lifted strands of her long hair to brush against his cheeks, the caress arousing his desire.

For a moment, Tianming experienced the illusion of being in another time and another place, as though he had returned to that college outing in the suburbs of Beijing with his classmates, returned to that happy afternoon he had spent by the side of Cheng Xin. But the lemon-colored water, the blue grass, and the varicolored pebbles around him reminded him that this was a different era in a different world, a planet three hundred light-years away and almost seven centuries later.

And a different woman.

Slanting rain, gentle breeze, no need to return home.*

Tianming didn't know why he'd thought of a line of Classical Chinese poetry, something that his parents, who had admired classical education so much, had forced him to memorize. He could no longer imagine going home. There was no home to return to; he could only endure the cold wind and rain on this alien planet.

What a fool! Tianming castigated himself. *Did I really think I was going to get another chance with Cheng Xin, my beloved, and make toy boats by a lake? Wake up!* The very idea that he might reunite with the woman of his dreams seven centuries later was absurd. The fact that he was now sitting next to a female of the same species was already an incredible miracle.

But a greater miracle had once been within his grasp. After being apart for seven hundred years, he could have seen that woman if only he had gotten here a few hours—even a few minutes—earlier. He could have spent the rest of his life with the woman he had been in love with for seven centuries on the shore of this lake, never again parting from her. The woman who sat next to him now, on the other hand, would have been only his wife's best friend and married to another man.

Even now, Cheng Xin was not so far from him, at most only a few hundred kilometers away. On clear nights, he could even see her spaceship orbiting this planet slowly. However, though he could admire her from afar, she was forever out of his reach.

He had once given her a star. But now, because of the sudden expansion of the death line, she would never be able to land on this world. She had become his star.

Tianming grimaced and glanced at the sky out of habit. Today, because of the rain and clouds, he could see nothing. But he knew that she was there, above the clouds, perhaps even drifting overhead at that moment . . .

**Translator's Note:* The line is from a poem about a fisherman out in the drizzle by the Tang Dynasty poet Zhang Zhihe (732–774 CE).

Tianming pulled his gaze back and realized that her eyes were still staring at him; he pretended not to notice. A pair of arms, like vines, entwined around his neck. He was readying himself to enjoy this moment of intimacy when the arms' owner spoke, asking a question that lovers across eons and galaxies and species and sexes had all asked: "Hey, who do you like more, me or her?"

"You, of course!"

"But in what way?" 艾 AA refused to give up. "You have to be specific! I thought Cheng Xin—" But her question was interrupted by a kiss. Numerous similar experiences had taught Tianming the painful lesson that there was no appropriate answer under such circumstances, nor was there any need to speak.

艾 AA gave in to the kiss, and once the kiss had ended, she did not pursue the previous line of questioning. Shyly, she bit Tianming's earlobe; a moment later, as though unsatisfied, she bit his shoulder, hard.

Tianming screamed and pushed her away. Hallucinations that had long been buried in his memory erupted forth, weighing down his consciousness. He had trouble breathing and could not think. He pressed his head between his hands in pain.

"I was just playing!" Although 艾 AA's immediate reaction was that he was being dramatic, when she saw the pallor in his face and the tremors that racked his body she realized that he was terrified, perhaps delirious. She had seen him going through such episodes from time to time. "Tianming, what's wrong?" she asked with concern.

Tianming stared back at her, confused and frightened, panting heavily. After a long pause, he asked, "You . . . are you real?"

"What are you talking about?" Now AA was frightened. She approached him, arms open for an embrace, but Tianming backed away and gazed at her suspiciously, his body crouched defensively. He repeated his question: "Are you a real person or just a hallucination? Is this whole world a trick in my mind?"

AA grasped the seriousness of the situation. Taking a deep breath, she spoke slowly. "I *am* real. Tianming, look at me. I'm standing right here in front of you. Every inch of my skin, every hair on my head—they're all real. The planet we're on is absolutely real. This . . . this is our world!"

"Our . . . world?" Tianming asked.

"Yes! Do you remember that day when we stood here waiting for Cheng Xin and Guan Yifan? We watched as their spaceship entered orbit around Planet Blue. You laughed like a child, holding my hand and telling me that you were going to surprise her, lead her into that marvelous little universe that even you had not seen. And then, all of a sudden, the death line expanded and the sky darkened; there was no more sun, no more stars. When you figured out what had happened, you just stood there like a zombie, not crying, not screaming. I didn't understand how much you loved her until I saw the depth of your despair."

"I do remember," Tianming muttered, but his expression remained far away.

"For three days and three nights, you didn't drink or eat and barely slept. I kept on telling you that they didn't die; they were just living in a different frame of reference, and maybe one day you would see each other again. But you didn't seem to hear me. Finally, on the third night, you cried. At first silently, and then weeping and sobbing, and finally howling and wailing. And I . . . I put my arms around you. And I heard you say to me, 'There are only the two of us on this planet! Only the two of us!' Do you remember what I said to you next?"

"You said, 'You are my Adam and I'm your Eve.'" Tianming closed his eyes, remembering.

"I don't know how I found the words." 艾 AA bit her lip and blushed. "Anyway . . . that was how you and I became a couple. We couldn't be free of the despair, of course, but on that day at least, we let go and . . . it was wonderful. The next day, you told me, 'From now on, this is our world.' Do you remember?"

A smile appeared on Yun Tianming's face, perhaps without him even realizing it. "Yes, of course."

"Then how can all of that be unreal?" AA asked.

Smiling encouragingly, she took a step toward Tianming. This time, he did not back away. She picked up his hands and wrapped his arms around herself as she hugged him, pressing her ear against his chest to listen to his heartbeat. Still confused, Tianming looked into the distance, allowing her to cling to him. Gently, she kissed his face, and gradually, hesitantly, Tianming returned her embrace. His gaze warmed and he returned her kiss, which she returned with even more ardor . . .

Tianming received the most primitive and most authentic proof of the reality of the universe.

The rain had stopped some time ago, and the blue grass swayed in the evening breeze. The light of dusk pierced the clouds and painted a golden edge on the azure hills.

What happened next would have been unimaginable on Earth: The blue trees and shrubs of the forest came to life. They stretched as they woke, turning hundreds of thousands of leaves toward the warmth of the setting sun, absorbing every drop of energy. A few branches, fighting for more light, shoved and jostled against each other, filling the air with a susurrating noise. Dragonfly-like amphibious insects took off from the lake and danced in the air, spreading their four transparent wings to absorb the nutrients released by the blue grass and singing in high-pitched chirps to attract mates. Insects of the opposite sex responded with their own songs, and then, pairs began the complicated mating dance above the lake, enacting the sacred ritual that allowed life to multiply and continue . . . all these sounds fused into one composition, Planet Blue's unique cantata of life.

At the heart of this new black domain, life seemed to go on as before, except for the intrusion of two wanderers from afar. They clung to each other, and they would remain on this world forever. But to this planet that had already existed for billions of years and would continue to exist for billions more, the pair were nothing—they would disappear in a flash, leaving no trace behind, like the ripples passing over the surface of the lake.

Gazing at the setting sun, Yun Tianming spoke softly. "I'd already thought of this world as a dream. AA, forgive me for my behavior earlier. Even now, I still can't tell if I'm truly awake. I can no longer tell when a dream starts or when it ends. All of this . . . seems to have no end."

"No end? What do you mean?" asked AA.

"How old are you now?" Tianming asked.

"I can't remember. At least four hundred," said AA.

"What if you don't count the years you were in hibernation?"

"I guess twenty . . . thirty something? I really can't remember," AA said.

"By the standards of the Deterrence Era, you're still very young. But do you know how old I am?"

"A smidgen over seven hundred, I'd say. But if you don't count the years of hibernation I don't think you're much older than I am."

"No." As he spoke, Yun Tianming's eyes seemed ancient. "My mind is at least several thousand years old, maybe even tens of thousands."

艾 AA found this incomprehensible. But instead of asking more questions, she listened.

With a grimace, Tianming explained, "I know it's hard to believe. Here's the difference between the two of us: I spent the vast majority of my life in a dream, a dream that lasted tens of thousands of years.

"From the first year of the Crisis Era, from the moment I—no, my brain—was frozen, I began to dream. Endless dreams filled my time as I drifted in the abyss of space. In retrospect, I'm sure much of that was false memory constructed later by my mind, since a brain kept near absolute zero could not possibly generate dreams . . . And then, once the Trisolarans captured me, they seized on dreams as their most potent weapon and employed them to stimulate me, to study me . . . to use me."

Tianming kept his voice calm, as though describing a stroll by the you now. There's no difference at the level of neural activity. They injected those nightmares into my brain and made them real by taking advantage of biological mechanisms to which I had no defense. I wasn't fighting illusions *with reality*; instead, I was making illusions to *fight reality*—a battle that I couldn't win.

"What use was it for me to conjure Cheng Xin? In response to my pleas, my tormentors could make her show up in my mind, giving me hope that a miracle had occurred, that salvation was at hand. But then they would turn the visitation into an even worse hell, one a thousand times worse than the one I had just suffered.

"In one dream, I lived together with Cheng Xin for ten years, and we even had a wonderful little daughter. But those ten years of joy and tranquility were but a prelude for the inferno to follow: A great famine struck the land, and all of us were so emaciated we were barely more than skin and bones, close to dying. Yet one day, somehow Cheng Xin made a pot of meat stew for me. I was baffled; where did we get the meat? After eating some, I discovered a clump of hair and a patch of skin in a corner of the kitchen. I was shocked. Cheng Xin then lifted something out of the pot for me with a ladle—it was round and fleshy, boiled for so long that it was almost falling apart . . . I recognized it as the head of my daughter. Smiling, Cheng Xin said to me, 'Delicious, isn't it? Have some more!'"

"Ah!" AA grabbed Tianming's arm, utterly nauseated. She could not imagine living through such a nightmare.

But Tianming continued to explain, almost cruelly, "The worst part was that even though I wanted to throw up and I was racked with grief and terror, my hunger seemed to have a mind of its own. I couldn't help it. Mouthful by mouthful, I ate my daughter, until I was so full that I burped. Once satiated, Cheng Xin and I even made love next to my daughter's bones before falling asleep.

"When I woke up, I found myself tightly bound and unable to move. Cheng Xin knelt down next to me and explained that she had to eat me to survive. As I watched in horror, she bit into my arm, tore off a piece of flesh with her teeth, chewed, and swallowed. She continued until all the flesh had been picked off the bones—"

AA could not stand it anymore. "Stop! Stop it! I beg you!" She turned around and retched, and her mouth filled with the foul taste of acid.

When she had recovered, she asked, "But why? Why did the Trisolarans torture you with such grotesque visions?"

"To understand humanity," Tianming answered. "If you think about it, it's not strange at all. Although the sophons helped them keep everything happening on Earth under surveillance, they couldn't understand our emotional responses or physical reactions without experimentation. The nightmare I just described to you wouldn't have struck the Trisolarans as a tragedy since they operated according to a moral code completely alien to us. They often consumed the flesh of other dehydrated Trisolarans, and so they were baffled by the human revulsion against cannibalism. I can tell you stories that are far more disgusting. For example—"

"Why don't we save such unpleasant stories for another time?" AA interrupted. She finally understood why Tianming never mentioned his experiences among the Trisolarans. "No matter what, Tianming, you have to remember this: You survived those trials and won their trust and respect; you inserted yourself into the heart of an alien society. Your sacrifices were worth it."

Tianming looked at her, grimacing. "Yes, of course my sacrifices were worth it. They brought about the destruction of Earth and the human race."

AA stared at Tianming in confusion. Taking a deep breath, he finally revealed to her the secret he had always kept from everyone. "Don't you understand, AA? The only reason that I could win the trust of the Trisolarans and 'infiltrate' their society was because I surrendered. The droplet attack that ended the Deterrence Era was, in large measure, my work."

If one were to pick a single individual to bear the responsibility for the destruction of humanity's cradle, the most appropriate choice would not be Cheng Xin, Yun Tianming, or anyone else whose decisions swayed the lives of billions. It would have to be Thomas Wade, who had dedicated himself to the task of saving the human race through a program of violent struggle. More than six hundred years ago, he had uttered the fateful words that determined the ultimate fate of two species.

"We'll send only a brain."

This stroke of genius propelled the Staircase Program out of its darkest moments and handed the Trisolarans a precious human brain specimen. Although the sophons were capable of observing the human brain in minute detail, such passive observation was insufficient to gain an in-depth understanding of the mechanisms of human cognition. Moreover, after Wallfacer Bill Hines's efforts at mental sabotage, humanity's leaders grew increasingly concerned with the dangers of neuroscience research. Researchers were forbidden to delve into the specifics of how bioelectric signals between neurons gave rise to thought, lest such research give the Trisolarans the capability to read human thoughts through detailed neuroelectric monitoring.

Two centuries after initial contact, human cognition still presented an impenetrable black box to the Trisolarans. The aliens desperately wanted to experiment on a live human. Their enthusiasm wasn't driven entirely by scientific curiosity; rather, it was out of a desperate, practical need for strategic deception.

Throughout the Crisis Era, the Trisolarans saw no need for practicing strategic deception against humans—just as humans needed only pesticides, not lies, to take care of troublesome bugs. However, that didn't mean the Trisolarans were unaware of the value of such deception against other targets. Ever since they had discovered the dark forest state of the cosmos, the Trisolarans had lived in a state of perpetual terror of the rest of the universe. They knew that countless hunters were concealed in the galaxy, and the previous communications between

Trisolaris and Earth were likely to be discovered and posed a threat for their own survival. Strategic deception was an important defensive weapon they had to consider, but to wield it, the Trisolarans first had to understand the only species known to possess such a capability—humans.

A branch of advanced knowledge known as "deceptionology" arose among the Trisolaran elite soon after Evans revealed this unique feature of human cognition. The Trisolarans at first hoped to learn this human skill quickly, but that hope was soon dashed. Theoretically, understanding the principles of deception posed little difficulty; one simply had to purposefully make a false statement, which would achieve the desired goal when the target of deception believed it. Unfortunately, the Trisolaran scientists soon realized that their species lacked the biological instinct for lying, and they could not put this simple principle into operation. It wasn't very different from how human scientists could describe the mathematical underpinnings for four-dimensional space in detail, but could not construct even very simple four-dimensional figures in their minds.

Like all sentient beings, the Trisolarans occasionally made mistakes, but as their language consisted of the electrical patterns of thought being emitted directly, there was no way for them to speak of a known falsehood while pretending it was true. If a Trisolaran believed that a statement was false, the cognitive markers were immediately exhibited externally. Although in certain special situations, such as technology-enabled long-distance communication, it was possible to manufacture the signals of false brain activity, the deep biological instinct of the Trisolarans, inherited from their long evolutionary march up from primitive life-forms, prevented them from taking such a step.

The Trisolarans had hoped that they could gain the ability to practice the art of deception by studying human history, including advanced works in politics, military strategy, commerce, and game theory. But they soon discovered that they could not understand human history, nor could they decipher theoretical tomes on these subjects by human authors. (To be sure, few humans understood those works either.)

They turned to works of fiction, which seemed easier to understand. For some time, various popular tales of deception were required reading for Trisolaran scientists and politicians. Books like *The Count of Monte Cristo, The Adventures of Sherlock Holmes,* and *Romance of the Three Kingdoms* became bestsellers. But the aliens didn't have the capacity to appreciate these books, either. Novels that humans consumed for entertainment and leisure appeared to the Trisolarans as abstruse, incomprehensible treatises. Even after years of study, the most intelligent Trisolaran strategists could understand only the simple deceptions presented in fairy tales like "Little Red Riding Hood." Such techniques were, of course, useless for devising grand strategies applicable to interstellar warfare.

After decades of fruitless effort, the Trisolarans had to give up the ambitious plan to fundamentally change their own nature; they redirected their efforts to devising computer simulations to generate potential strategic deception scenarios. However, computers were capable of nothing more than reproducing and extending the abilities of their creators. In order to endow computers with special skills, it was necessary to write the requisite software; and to write such software, it was necessary to understand the relevant principles in depth. If human beings were not capable of coming up with a proof for Goldbach's conjecture, they could hardly expect computers produced by humans to calculate such a proof. Similarly, since the Trisolarans did not understand deception, neither did their computers.

Finally, after years of concentrated development and repeated trials by generations of the best Trisolaran minds—aided by access to data equivalent to the storage capacity of all human libraries—the most advanced Trisolaran computers attained the ability to practice deception at the level of the average twelve-year-old human, although such performance was only possible in environments familiar to humans (since

all scenarios used to train the computers were derived from such environments). Such skills were of limited applicability to potential conflicts
between the Trisolaran civilization and other undiscovered alien civilizations. In many cases, computers running deception software could
not even carry out a sensible conversation, failing the basic Turing test.

After having wasted so many years on a wild-goose chase, Trisolaran
scientists concluded that in order to acquire the capacity for strategic
deception it was vital to study an actual human specimen. Before the
Trisolaran Fleet reached the Earth and conquered it, the only available human specimen was Yun Tianming's brain, which had already
left the Solar System. At the end of the Crisis Era, the Trisolaran Fleet
diverted a ship for the sole purpose of intercepting the probe carrying
the brain of Yun Tianming.

Humanity then mistakenly interpreted the departure of this ship as
an attempt by the Trisolarans to seek peace in the face of overwhelming human strength, and this misinterpretation then indirectly led to
the destruction of the human fleet at the Doomsday Battle. In that
sense, this act of unintended "strategic deception" by the Trisolarans
was rather successful.

The Trisolaran Fleet succeeded in capturing the probe with Yun
Tianming's brain only after Luo Ji had established strategic deterrence.
By then, Earth and Trisolaris were locked in a delicate balance of power.
After years of being blocked by the sophons, Earth's technological
development took off by leaps and bounds; Trisolaris, on the other hand,
saw its advantage slip day by day. The primary target for Trisolaran strategic deception was no longer some unknown alien species in the future,
but humanity. Although there were still some spiritual successors of
the ETO on Earth willing to plot and scheme for the aliens, the Trisolarans were unwilling to engage in any trickery right under the eyes of
humans and risk triggering a universal broadcast. Probing and understanding Yun Tianming thus took on an unprecedented importance.

It took the Trisolarans about ten Earth years to figure out the basic
structure of Yun Tianming's brain. Taking into account Trisolaran

efficiency—which far exceeded that of humans—their progress was equivalent to a century's worth of work by humans. They constructed a simulated body for the captured brain so that it could experience sight, sound, touch, taste, smell, and then they studied it to understand how sensory signals were generated and transmitted.

Next, the aliens tried to interpret the information contained in Tianming's memories. To accomplish this feat, the Trisolarans stimulated the language center of Tianming's brain at the appropriate times so that he would tell them what he was seeing, what he was hearing, what he was thinking, and so on. Although they still couldn't read his thoughts directly, by means of trial and error with different stimuli, they learned to inject any information they wished into his brain, and then observed his responses through his narration.

At first, the Trisolarans were very careful with their test subject, and the experiments were gentle and mild. Indeed, they fed Tianming many beautiful sights and comforting scenes. These experiments left illusory memories in Tianming's mind of dreaming during his long flight through the darkness of space. But as the Trisolarans mastered the details of Tianming's brain, their experiments grew crueler and more violent. Many times, they pushed Tianming to the precipice of mental breakdown, but they knew enough to stop just at the edge and to calm him with tranquilizing chemicals, giving Tianming a chance to recover.

Although they learned to read Tianming's thoughts with relative precision, the Trisolarans discovered that due to the unique neural topology of each individual, what they learned from him was applicable to other humans only at a very basic level. The neural structures and patterns for higher thought they learned belonged to Tianming alone. The Trisolaran dream of reading all human thought remained out of reach.

The individuality of experience and memory thus preserved the black-box nature of human thought. If the Trisolarans had had access to thousands or millions of test subjects, they probably could have broken through this barrier as well. Alas, the Trisolarans had only Yun Tianming.

Still, what they accomplished with just one brain was immense.

With seven Earth years of additional, concentrated study of Tianming's brain, the Trisolarans completed the first digital model of the organ. This model contained all the information in his mind at the quantum level and could be used to simulate his basic thoughts. After the Trisolarans deleted all the "useless" human sentiments and sense of belonging from this digital brain, they filled it with their own data, hoping that the machine mind could then help the Trisolarans with devising plots and schemes. The Trisolarans called this invention "cloud" computing, because it concealed the light of truth like a cloud and because "Yun" in Chinese meant "cloud."

As Trisolaran civilization grew increasingly commercialized, low-cost versions of Yun Tianming's simulated digital brain found applications as consumer technology. The Trisolarans installed these cloud-computing devices on their organs of cognition and relied on them to disguise their own true thoughts, thereby achieving novel effects impossible for the unenhanced Trisolaran.

For example, a traditional conversation during the Trisolaran mating season might go something like this:

"My dear sex-one entity, this humble sex-two entity wishes to join our bodies." The imploring Trisolaran would wave its feelers in a gesture of desire. (Like humans, the Trisolarans are also divided into two sexes, though they are entirely different from human sexes.)

"Get away from me, you ugly thing! The very sight of you makes me wish to expel fecal matter!" The other Trisolaran would release thought waves that indicated extreme disgust.

Such honesty from the second Trisolaran often led to fierce fights between the two parties, an unfortunate state of affairs no one desired. The invention of cloud computing allowed uninterested Trisolarans to answer in a more indirect manner.

"Thank you! I think you're wonderful. But I don't think I'm good enough for you."

The imploring Trisolaran would then leave, satisfied and proud, perhaps even happier than if it had mated.

This was without a doubt a major improvement in Trisolaran society, but some other applications of the technology did not seem so wonderful. Due to the lack of deception and the almost eidetic memory of Trisolarans, there was no cash or coinage on Trisolaris. Most business transactions were not even recorded, but involved only the recitation of desired prices and remaining balances. A typical Trisolaran market exchange, described below, was practically unimaginable for humans:

"I'd like to purchase this rapid-action dehydrator. I still have 12,563 credits. I'll now pay you 231 credits, leaving me with 12,332 credits."

"Agreed. I had 73,212 credits. I've just received 231 credits, giving me a total of 73,443 credits."

"Done. I'll now take the rapid-action dehydrator and leave."

In reality, market exchanges didn't involve such ponderous dialogue. The two parties simply projected their separate calculations and observed the changes in the counterparty. If one side made a mistake, the other side would immediately correct it. But cloud computing allowed a Trisolaran to disguise true thought waves and project falsified results. A poor Trisolaran without the funds for luxuries could claim to be a billionaire, and no matter what they bought their account balances never decreased. Merchants could similarly claim that the basest goods were really special high-quality specimens and jack up the prices.

The popularity of cloud computing almost led to the total collapse of the Trisolaran economy. The Trisolaran government had to ban the direct installation of cloud-computing devices on organs of cognition on penalty of immediate dehydration followed by incineration. To enforce the ban, cloud detectors were installed in various locations. Finally, market order was restored.

But even if cloud-computing devices could not be integrated directly with Trisolaran thinking, it was fun for the average Trisolaran to converse with an imitation Yun Tianming brain. If one controlled for the relative slowness of human thought and the pronounced forgetfulness, a human was not unintelligent compared with a Trisolaran. In fact, the human mind possessed some qualities that were unmatched by the Trisolaran mind. Other than being deceptive, a human was also sensitive to nature, curious, imaginative, and creative—unpredictably so. In some sense, mastering human thinking processes—specifically Yun Tianming's mind—was the key to the Trisolaran technology explosion at the end of the Deterrence Era, culminating in the invention of curvature propulsion.

This was the real reason for the high honor and genuine gratitude the Trisolarans accorded Yun Tianming. Later, after he demonstrated loyalty to Trisolaris, they granted him a very elevated social status.

Cloud computing nonetheless proved inadequate for directly advancing the strategic goals of the Trisolarans. The second-generation simulated Yun Tianming brains used digital models specifying quantum-level details. But just as Hines had discovered during the Common Era, human thought was affected by quantum uncertainty. The Trisolarans couldn't replicate the activities in Yun Tianming's brain at the quantum level, so they couldn't master the essence of human thought. To achieve the level of complexity and intricacy characteristic of true human cognition, they had to rely on a genuine human brain.

After three generations of experimental cloud computing, the Trisolarans had to admit that simulation was no answer. They settled on the last choice available to them: wake Yun Tianming from his endless dreams and, by coercion or inducement, make him serve Trisolaris.

Yun Tianming paused in his story. AA stared at him, her face tense. "And did you . . . did you agree?" She held her breath, afraid that his answer would dash her hopes.

Tianming shook his head, but AA wasn't completely relieved. She had guessed the answer: He had at first refused, but after a regimen of nonstop, inventive torture, in the end he gave in. She knew that there was a limit to the suffering a mind could endure, and she wasn't so naive as to despise him for it. Still, deep in her heart, she found it hard to accept that the man she loved was responsible for the destruction of humanity. She did not want to hear any more.

"I'm cold," she said, shivering and hugging herself. "Why don't we return to the spaceship?" The sun had already set, and the eerie starlight of the black domain lit up the heavens. The temperature dropped precipitously, and AA hadn't a stitch of clothing on.

Not too long ago they had welcomed summer on Planet Blue. Their initial judgment of the climate on the planet had been slightly off. Due to the extreme eccentricity of the orbit, the planet's coldest season left almost two-thirds of its surface in a condition akin to Antarctica on Earth, but during the hottest season, parts of the planet reached fifty degrees Celsius. As the heat was simply too much to bear, the two decided to discard their clothing and live in a prelapsarian manner. But seasons on Planet Blue changed quickly, and after a few storms, it was now chilly autumn.

Tianming twisted a ringlike ornament on his finger—the only item of clothing or jewelry he wore—and a protective force field with a radius of three meters appeared around them. The temperature within the field quickly rose to a comfortable level. AA could see no obvious heat source. She gave a wry smile. Humans during the Deterrence Era could manipulate force fields with the same precision, and such technology was used to maintain an atmosphere suitable for life in space without the use of physical barriers. However, humanity accomplished the feat only with the aid of enormous machines that consumed a great deal of energy, while Yun Tianming did it with nothing more than a ring on his finger.

She did not know where Tianming had acquired the advanced technology he brought with him. Although his ship couldn't escape the black domain, it was able to satisfy virtually all their other needs. Even on this desolate planet, the two of them lived a life of relative ease that rivaled conditions back in the Solar System.

A few days earlier, while bathing in the lake—the water did contain some trace metals, but was safe enough to bathe in—she had been reminded of the time in her life when she and Cheng Xin had experimented with antique bath soap bars. She told Tianming the story, and then, half joking, she said, "Oh, I wish I could get a bar of sweet-smelling bath soap! Wouldn't it be nice to take a bubble bath here?"

She wasn't serious, of course, but to her surprise, Tianming entered his ship and returned a few minutes later to toss her a bar of soap. The fragrance was even stronger than the bar she had found in the museum hundreds of years ago. She had no idea how Tianming had managed it.

There was also the miniature universe that Tianming had brought as a gift for Cheng Xin. She had seen the floating rectangular outline with her own eyes. Although she had never entered it, the very concept seemed to her an almost inconceivable invention. A small, self-contained universe that existed independent of the larger universe around? How could the Trisolarans possess such advanced technology? If they did, they wouldn't have worried about the destruction of Trisolaris, because moving to mini-universes would have solved all their problems. So how did such a marvel end up in the hands of Yun Tianming?

She changed her mind. "I'm warm now. Why don't you continue? It's better to let it all out. No matter what, I'm on your side."

Tianming lifted his face to the sky, deep in reverie. Only after a long pause did he speak again. "I'll tell you about the day I woke up, a day I will never forget."

Tianming woke up and saw that he was lying in bed.

He had a body.

It must be a clone, he realized. This was a body without cancer cells, and he felt healthier and stronger than he had on Earth. Everything around him was automated; he didn't see any Trisolarans. *Perhaps the extraterrestrials don't want to reveal themselves to me, lest their frightening alien appearance become a barrier for effective communication.*

He got up and surveyed the room. There was a door, unlocked. After a moment of hesitation, he pushed it open, stepped through, and found himself in a garden. It was filled with sights familiar to him from the Common Era: an open lawn, a bridge over a thin stream, a rock formation, a small pagoda . . . replicas made by the Trisolarans based on their understanding of Earth. The garden was surrounded by a tall wall that blocked his view of what lay beyond. Puffy clouds drifted in the clear sky, and the sun was bright and warm.

He figured that this whole place was just a part of a Trisolaran ship, which had been modified into a comfortable cage for him. The sky was probably the result of holographic projection. How did the Trisolarans plan to communicate with him?

A line of text appeared in the sky: "Dear Mr. Yun Tianming, welcome to our world."

The greeting, which was the first time the Trisolarans had talked to him, shocked him. But he maintained a calm demeanor and nodded. "How are you?" he asked.

"Fine." The Trisolarans got right to the point. "We woke you because we need you to help us complete the plan for the conquest of Earth."

This is it.

A complicated smile curved up the corners of Tianming's mouth. He wasn't entirely surprised by the request. When he had refused to pledge his loyalty toward the human race at the United Nations, he had known such a day might come. It was time to make a decision.

"Why should I betray my people?" he asked coldly.

"Divisions between species do not represent unbridgeable gaps. On Earth, many have already pledged their allegiance to us without our asking."

"I'm sorry, but you're severely mistaken if you equate me with those pathetic cowards in the ETO."

The Trisolarans weren't angered by his response. "We all know that humans on Earth didn't treat you with kindness. It was no coincidence that you came to be among us. For the last few years, by studying your brain and mind, our society has already made great strides, and your name is highly esteemed by the Trisolaran people. If you agree to help us, you will become the most honored citizen of Trisolaris, with privileges second only to the princeps. We understand that our material goods may be of no interest to you, but once our fleet arrives at Earth, you will have the resources of the entire planet at your disposal, and you can have whatever humans dream of."

Tianming sneered. "What would I do with any of that if humanity is exterminated?"

"We won't eradicate all humans; your species will certainly continue. The need for scientific research alone requires a small number of humans to be preserved—say, in the range of a few hundred thousand to a few million. We'll set aside a reservation on Earth for them, and we'll make you their absolute ruler. With the help of our advanced technology, you'll live better than any king or emperor in the history of your world."

Since the Trisolarans were incapable of lying, Tianming knew that their promises were genuine.

"What if I refuse?" he asked.

"We would be sorry to hear that. But we won't do anything to you . . . except return you to sleep in our dreams."

Tianming trembled uncontrollably. He knew what the Trisolarans were promising: a perpetual nightmare from which he would never wake up. This was far worse than any physical torture they could devise.

Tianming had had enough. Why should he continue to live in that hell in his head? For the sake of his human compatriots? What was humanity? They were the ones who pulled him out of a quiet end in euthanasia, cut out his brain, froze it in a space probe, and then sent it here to a fate worse than death. Why should he care about them?

The dark thoughts flitted across his mind, demanding that he not be foolish. Tianming knew that the Trisolarans were waiting patiently for his answer.

"I'm sorry, but I have to say no," he said. He didn't know exactly why he chose to resist. He knew that if he yielded, even if every human being on Earth cursed his name, he wouldn't have felt guilty at all. This wasn't a burden that he should have been made responsible for. Perhaps he refused not out of any sense of duty, but because of an anachronistic sense of nobility.

To hold on to one's independent will, to refuse to submit to enslavement, to despise enticements as well as threats—such was the dignity and pride of each individual human being. This was something that the Trisolarans, guided by the philosophy of survival above all else, could never understand and perhaps did not want to understand.

"Do you need more time to consider our proposal? We have noticed that humans seem to require some time to think before making important decisions."

"There's no need," Tianming said.

He wasn't sure how much time had passed.

He found himself standing on a tree-lined path with golden leaves drifting down around him. It was fall, and he was next to the open lawn at the heart of his college campus. A few students sat on the grass, reading; in the distance a couple held each other tightly; on the basketball court next to the lawn a group of athletes played, cheering and shouting . . . Aimlessly, he walked along the path. He decided that he must still be a student here, but he was too shocked to think about how he had returned.

The whole world seemed to brighten as a familiar figure appeared at the end of the path, gradually growing as the distance between them closed: a young woman dressed in a pale yellow windbreaker. She stopped in front of him, a smile on her face.

"You came," she said.

Tianming heard the affectionate tone in Cheng Xin's voice. He saw her take his arm and lean against his side as though they were lovers. He was perplexed. *When . . . how . . .*

Love and tenderness filled his heart, but he immediately realized that it was all too perfect and too sweet to be true. With a deep shudder, he realized that this was yet another dream, the beginning of another horrible session of torture.

"No!" he cried out. But he didn't wake up. Cheng Xin gazed at him, puzzled.

Anxiously, Tianming looked around. Was the sky going to open up and rain down blood? Would the earth crack under his feet? Would all those students around them turn into zombies and attack him and Cheng Xin? For that matter, was Cheng Xin about to turn into a mummy with wispy white hair or a monster with bloody boils all over her body? Would the two of them be buried alive or slaughtered in cold blood? What kind of horrors and evil lay in wait for them in this dream of paradise?

"What's wrong, Tianming? Are you all right?" Cheng Xin asked, concerned.

He gazed into her clear and innocent eyes; he could not imagine the trials and tortures that would be inflicted on her. He fell to the ground, unable to bear this twisted version of "life."

"Stop it! Please. Please don't make me dream any more. I . . . I will cooperate. Do you hear me?!"

Everything around him disappeared. Tianming found himself lying in bed in the room in which he had awakened earlier. Sweat drenched his body.

"I will ask for only one thing," he said. "I want to dream of being together with Cheng Xin every night. Dreams of happiness, not nightmares."

"That's not a problem at all," replied the Trisolarans with a line of floating text. Tianming imagined the alien sneer on the faces of the

Trisolarans behind the text: *You're nothing but a bug. No matter how you struggle, in the end we will win.*

Though he paused in his account, Tianming remained mired in reminiscence. From behind, 艾 AA wrapped her arms about him and muttered, "It's not your fault. It's not." But she couldn't sort through her own complicated emotions; a sense of dread and bitterness grew in her heart.

The hero she worshiped turned out be as vulnerable as any ordinary human.

Tianming gave another wry smile. "My story isn't so simple."

Having reached an understanding with him, the Trisolarans gave Yun Tianming all the data and references he requested. In total, the information amounted to the capacity of a large library. After perusing the files for some time, Tianming explained that the task of helping the Trisolarans deceive humans was extremely difficult, and he needed time to think.

The Trisolarans left him alone. Tianming paced back and forth in his artificial environment, sitting down to rest from time to time. There was a seven-story pagoda in the garden, and he climbed to the top to survey his world from that elevated perch, deep in thought.

The next day, he returned to the top of the pagoda and sat there for about an hour. The Trisolarans did not bother him. He concluded that perhaps the Trisolarans had relaxed their vigilance against him.

On the third day, he climbed the pagoda again as before, but when he had reached the top, he leapt over the guardrail and plunged toward the ground more than twenty meters below.

He had planned the entire sequence of initial refusal, surrender in the dream, and postdream proposal to collaborate; the goal of his deception was his own death. The gravity here was similar to gravity on

Earth, and he had thought long and hard about where and how to make his leap. He was accelerating toward the ground with his head first, and as soon as his skull cracked open, his brain would be splattered. No matter how advanced Trisolaran technology was, he suspected that they couldn't put back together *this* cracked egg. The only fear he had was that the Trisolarans might possess the ability to generate a force field in midair to prevent him from striking the ground.

As the ground neared and filled his sight, he barely had time for a flash of relief and joy before it all went dark. Tianming was the happiest suicide in the history of the world.

"So how did they revive you?" AA's voice trembled. The knowledge that Tianming had survived the suicide attempt couldn't dispel a nameless terror from her.

"I woke up again and found myself, unharmed, lying in that same room. Everything had been reset," Tianming said.

"How . . . how was that possible? Do you mean . . . oh—" AA had guessed at the truth.

"That's right. I never jumped off the pagoda." Tianming's face now held a self-mocking expression. "There was no pagoda, no 'waking up,' no cloned body. The entire experience was nothing more than another dream injected into my mind by the Trisolarans. They didn't care what I did, because I was never in any real danger. This wasn't a deliberate act of deception on their part; they didn't inform me of this detail because they didn't think it was important. Although communicating with me through a dream had been done out of convenience, the Trisolarans later told me that they were impressed by my attempt at deception followed by suicide, a trick they could never have devised. If they had truly revived me in a cloned body, they suspected that they wouldn't have been able to stop me. This only reassured them that I was the right person to carry out strategic deception. Ironic, isn't it?

"After that, the contest of wills between the Trisolarans and me heated up. Since I refused to collaborate, they invented a variety of cruel nightmares to punish me. Whenever I couldn't take it anymore, I would agree to help them and then come up with excuses for delay or bad suggestions. Of course, such tricks became harder and harder to pull off, because the Trisolarans had studied my brain for such a long time that my thoughts were comparatively more transparent to them than other human beings'. Deceiving them grew increasingly difficult.

"On the other hand, my mind also grew more inured to various scenes of horror and mental tortures, and I even learned to consciously override some of the sensations of physical pain they injected into me. Finally, they grew tired of this cat-and-mouse game, and decided to bypass my consent and use my brain directly."

"Use your brain directly?" AA asked.

Tianming explained that the human brain was to some extent a problem-solving machine. When stimulated, it responded in certain predictable ways. Much of the process didn't require the participation of consciousness. Many important cognitive tasks were carried out subconsciously, with consciousness only providing supplemental functions like monitoring, storing, organizing, and refining. Nonetheless, if a person was unwilling to cooperate, they could consciously disrupt the nearly automatic processes. In order to make Yun Tianming's brain serve them subconsciously, the Trisolarans carefully isolated his consciousness from the rest of his mind, and then used their computers to control and direct what remained of his cognitive functions.

The test, however, resulted in a failure. The Trisolarans discovered that a computer could not substitute for the reflective and refining functions of consciousness itself, especially not a Trisolaran computer that was ill-matched to human minds. The Trisolarans had to make all of Tianming serve them, including his conscious will.

So, the Trisolarans resorted to other techniques to induce some semblance of cooperation. For example, they used drugs to bring Tianming's brain into a hallucinatory state and attempted to question him for ideas on strategic deception. However, Tianming's confused and unfocused mental state while drugged prevented him from giving useful suggestions.

The Trisolarans also tried a technique that Tianming later dubbed "soul-shock therapy." This involved injecting questions into Tianming's brain and forcing him to think about how to solve them. Whenever Tianming tried to resist, his brain center emitted a specific signal, which triggered a "soul shock," a powerful surge of stimuli that caused Tianming extreme mental anguish and the sensation of physical pain. By this means, the Trisolarans hoped to remove his resistance through aversive conditioning.

They were somewhat successful at first. But eventually Tianming learned mental techniques familiar to yoga and Chan Buddhism practitioners. Instead of actively resisting, Tianming made his mind go blank. By not thinking of anything, he created a hidden partition in his mind in which thoughts could continue without interruption. He also developed the nearly superhuman capacity to endure the painful tortures the Trisolarans subjected him to without breaking down.

The average person used only a small part of the potential of their brain, and the cruel Trisolarans unintentionally forced Tianming to realize more and more of his mind's infinite potential. Despite repeated all-out assaults in this epic of *psychomachia*, the technologically far superior Trisolarans failed to breach the fortress Tianming had constructed in his mind, and had to admit defeat.

AA was now even more baffled. "If the Trisolarans couldn't conquer your mind, why did you surrender to them in the end?"

"What do you think is the key to a successful lie?" Tianming countered.

AA hesitated. "I guess . . . to account for the details? Or maybe to understand the other side's psychology?"

"No. It's sincerity. To be so sincere that even the liar believes it." Tianming sighed.

The Trisolarans were not of a single mind. Encounter with human civilization had shocked their society to the core. The early years of the Deterrence Era, when Tianming and the Trisolarans struggled over his soul, also saw Trisolaran society face its own unprecedented crisis. The creation of the deterrence system put the dream of Earth's conquest out of reach, and the sense of defeat led to social instability. The popularity of Earth culture and the advent of cloud computing further buffeted the foundation of traditional Trisolaran society. Gradually, the sparks of revolution spread both on Trisolaris and in the Trisolaran Fleet. And soon after, an unexpected Chaotic Era struck, leading to social collapse and the turbulence of the Trisolaran Revolution.

Because they lived in such an inhospitable environment, stability was the overriding goal of Trisolaran political philosophy. Throughout Trisolaran history, there were few events that could be classified as true revolutions. Even if there had been seeds of rebellion, the Trisolarans' inability to lie meant that revolutionary techniques such as secret plots and underground organizations were inapplicable—it was impossible for Trisolarans harboring rebellious thoughts to disguise them, and they would have been prosecuted for their thought crimes long before they could put them into action. It wasn't until the Trisolarans encountered humans that they realized that a secret organization aiming to change the status quo was even possible.

But now they had cloud computing. Although the devices were forbidden to ordinary citizens, government research institutes and the military still possessed some. The revolutionaries took advantage of the deceptive capabilities of these devices and remained undetected until the period of instability between the Stable Era and the Chaotic Era, at which point they instigated a riot that snowballed out of control. The revolution succeeded beyond their wildest dreams because the ruling elite were completely unprepared, and the old order collapsed overnight.

The rebels overthrew the old princeps and nobles on Trisolaris, and renounced plans for a strategic counterattack against Earth. The new government held romantic notions about Earth civilization, and the new leaders desired to maintain peace with humanity in exchange for a new home on one of the other planets in the Solar System. Through the use of instantaneous sophon communication, they took charge of the Trisolaran Fleet. Although the fleet was dominated by hawks who preferred to conquer Earth and exterminate humans, they obeyed the orders of the new government. Obedience was the instinctive reaction of most Trisolarans, who had no tradition of saying one thing while planning another.

On the Trisolaran ship, Tianming's understanding of the details of the revolution was limited, but he quickly sensed that something seemed to have changed among his Trisolaran captors. The tortures they subjected him to slackened and then ceased. After some time, the Trisolarans reestablished contact with him and informed him that there had been a change back home on Trisolaris. They now wished him to serve as a bridge between the two peoples and build trust and friend-ship.

"Wait a minute!" AA cried out. "This must be a trick! Did you be-lieve them?" Although AA had once been a believer in the "friendly" nature of the Trisolarans, the experience of the alien conquest of Earth had completely shattered such faith. She could never trust anything the Trisolarans said.

"No, it wasn't a trick," Tianming said, shaking his head. "If the Triso-larans were capable of devising such an elaborate plot, they would have had no need for my services. If I had believed them, then per-haps I really could have helped the two peoples to find a way to live together in peace. But history is full of unexpected turns and ironic twists . . . I missed the opportunity."

Tianming had refused to believe the Trisolarans' sincerity and had continued to refuse to cooperate. This time, the Trisolarans, beset by all the problems in the wake of a revolution, left him alone to dream on in his long sleep. They didn't torture him with manufactured night-mares, and they didn't wake him. From then on, Tianming lived in his dreamworld, and he had no idea how much subjective time he lived through. It might have been two thousand years, but it could also have been five thousand or ten thousand.

"How many years was it really?" AA asked.

"Given that there are no objective markers such as sunsets or sunrises, I can't tell you for sure. In reality, perhaps about twenty years had passed in the real world, but it felt to me like thousands of years. In one dream, I even founded a civilization and observed its rise and fall—"

"They trapped you in a dream for thousands of years? That . . . that is even more cruel than a life sentence!" AA was enraged.

"Not at all," Tianming said. "I count that long dream as the happiest period of my life. No one bothered me as I lived in my own mind. This was a happiness I never enjoyed even back on Earth.

"After so many years in the crucible of Trisolaran mental torture, my mind had been refined into a keen instrument. Not only did I wield it to create an unimaginatively vast interior landscape, I was also the master of this fresh domain. I could use my will to drive and describe the details of every dream. The education in classical literature that my parents had forced on me in my youth turned out to be incredibly helpful, and provided me with the raw materials for the construction of my dreamworld. Sometimes I set off with the heroes aboard *Argo* in search of the Golden Fleece, ready to slay sea serpents and fight monsters; other times I followed Gringoire through the dark alleys of medieval Paris, listening to the tolling of the bell by Quasimodo; still other times I rode cloud carriages drawn by flying horses and traversed thousands of snow-topped peaks to visit Queen Mother of the West in the Kunlun Mountains . . .

"I was not a mere visitor to these worlds, but a creator. I conceived every detail of these universes: the Jerusalem of the New Testament, the Hell and Heaven of *Divina Commedia*, the Bianliang of *Along the River During the Qingming Festival*, the Heavenly Palace and the Buddha's pure land as portrayed in *Journey to the West* . . . I also invented many marvels that had never been portrayed before: kingdoms found in flower petals, universes bound in nutshells, seafloor metropolises and gardens floating in space . . .

"As a creator in dreams, I did not need to understand technical details or follow scientific laws. All I had to do was to imagine it, and it was so. Let there be light, I declared, and the universe was luminous. I devised buildings that could not exist under mechanical principles, but they were magnificent, august, sublime. I constructed wonders that scrambled time and space: a Venice in the desert, a primeval forest at the heart of a metropolis, waterfalls that hung from the stars to the earth, tropical islands suspended in air . . .

"I also populated my worlds with colorful characters and astounding tales: war among the gods, mysterious treasures, legendary heroes, youthful adventures, love that seared the soul and shattered the heart . . . indeed, most of the hundred-plus fairy tales I told the Trisolarans later were first conceived of during that time."

"I had no idea," exclaimed AA. "I thought you worked hard to invent all those other fairy tales in order to disguise the fact that the three stories you told Cheng Xin held secrets."

"The work wasn't that hard," said a smiling Tianming. "When you have only limited time, somehow all you want to do is to procrastinate, nap, waste time. But when the time available to you is unlimited, you don't want to do anything else except create. Those fairy tales were an insignificant portion of my output."

"Why don't you tell me one of your romantic stories then?" AA said. She was so entranced by his account that she had forgotten the purpose of Tianming's story. Tenderly, she wrapped her arms about his neck and leaned on his shoulder.

"All right. But let me think about which story to tell you . . . Oh, I know. I'll tell you one of my favorite tales.

"In ancient China, at the source of the Yangtze River, there was a Tibetan boy who lived in a village at the foot of the Tanggula Mountains. The boy liked to imagine the world outside the mountains, which he had never left. One day, a merchant from China's heartland passed through the village. The boy followed the merchant everywhere and asked him about the sights he had seen. The merchant told the boy that the stream passing by their village flowed east to join many other streams and brooks, grew wider and deeper, progressed between peaks and over plains, through canyons and around hills, and after a journey of twelve thousand *li*, plunged into the endless sea as the mightiest river in the land.

"The boy didn't know what a sea was, and so the merchant told him that it was a body of water so large that a ship could not sail to its edge. The whole world's rivers commingled there into a mirror broader than any land, reflecting a blue as pure as the sky. Next to the sea, situated in the lower reaches of the Yangtze River, was the Jiangnan region, a land of verdant hills and misty lakes, where painted pavilions and delicate houses dotted the countryside like figures in a painting or words in a poem. Women dressed in flowing silk dresses oared elegant barges over the placid waterways, singing folk ditties in the gentle, refined accents of the Wu topolect . . .

"The boy was utterly entranced by the merchant's tale, and he wanted to follow the man to Jiangnan, but none of the villagers believed the merchant's fantastical descriptions, and the boy's parents refused to let him go. Finally, the merchant had to leave, but he left the boy with a small bottle from Jiangnan. The boy then wrote a letter in Tibetan that described his dreams and fantasies and sealed it into the bottle along with a piece of pure jade from the nearby mountains. He set the bottle down in the stream by the village and hoped that the river would bring it to Jiangnan, thousands of *li* away.

"Half a year later, as a lonely girl walked by the shore of the Yangtze outside the walls of Jiankang, the City of Stones and the largest metropolis in the world, she saw a bottle bobbing in the river—"

Tianming stopped because he saw the look on AA's face, a look of horror at the realization of a cruel secret.

"That's . . . that's *A Fairy Tale of Yangtze!*" she finally cried out. A few hundred years ago, she had played the popular and award-winning film for Cheng Xin. Since she had spent the vast majority of the intervening centuries in hibernation, the film was still fresh in her mind.

You live at one end of the Yangtze, and I the other.

I think of you each day, beloved, though we cannot meet.

We drink from the same river . . .

She had been so excited to share the film with Cheng Xin, telling her that it was an amazing artistic creation by the Trisolarans. But now Tianming was telling her that the story had been woven by him in a dream . . .

"That's right, I'm telling you the story of A *Fairy Tale of Yangtze.*" Tianming's tone was calm as he continued his revelation. "That film and the vast majority of so-called Trisolaran artistic creations were dreamed up by me. The Trisolarans gained the trust of humanity with my dreams."

The Trisolarans' strategic goal was to destroy humanity's gravitational-wave universal broadcast system without triggering a broadcast, thereby ending the deterrence standoff. A prerequisite for reaching this goal was to induce humanity to elect as the Swordholder someone as kindhearted and weak as Cheng Xin. And the only way to accomplish *that* was to persuade humans that the Trisolarans no longer posed a threat.

There were many ways to lull humans into thinking that the Trisolarans had been defanged, but the most effective was to build trust and goodwill. In order for humans to trust aliens, the humans had to be made to feel a sense of empathy with the aliens, to think "we are all the same."

The chain of reasoning so far had long been the consensus of Trisolaran strategists after many rounds of theoretical debate and deduction. But they could not see how to accomplish the first link in the chain: changing the human perception of Trisolarans as irreducibly alien. The differences between the two civilizations were too vast. At the beginning of the Deterrence Era, the Trisolarans, lacking experience, had revealed some true facts about their social organization to the humans. For example, Trisolaran parents, after joining bodies in mating, would essentially die as they "exploded" into baby Trisolarans. As another example, aged and disabled Trisolarans were forcibly dehydrated and incinerated to improve social efficiency. These facts caused humanity to view the Trisolarans with great horror and disgust. The famous one-liner that had once been used by Trisolarans to describe humans was turned around and applied to the Trisolarans.

You're bugs!

The Trisolarans had used such a description for humans to summarize the vast gulf between the two civilizations' scientific knowledge and technology levels. But as used by the humans, the sentiment was also imbued with moral and cultural disgust. Once the peaceful Trisolarans took power on Trisolaris, they attempted to improve relations between the two peoples, but the weight of history and the cultural gap meant that their efforts had little effect. Trisolarans were a rational species little affected by emotions and sentiments in their decisions, but humans could not forget the atrocities committed by the Trisolarans during the Doomsday Battle. The intensity of this human hatred seemed to the Trisolarans completely irrational, and they could not understand how to deal with it.

And so the Trisolarans remembered Yun Tianming and hoped to discover the secret of overcoming this obstacle in his mind. They recorded all of his dreams, which they viewed as a treasure trove. Tianming himself became an idol for Trisolaran fans of Earth culture. After suitable processing, his dream creations were released as literary and visual compositions to wide acclaim among the Trisolarans. And after some careful adaptation, these works were transmitted to Earth under the guise of Trisolaran creations.

It was unclear whether the Trisolarans intended to deceive humans from the start. Sending Tianming's works to Earth probably began as a simple gesture to demonstrate their goodwill. In addition, due to the

extreme collectivist nature of Trisolaran culture, the concept of author-
ship was almost absent among the Trisolarans. Once they had slightly
adapted Tianming's dreams to their own tastes, they naturally felt that
the dreams could be called their own. By then the Trisolarans had more
or less learned the basic idea of keeping secrets, and so when humans
inquired after the source of these artistic works, they didn't give a direct
answer; such omission was the height of their capacity for deception.
Humans, of course, could never have dreamed that the Trisolarans possessed a human brain that was unconsciously churning out works of art
for them, and came to the natural conclusion that the Trisolarans themselves were the artists.

That Tianming's dreams were imbued with so much humanistic
value and so rooted in Earth culture should have aroused suspicion
among the humans, but the overconfidence of the Deterrence Era and
the Trisolarans' genuine admiration for Earth culture led to a blind-
ness on Earth. Humans believed that although their culture was still
but a budding sprout in the dark forest, they had mastered universal
moral values that were applicable everywhere in the cosmos regardless
of time or space. That these barbaric aliens would express such admiration for Earth culture and imitate it was perfectly natural. The very
proof that Earth values were universal was provided by the fact that the
Trisolarans, another advanced civilization, generated similar art as the
Earth's when stimulated in appropriate ways. Moreover, the Trisolarans
did add a few Trisolaran elements in the process of adaptation. Mixed
in with a few genuine Trisolaran works of art done in imitation of Earth
examples (though they were not of the same quality as Tianming's
dreams), the result was a story that compelled the belief of humans on
Earth.

As she listened to Tianming's explanation, AA recalled another "humanistic" Trisolaran creation.

"Wait a minute . . . Did you also have a hand in the creation of
Sophon?" AA shuddered as she thought of the Trisolaran "ambassador"

who appeared sometimes as a ninja and other times as a classical Japanese beauty.

Tianming's expression was a bit awkward as he nodded. "Yes. Sophon came out of my dreams as well . . ."

Since Tianming had lived a socially awkward and isolated life on Earth, few female figures appeared in the visions his brain spun on the Trisolaran ship except for his mother, his sister, and Cheng Xin. But one other woman appeared often in his imagination, sometimes gentle and shy, sometimes passionate and bold. The Trisolarans were very interested in this mysterious woman, and after much research by the sophons, they discovered that she was a Japanese actress from the Common Era by the name of Ran Asakawa. During college, Tianming had often enjoyed her clips online in his dorm room when he was alone, and after he started working he had bought a box set of all her films. Ran was apparently the representative of an aspect of Japanese culture that was extremely popular in much of Asia during that era.

The Trisolarans had not initially paid much attention to Japan, but Tianming's dreams led their strategists to focus on this geographically confined state. They learned that the Japanese islands were subject to extreme natural disasters. Located on the fault line between two tectonic plates, the islands were often struck by earthquakes, tsunamis, and volcanic eruptions. A major tsunami near the end of the Common Era had taken the lives of tens of thousands . . . Many Japanese leaders had expressed concern that the islands were not a stable environment, and over Japan's history had launched multiple invasions of the mainland. Many humans spoke of the Japanese people as hardy, orderly, disciplined . . . Clearly, the Japanese experience could be quite illuminating for the Trisolarans.

Most instructive of all, decades before the birth of Yun Tianming, Japan had initiated a bloody invasion of Yun Tianming's homeland, China, resulting in deep animosity between the two nations—yet within decades Japanese entertainment products had swept China, and millions of young Chinese worshiped Japanese culture and followed Japanese stars, greatly ameliorating the historical enmity. This led numerous Trisolaran scholars to conclude that in order to induce humans to forget the historical wounds of the Doomsday Battle, the Trisolarans should imitate Japan's success.

Thus, Sophon appeared as a Japanese woman modeled after Ran Asakawa.

"Ah!" AA exclaimed. "After Cheng Xin met Sophon, she told me that the robot reminded her of a foreign actress from her time, but she didn't tell me who. I didn't realize that you and she were both fans of the same actress."

"Cheng Xin was a fan of Ran Asakawa?"

"Why are you so surprised?" AA wasn't sure why Tianming's tone was so odd.

"Um . . . never mind." Tianming grinned awkwardly and shook his head.

Sophon's presentation achieved great success on Earth. In the middle years of the Deterrence Era, the trend was for growing valorization of traditionally "feminine" qualities, and Sophon's ultra-feminine act played to the taste of the time. Her dress, makeup, and jewelry all became marks of fashion. The appearance of Sophon accelerated the trends she was playing into. Many humans came to the conclusion that if the once brutal, savage Trisolarans were choosing to adopt such an image of nonthreatening, gentle femininity, it was a sign that a similar evolution among humans would be most in line with the universal values of civilization. That classical line from *Faust*, slightly modified, became the symbol of a new conception of cosmic civilization:

"The eternal feminine draws us as well as the Trisolarans ever onward and upward!"

Soon, however, the Trisolarans were no longer willing to be led by human civilization.

The Trisolaran reform movement didn't last long. Blindly introducing and imitating Earth culture was not useful for solving the many

practical problems facing Trisolaran society. The Chaotic Era wasn't
going to go away just because of the advent of a "humanistic" society.
On the contrary, due to rising individualism on Trisolaris, the old au-
thoritarian, militaristic chain of command had broken down. During
the Stable Era, various factions pursued their own goals, leading to the
fragmentation of Trisolaran society. Once the Chaotic Era arrived, the
factions fought against each other with no coordination, leading to
the deaths of billions. After twenty years of living under the new re-
gime, the average Trisolaran had little good to say about the way things
were going, and many even contemptuously called the Trisolaran government "Government of the Earth bugs, by the Earth bugs, for the
Earth bugs."

The reformists tried to solve their political difficulties by introducing democratic elections—another import from Earth. But the result
was not what they expected. Candidates representing the ancien régime
received the vast majority of votes and swept back into power, immediately purging and punishing the "pro-Earth" faction. After decades of
tumult, the Trisolarans had seen enough of the weaknesses of human
values, and the old yearning for military dominance came back into
fashion. Once again, the plan to engage in strategic deception and attack Earth was on the agenda.

The new hawks discovered, to their delight, that the grand strategic
deception had somehow already succeeded. Humans were now of the
general opinion that the Trisolarans were a friendly and kind species.
The key ingredients of the success of this strategic deception were none
other than Yun Tianming's artistic creations and the once-sincere
admiration of the Trisolarans for Earth culture.

Continuing the deception didn't pose a great difficulty. The Trisolaran scholars came to the conclusion that the self-defanging of human
society was an irreversible trend that would continue unabated for at
least a century more. With greater than 90 percent certainty, the com-
placent humans would elect as their next Swordholder someone
gentle and kind, and there were still many more artistic creations in

Tianming's brain that could be employed as opiates for the humans. The Trisolarans might still be relatively naive when it came to schemes and plots, but they knew enough to let Sophon keep on arranging flowers and performing tea ceremonies to please the humans.

This was also when Trisolaran scientists first successfully tested lightspeed spaceships with curvature propulsion. Humans in later ages were sometimes puzzled by why the Trisolarans were still intent on conquering Earth if they possessed such advanced technology. The answer came down to the persistence of the Trisolarans. The First Trisolaran Fleet had already been launched to conquer Earth, so they might as well finish their mission. The lightspeed ships provided an additional bit of insurance. Even if the plan for conquest failed and humanity initiated gravitational-wave universal broadcast, the Trisolarans figured that they had almost 150 years to produce massive lightspeed ships to evacuate the vast majority of Trisolarans from their home world before the arrival of any dark forest attack. Based on how long it took for Luo Ji's "spell" to take effect, this was a reasonable estimate.

No one could have predicted how quickly the dark forest strike would follow the subsequent universal broadcast. It was only three years before Trisolaris was obliterated.

As plans for the conquest of Earth proceeded apace, the Trisolarans finally decided to awaken Tianming. They had no more need to study. The satisfied Trisolarans informed him that they wanted him to see the benefit of actively collaborating with them, but if he insisted on being contrary, they wouldn't force him. Due to his many "contributions" to the success of the Trisolaran deception of Earth, the glorious and generous Trisolaran civilization was happy to allow him to live out the rest of his life in peace. He could choose to do it as a dreaming brain, or he could even join Trisolaran society as a full-fledged member.

If Yun Tianming chose to collaborate, he would give the Trisolarans some advantages. He could, for instance, suggest better ways for them to disguise their true intentions. The Trisolaran scholars calculated that the probability that a strike against Earth at the moment of the next Swordholder handover would succeed was 87.53 percent. If Tianming chose to help them, the probability of success increased to 93.27 percent. If Tianming collaborated, the Trisolarans were willing to leave about ten million humans alive after the invasion and pen them in Australia. This was a breeding population more than sufficient to preserve the seeds of human civilization.

If Tianming refused to collaborate, the Trisolarans were happy enough with their 87.53 percent probability of success. And once they conquered Earth, they would engage in a program of total extermination of all humans and other Earth organisms—though for scientific research purposes they might preserve a few specimens and a genetic databank. They would, they vowed, not only eliminate humans from the Solar System, but launch droplet strikes against *Blue Space* and ensure that human bugs did not survive anywhere in the universe.

"That's an impossible choice!" AA couldn't help interrupting. She saw that no matter which path Tianming chose, he would be judged to have committed crimes against humanity. The only way out was if the humans could somehow seize the slight advantage provided by Tianming's noncollaboration—reducing the chances of Trisolaran success from 93.27 percent to 87.53 percent. But such hope was too dim to be relied on.

"If you had been in my place, what would you have done?" Tianming asked.

"I . . . I don't know. I can't choose." AA shook her head.

"What if you had to answer?"

After a long silence, AA answered. "I . . . I would collaborate."

Such was Tianming's choice as well. Collaboration would ensure the survival of at least a small population, and it was the only way to pass on a warning to the humans. After using sophon surveillance to verify that the Trisolaran claims of conditions on Earth and the fleet's readiness for war were true, Tianming continued to negotiate with his Trisolaran captors. He extracted from them the promise to increase the postconquest human reservation population to fifty million. Only then did he pledge fealty to Trisolaris.

The Trisolarans had no tradition of loyalty oaths or anything equivalent. Because their thoughts were transparent, determining whether someone was loyal was not a problem they ever needed to solve. Since Tianming was not a transparent Trisolaran, however, they wanted a ceremony to mark the special occasion. They scoured records of the ETO from centuries earlier to design a special oath-taking ceremony that could be broadcast to all Trisolarans on Trisolaris and in the fleet. Facing a camera, a grim-faced Tianming raised his fist and declared, "Eliminate human tyranny! The world belongs to Trisolaris!"

One wonders what Ye Wenjie, Mike Evans, and all the other pioneers of the ETO would have thought of that moment.

The Trisolarans also carefully examined Tianming's brain activity to ensure that they weren't being deceived. But after decades of fighting Trisolaran torturers for his own soul, Tianming had learned to disguise his deeper thoughts from Trisolaran probes: He simply tapped into the natural human instinct for self-deception. He had only to recall all the ways he had been mistreated and used by humans back on Earth and imagine the wonderful life he was going to lead as king of the surviving humans. The Trisolaran scientists observing his brain saw fear, anger, and finally surrender based on cost-benefit analysis. Tianming helpfully organized these superficial thoughts into layers: resentment toward humanity and despair, shame at his betrayal, self-justifying arguments, and greed for all the benefits he was going to enjoy later. The thoughts matched what the Trisolarans knew of human psychology and convinced them that Tianming's collaboration was genuine.

Even after he had sworn the oath of loyalty, however, the Trisolarans still refused to show themselves to him. He had never once laid eyes on a Trisolaran. The Trisolarans explained to him that because their two species lived in such different environments, physical presence in the same space would require substantial work. Besides, the two sides could communicate effectively at any time through virtual windows appearing out of thin air, rendering face-to-face meetings unnecessary. Tianming puzzled over why the Trisolarans refused to let him see them and prevented him from looking up any images of Trisolarans. Eventually, he put the riddle aside, as he had more pressing matters to worry about.

The main tasks required of Tianming were creating additional works of art for human consumption, revising and adding polish to diplomatic communiqués from Trisolaris to Earth, and directing some nonofficial exchanges between the two worlds. His existence had to be kept hidden from the humans, and everything he did had to go through a special censoring group of Trisolaran officials to prevent him from secretly passing on intelligence information. Of course, this was exactly what Tianming intended to do: warn humanity that the Trisolarans were intent on conquering Earth.

Tianming soon discovered that the Trisolaran censors were as unskilled at counterdeception as at deception. They could not tell when messages contained hidden meanings, and so it was easy to slip warnings past them in his work intended for humans. During the next decade, Tianming warned humanity many times, often through Sophon herself.

"What?" AA was shocked. "But I don't remember any such warnings!"

"I sent plenty of secret messages! For example, do you remember the science fiction novel *The Trojan Nebula*? It's a retelling of the classic tale of the Trojan War in a space opera setting. I deliberately emphasized the plot point where the space Greeks only pretended to give up, but then used gifts to the space Trojans to disguise their plot of conquest. The book sold well on Earth, but no one seemed to understand the real theme."

"Oh, so that's what that book was about!" AA was amazed. "I did think the book was probably trying to make some political point, but

I thought it was about how Luo Ji and Zhang Beihai had only pretended to give up or run away from the Trisolarans in order to use plots and schemes to triumph over the Trisolarans in the end. I had no idea you meant the opposite."

"Your interpretation was shared by nine people out of ten on Earth." Tianming sighed. "Arrogant humans always imagined themselves as the victors, even when reading fiction. I realized after a while that such hidden messages were too obscure to be of use. As the years went by, I was running out of time. Finally, I took a big risk and wrote a film script that laid out the truth in plain sight: *The Betrayal of Heaven*."

The Betrayal of Heaven was an alternate history tale. In this fictional universe, shortly after the establishment of dark forest deterrence the Trisolarans murdered Luo Ji through a series of clever plots and then invaded Earth. The scenes involving the conquest of Earth by the Trisolaran Fleet were extremely brutal and shocking. Tianming thought he was being too obvious and was prepared to die when the Trisolaran censors reviewed his work. However, the Trisolarans not only approved his script, but even turned it into a holographic film for transmission to Earth. The film did cause a great deal of controversy and debate on Earth, but not in the ways Tianming intended. Critics praised the film as a "profound distillation of Trisolaran rumination on the horrors of their warlike past and the depth of their commitment to humanistic values." It won Best Picture at the Oscars, and Sophon, dressed in an elegant kimono, accepted the award on behalf of Trisolaris.

Not all blame could be laid at the feet of human arrogance and stupidity. The film was a paradox. Since it was presented to Earth as a Trisolaran creation, the more it showed the Trisolarans to be cruel and bloodthirsty, the more humans viewed it as the Trisolarans engaging in honest reflection. Moreover, since everyone knew that the Trisolarans were incapable of lying, the idea that it represented some kind of elaborate Trisolaran plot was unthinkable. Although a few suspicious humans who advocated a hard line against the Trisolarans claimed that the film was a confession of the Trisolarans' true intentions, most people ignored these Cassandras.

But Tianming had one more trick up his sleeve.

Besides composing novels and scripts, Tianming was also tasked with helping Trisolaran scientists come up with false fundamental scientific theories to give to the humans. To be effective, such theories had to appear correct while being wrong, and such advanced deception was beyond the capacity of almost all Trisolaran scientists. They thus left the job to Yun Tianming. But Tianming had only a college degree from the twentieth century, and it was difficult for him to grasp many advanced scientific concepts.

He took inspiration from the *wuxia* fantasy novels he had read during his youth, in which evildoers would sometimes kidnap heroes and force them to teach them supersecret, advanced martial arts skills. The heroes would pretend to teach them these techniques, but alter key breathing instructions or meridian *qi* flow paths to sabotage their efforts. Tianming took real Trisolaran scientific theories and altered the numbers in them—adding a zero to a quark-related constant here, erasing a radical sign from a formula relating to space curvature there, and so on. Given the rate that human science was progressing, it would take them decades before they could experimentally falsify any of these numbers. After the Trisolaran scientists learned his technique, they hailed him as a genius. What Tianming did wasn't difficult, but the scientists were disgusted by the very idea of having to deceive anyone with made-up numbers. Whenever they had to do such a thing themselves, they felt the urge to expel fecal matter.

"So that explains it!" AA said. "When I was working on my Ph.D. dissertation, I was confused by how a constant provided by Trisolaran scientists just didn't fit. I worked and worked at it, and had to give up in the end. I almost failed my defense because of it. It's all your fault!"

Tianming smiled helplessly. "That was actually a deliberate plant from me intended as a hint. While most of my changes could not be experimentally falsified for many years, there were a few changes I

made that could be shown to be nonsense through theoretical deriva-
tion alone. I was hoping that these could serve as clues for human
scientists and alert them to be vigilant against Trisolaran treachery."

"Oh, you idiot!" It was now Dr. 艾 AA's turn to lecture him. "This is
because you only have an undergraduate degree and don't understand
how academia really works. Your way of dropping hints is useless. Even
if someone managed to experimentally falsify your numbers, the immediate response from the professors would be to question whether the
experiment had been designed and conducted correctly. How could
you expect an experiment to disprove theories handed to us by Trisolaran scientists, widely accepted as being at least several centuries ahead
of Earth scientists?

"Other labs wouldn't bother trying to replicate your result, and even
if you could somehow get others to repeat the experiment and show
that the number was wrong, the established theoreticians would come
up with one supplemental theory after another to explain away the dis-
crepancy. They'd built their entire academic reputation and careers
on Trisolaran theories, and they'd defend their paychecks to the death.
Even if they ran out of explanations, they'd demand that you provide
a better theory that could explain the results. And God help you if your
new theory had even one imperfection. They'd attack you like a swarm
of bees and focus on that one weakness and ignore the rest of it. And
even then, you'd be lucky. The most likely result is they would just ignore you as a mere upstart. To get the entire scientific establishment
to recant would require all the old tenured professors to die of old age."

In any event, all of Tianming's attempts at warning humanity failed.
His collaboration did in fact increase the chances of the success of
Trisolaran deception. The silver lining was that it got the Trisolarans
to believe that he really was loyal to the interests of Trisolaris. Tianming's status in Trisolaran society shot up, and shortly before the final
invasion, he gained the authority to direct the sophons to observe Earth
wherever he wanted, though he still couldn't initiate contact with the
humans.

"That was when I saw Cheng Xin being awakened from hibernation. After that, I was with the two of you constantly—"

"I think you mean that you were with *her*," said AA. "I was the third wheel without knowing it."

Her outburst of jealousy was actually rooted in a secret only she knew, a secret concerning Cheng Xin and Yun Tianming. The secret had started two hundred years before her birth, during the Common Era, when aliens existed only in science fiction.

It involved someone who was AA, and also not AA.

"I really did mean both of you," Tianming said. "AA, during all these years you were always by Cheng Xin's side, and I knew you like a best friend. Actually, come to think of it, I felt a sense of familiarity with you as soon as I saw you—"

"Are you telling me I reminded you of Ran Asa . . . something?" AA interrupted.

"Of course not! I don't know how to explain it . . . Maybe you just have a natural charisma that makes people feel close to you. You were always running around, and sometimes the sophons couldn't even keep up—"

"Wait a minute. You were watching us all the time with the sophons?"

"That's right. Through the sophons, I was by your side throughout all the years of your suffering. I experienced your trials and tribulations as though I was there myself," Tianming said. "I know everything. I've always been with you."

This line had deeply moved Cheng Xin when he said it to her, but AA's reaction was completely different. She gazed at Tianming with narrowed eyes. "Did you watch us while we were in the shower? While we were changing?"

Tianming's mouth hung open. He had not expected this development.

"Hey, answer me!"

"No. Really no!" Tianming protested, hoping AA was joking. AA continued to gaze at him suspiciously, and Tianming flushed. "All right.

I confess. I . . . I did look in on Cheng Xin a few times while she was . . . but it was to protect her! I really didn't look at you at all!"

"Oh! So, I was not even attractive enough for you to sneak a peek?" Somehow AA had grown even more angry.

"Um . . . okay, let me amend that." Tianming had no idea how to get out of this minefield. "In Australia, one time, when you two were both in the shower . . . you remember how so many people wanted to harm Cheng Xin back then—"

"So, you did look! You bastard!" AA raised a fist, ready to punch him.

Tianming decided that there was no way out of this trap except to pull AA into another kiss; at last, his answer was satisfactory.

Some time later, Tianming asked, gingerly, "So, you're not mad anymore?"

AA giggled.

"Oh, it's just too easy! Did you think I was really mad? Only you Common Era men think this is a big deal."

Tianming held her and gently kissed her forehead. Tenderness filled his heart. He knew well that AA was trying to keep it light, but the reality was that they were reliving the most harrowing period in human history. Her jokes were intended to relieve the oppressive psychological weight of history, but it was a burden he couldn't set down.

"You were saying that you kept watch over us," AA said. "But not long after Cheng Xin woke from hibernation, that madman Wade almost killed her. Did . . . did you see that?"

The grin on Tianming's face disappeared, and sorrow and guilt took its place. AA immediately regretted it.

"I'm sorry, Tianming. I know it wasn't your fault. You were light-years away and all you could do was to watch helplessly. It must have felt terrible. Don't blame yourself. After all, Cheng Xin ended up all right."

Tianming let out a laugh that was closer to a sob. Under the eerie black domain sky, the sound seemed even more pitiful. "Helpless! Oh,

I wish I was helpless. If I really couldn't do a thing, it would have been a great fortune for humanity. But I was responsible for eliminating the last opportunity for Earth to escape total destruction. Tell me, why shouldn't I blame myself?"

"What are you talking about?"

Tianming's answer shocked AA to the core. "On that day, I saved Cheng Xin."

The other half of the truth behind that failed murder four hundred years ago would be revealed only now.

"Once Cheng Xin awakened from hibernation, I kept on watching over her. I missed her so much that her every gesture and expression seemed entrancing. After being apart for several hundred years, I never imagined I'd see her again in this manner. Though light-years separated us, I felt I was right next to her. For a few days, I did nothing but watch her, until she got that phone call from Wade in which he disguised his voice as yours."

"The phone call . . ." AA struggled to remember.

"Since the caller invited her to meet at an out-of-the-way spot, I grew suspicious and used the sophons to trace the call. Soon, I found that the caller wasn't you at all, but Thomas Wade with a voice mask. I didn't know who he was, of course, but the sophons soon discovered his real identity and other activities. I immediately recognized his motive: He wanted to be the Swordholder.

"When I found out the truth, I was stupefied. I had been so absorbed with Cheng Xin that I failed to notice that she was already being discussed as the most favored candidate for the Swordholder. What an improbable occurrence. Everything had happened because I gave Cheng Xin that star, our star. Cheng Xin could have lived out the rest of her life in peace, but because of that star, she had become a saintly woman possessing a whole world in the eyes of the worshipful public. They even saw her as an embodiment of the Virgin Mother!

"I knew very well that Cheng Xin was exactly the kind of Swordholder the Trisolarans were waiting for. As soon as she won the election, the Trisolarans would attack without hesitation. They believed that she was incapable of pressing the button to initiate the broadcast. And because the Trisolarans believed this, it was irrelevant whether Cheng Xin would push the button at the decisive moment—whatever she chose, it would be too late. Humanity was doomed.

"Because of a star, I pushed my beloved onto the path that would lead to her destruction, as well as the destruction of the human race.

"I followed Wade and saw him conceal an antique pistol under his jacket before he left for the meeting place. I didn't know everything about him, and so I harbored the hope that he was going to use the gun merely as a way to threaten Cheng Xin. He would not use it if she agreed to exit the race. I actually hoped that he would succeed in convincing her to withdraw, which would be better for her, better for humanity, better in every way.

"But then I saw Wade point the gun at her before even speaking, and I knew I was wrong. Thomas Wade was not someone who merely threatened. Laws and morals were no restraints for a man like that, who would pay any price to achieve his goal. Even if she agreed to withdraw, Cheng Xin might tell others what he had done. But a corpse told no tales.

"And the goal he had in mind—to become the Swordholder and eliminate the Trisolaran threat—was also one that I wanted to come true. Ironic, isn't it?" Tianming's smile was bitter.

"But what could you do?" AA asked. "The sophons could do nothing at that moment."

"That's not quite right. Though subatomic in size, the sophons could affect the world in tangible, visible ways. For example, by repeatedly striking the retinas at a high speed, the sophons could cause people to see images. This was a technique used back in the last years of the Common Era. I didn't have the authorization to direct the sophons to do such a thing, or I would have reported Wade's plans to the police, even if that meant exposing my identity. However, I could report what I saw to the Trisolarans. This involved no delay at all, because they had

installed a chip in my brain. If I directed my thought at them, the Trisolarans would understand the situation right away and guide the sophons to protect Cheng Xin."

"But even if you hadn't told them, didn't the Trisolarans keep all the
Swordholder candidates under surveillance?" AA asked.

"They should have. But you have to remember that the Trisolarans
still lacked in-depth understanding of human society. Even if they had
kept Cheng Xin under surveillance, a simple trick like Wade's fake
phone call would have taken them a long time to figure out, and would
have required the use of cloud computing. They wouldn't have responded quickly enough. Also, they had to be cautious. If they were
found to be interfering in the elections using the sophons, that would
have made humans far more vigilant against Trisolaran influence. At
least based on what I knew at the time, only sophons under my control
were at the site of Wade and Cheng Xin's meeting.

"I don't know if the Trisolarans would have done something if I had
not alerted them. But the fact was: In the end, I acted.

"So many thoughts went through my mind at that moment. Other
than my love for Cheng Xin, I had numerous other reasons to save her.
Cheng Xin had a gentle heart, but her will was iron. Who could say
for sure that she wouldn't be a capable Swordholder? Maybe she would
keep the Trisolarans in line even more effectively than Wade. And even
if Cheng Xin was a bad choice, if humanity was set on electing her,
with her out of contention maybe they would elect someone else just
like her. Wade and his supporters still had no chance. Fundamentally,
Cheng Xin's death wouldn't have altered humanity's fate."

"I agree, Tianming. You made the right choice. You were dealing
with history, with the collective decision of all of humanity that set
them on their path to doom. Cheng Xin's own death wouldn't have
changed things," AA comforted.

"I didn't know if I was right, but I knew that I wasn't thinking ra-
tionally. I was just trying to look for excuses to save her. It was . . .
self-deception. After I realized that, I made the decision—or maybe

it's more accurate to say that I thought I made the decision—to sacrifice my beloved and protect humanity. I was already a criminal, and I wanted to carry out my last duty to the human race.

"And so, I watched as Wade shot Cheng Xin. But he didn't aim for her head. His shot shattered her left shoulder instead. I knew that it wasn't out of mercy; the madman enjoyed the suffering of others.

"But Wade didn't realize that he had made a fatal mistake.

"I had thought after enduring so much torture and pain, I would be able to bear any loss. I thought I could watch my beloved die in front of my eyes and still hold fast to my faith. But when I saw blood pouring from Cheng Xin's shattered shoulder, a heartrending love seized me. Rationality and sense of duty disappeared. I knew only that I could not let her die no matter what. Even if all of humanity would die because of my decision, I didn't care. As long as she lived, I was willing to commit the greatest sin in the world.

"Without hesitation, I directed my brain implant to issue a warning to the Trisolarans and send them the feed from the sophons. 'You must stop Wade and save Cheng Xin. Without her your plot will not work.'

"And then Wade made his second shot.

"Wade had aimed his gun at Cheng Xin's head, but somehow, his hand drooped a fraction of an inch at the last second, and the bullet pierced Cheng Xin's belly instead. My sophon informed me that a different sophon had arrived on the scene at lightspeed and was active around Wade's eyes at the moment of the second shot. Clearly, that sophon had been interfering with Wade's sight, causing his aim to be off. Due to the lack of time, the sophon had not been able to make Wade miss Cheng Xin completely."

A puzzle that had long bothered AA was finally resolved. By the time Wade attempted to assassinate Cheng Xin, he had already lived long enough during the Deterrence Era to know that advances in medical technology meant that a head shot was the only way to ensure her death. His first shot could be explained as a manifestation of his cruelty and perhaps as an attempt to disable Cheng Xin's ability to fight back, but his second shot should not have missed. Given his high intelligence and professional skills, it was an inexcusable error. She had later discussed this puzzle with Cheng Xin, and they could find no reasonable answer except the rather strained explanation that perhaps Wade, as a man of the Common Era, was entranced by Cheng Xin's beauty and could not bear to ruin it by shooting at her face. They never could have guessed that the truth involved Yun Tianming directing the sophons to interfere from light-years away.

"The sophon's interference with his sight was very subtle, and based on records of Wade's interrogation, he did notice that his vision had seemed to waver for a split second, which he attributed to his age and nerves. He wasn't very focused on the second shot anyway. Rather, he was upset that his third shot had been a dud. He was certain that if the third shot had fired, Cheng Xin would have died. In the end, he called it all just a series of unfortunate coincidences.

"The dud was indeed a coincidence that also disguised sophon involvement. But in truth, even if he had been able to fire the third shot, the bullet would have simply swept by Cheng Xin's ear. By then the sophon had already created a perfect illusion in his eyes."

There was a kind of perfect symmetry to Wade's failure. He had been responsible for picking Yun Tianming's brain to be sent into the abyss of space, and that very brain, ultimately, frustrated his plan and pushed humanity toward the abyss of annihilation through the unpredictable currents and eddies of history.

"And so, I saved Cheng Xin but also ruined the last hope for humanity. What happened after that . . . you already know."

Tianming dropped his face into his hands and sobbed.

"Oh, I'm so sorry, my darling . . . It's not your fault. You did everything you could." AA's words of comfort came from the heart. After hearing his incredible tale, she really didn't blame him; instead, she loved him even more.

When did I fall in love with such a man, strong and fragile at once?

艾 AA didn't know the answer to her own question. She only knew that the fate she had struggled against for so long had finally arrived. She was going to put aside all doubt and love him with her whole heart. She had to awaken his love with her own, to rebuild his strength with her own.

Should I tell him my secret? AA started to speak, stopped, started again, and stopped again. Through the years, she had lost count of the number of lovers she had taken, but she had never been so nervous as now. She knew that her secret was extraordinary, and would change the way he understood the intertwined history between the three of them as well as the inflection point of humanity's fate. She needed Tianming to understand and forgive her secret, or else the two of them would never share true intimacy, no matter how long they lived together.

She remembered what she had told Cheng Xin back when they first met during the Deterrence Era: "You're thinking of him again, aren't you? This is a new age, a new life. Forget about the past!"

She had been wrong, utterly wrong. Fate liked to play games, and the past, as Faulkner said, was never dead; it wasn't even the past. It always returned and forced you to confront it. That was true of Cheng Xin, of Yun Tianming, and certainly of her.

But perhaps now was not yet the time . . .

Tianming was still lost in the pain of the past.

He spoke to AA next of the ten momentous minutes after the Sword-holder handover ceremony, when the droplets launched their attack against Earth. Although by then the destruction of Earth was already a fait accompli, he kept on hoping that Cheng Xin would press the button and force the Trisolaran bugs to experience the same despair of losing everything in their desperate gamble. At least then he would experience the pleasure of vengeance for the suffering he had endured for the last few decades. He wanted to watch the Trisolarans face the reality of their own end and to see their pain and regret.

He watched Cheng Xin, knowing that all the Trisolarans on the home planet and in the fleet were also watching. One minute passed. Another. Cheng Xin trembled, her hand hesitating over the button. His heart and the whole Trisolaran world trembled with her, but the outcomes they wished to see were polar opposites.

Press it! Damn it. Why don't you press it? Press the button and give voice to justice. Press the button and punish evil. Let them die with us. His voiceless scream echoed in his mind.

But in the end, Cheng Xin did not push the button. Instead, she tossed the trigger away. She stopped shaking, and a preternatural calm came over her. She had made her decision.

The air around Tianming filled with text messages from his Trisolaran colleagues. *Did you see that? Tianming, we won! We won! She couldn't do it. The Earth is ours!*

For a species that despised emotions as much as the Trisolarans, this was an unprecedented display of joy.

Tianming hated Cheng Xin then for the first time. *Why are you so weak? Why won't you at least give us the satisfaction of mutual destruction? Why are you protecting these faithless bugs? Send them to the grave with us! Are you a human being or an alien?*

Somehow, he again recalled that college outing to Miyun Reservoir. On that trip, Cheng Xin had picked up a caterpillar wriggling along the trail and gently deposited it on the grass so it wouldn't be stepped on. Several of the other girls shrieked in disgust, but Tianming had been deeply touched. Because of Cheng Xin, he memorized the identifying characteristics of the caterpillar and later looked it up in a thick reference book in the library. The caterpillar was the larva of a plain gray moth, without the colorful wings of butterflies.

The moth belonged to an ancient branch of the Lepidoptera order, tracing its fossil lineage all the way back to the Jurassic period and even earlier. When the first ancestors of that caterpillar saved by Cheng Xin had wriggled over the soil of Pangaea and spread their fresh wings in dinosaur-filled jungles, there had been no civilization on Trisolaris, and humans would not arrive for eons. The moth had certainly a more ancient claim to the right of existence on Earth. But during the last few decades of the Common Era, human activity had destroyed its habitat, and the species was on the verge of extinction. No live specimen had been seen for many years by the time of their college outing.

Cheng Xin had saved a precious life.

After that, whenever Tianming thought of how Cheng Xin might have saved an entire species, a certain sweetness filled his heart, as though he'd had something to do with it. He imagined the caterpillar turning into a moth, finding a mate in the mountains near Beijing, multiplying for generations, thereby continuing an ancient lineage . . . and Cheng Xin was their protector, their goddess.

He could never have imagined that such an insignificant event was a preview of the fate of two worlds.

No matter how much he thought about her, Tianming did not understand Cheng Xin completely. All he knew was that the woman he loved had not changed over the course of two centuries. She wasn't at fault; those who made her the Swordholder—including himself—were at fault. In a moment, his hatred had turned into self-loathing and guilt.

Messages from other Trisolarans continued to swarm the air around him. This species, so lacking in emotional intelligence, now thought of Tianming as one of theirs. They shared their joy with him without reservation and mocked and ridiculed Cheng Xin.

"To be honest," they told him, "we really had no faith in the princeps's plan back when it was first announced. For decades, Luo Ji had been our nightmare. We knew of no way to defeat him. But his successor! Oh, how weak! How silly! Tianming, thank you! Thank you! You helped us deceive the humans. The pleasure we experienced when that foolish female bug tossed away the trigger for the universal broadcast was greater even than joining during mating! But what was that female bug thinking? Since you were once also a bug from Earth, can you explain her thoughts to us?"

The entire Trisolaran world hung on his answer.

Tianming suppressed the tumult in his heart and said, simply, "She loves you."

"Love?" The Trisolarans were confused. "Are you talking about . . . that emotion that encourages altruistic behavior in order to enhance the reproductive fitness of the species? We experience such emotions, too. But how could such an emotion be applied to an alien species from across the stars? Such an act has no benefit to the reproduction of her species!"

"A man once said, 'Love your enemies, bless them that curse you, do good to them that hate you, and pray for them which despitefully use you, and persecute you.'"

"What . . . what nonsense is that? That sounds like a paradox."

"No, this is a lesson from one of the greatest teachers of our species. Many still believe that this is the greatest truth in the universe, far more important than mere survival."

The Trisolarans did not respond for some time, as though sensing the spiritual power in those words. After a while, they said, "If every species in the cosmos believed this, perhaps there would be no dark forest."

"Perhaps," Tianming said. He gazed at the darkness of space outside the portholes, and he suddenly wondered whether the dark forest existed in only this dim corner of the universe—perhaps only this galaxy, or maybe even the few hundred square light-years at the end of one spiral arm. In the rest of the grand universe, the light of love had long illuminated every leaf, every blade of grass, every trail in the forest. What would such a sunlit forest look like?

He smiled wryly. Such a puzzle was not his to solve. His fate was to follow the Trisolaran Fleet back to the Solar System, where he would live out the rest of his life on Earth as the greatest traitor to the human race. He would endure hatred and contempt all his days, assuming he wasn't killed soon by an angry mob. He would never see the universe outside the region dominated by the war between Earth and Trisolaris. What was the point of thinking about anything else?

At that moment, completely unprepared, he had entered the sunlit forest. And everything—Earth, the Trisolarans, the whole universe—changed.

"What is the sunlit forest?" AA asked. "Does this have anything to do with the mini-universe?"

"I . . . don't know." Tianming shook his head.

He really didn't. But in that moment, his surroundings had glowed as though suffused by a sudden beam of sunlight—no, the light of a thousand suns. He saw that he and the ship he was on had been transported from the abyss of deep space to some indescribable *there*. An infinite space—no, an infinity of worlds—opened for him. If forced to put what he saw into words, he would have said that it was like what an ant must see upon suddenly emerging from a dark tunnel into a bright garden. Every flower petal, every leaf, every dew puddle was a grand world to him, and in that moment, he saw . . . *everything*.

"You entered four-dimensional space!?" Tianming's description reminded AA of the adventures of *Blue Space*.

"No, it's not a higher dimension. I was still in the three-dimensional world, and I've never been to four-dimensional space. But I think that sense of indescribable magnificence I experienced surpassed even four-dimensional space. It's . . . it's . . . it's like what Plato said. Emerging from the dark cave, I saw reality; I saw the infinitely beautiful ocean itself . . ."

AA had never read Plato, but she soon found a suitable comparison. "Is it like the first time you saw me?"

Tianming laughed and kissed her.

After his eyes adjusted to the sudden light that transformed the world around him, the first concrete thing Tianming saw was a solid figure that glowed with a silvery light, suspended before his eyes. At first glance, the figure seemed to be a nearly perfect ringlike structure containing an infinite number of circles of an infinite variety of sizes. But closer examination revealed that the circles were not perfect, because each circle itself was made up of hundreds of thousands of tiny circles, and the circles were connected to each other with complex, subtle structures. The circles appeared at first to be made from translucent lines that glowed with a soft light, but looking closer, he saw that each curve was itself a solid figure with an extremely complex, refined internal structure. It seemed to him that each part of the figure also encompassed the whole, and no matter how closely he looked, he found yet more detailed structures; the level of detail exceeded the capacity of his eyes.

"You mean like a fractal?" AA struggled to map Tianming's description to her own scientific knowledge.

"No, not a fractal. But I guess that's a barely adequate analogy . . . Imagine a blooming rose, and this rose forms a part of one petal of another, much grander rose, and the larger rose is in turn just part of the petal of yet another, bigger rose. Repeat this process to infinity. And then, if you examine the rose you started with, you find that it is formed from smaller roses, each of which is made of yet smaller roses, and so on ad infinitum. Marvelously, each rose in this image is different in shape, size, appearance—as though they belonged to a billion billion different varieties . . . I can't do better than that."

AA shook her head in confusion, unable to imagine what that would look like.

Tianming had dared not gaze at the figure any longer. Its soul-wrenching beauty threatened to overwhelm his identity. He shifted his focus and realized that the circular figure was itself part of a much larger circular structure in midair that filled the entire interior of the ship and continued through and beyond the hull. As in the analogy of the rose, the figures at each level were similar to the figures in the previous level, yet completely different.

As Tianming looked around, he noticed that the entire Trisolaran ship had been transformed by the marvelous circular structures into what seemed to be semitransparency, but wasn't; the bulkheads and hull were still opaque, and he could see their surfaces clearly, but he could see what lay beyond equally clearly, as though images captured by different eyes were stacked together. And what he saw involved far more than two eyes! He could see "through" bulkheads and other barriers and view each nook and cranny of the ship—including places he had never seen—but at the same time he could also see the bulkheads and barriers themselves.

Later, when Tianming found out about high-dimensional space, he wondered if he had indeed been to such a space during that time. But ultimately he came to the conclusion that that was not the case. The incredible structures he saw around the ship were still clearly three-dimensional, though nothing could block his view.

The infinitely rich and complex glowing structure spilled out of the Trisolaran ship in all directions without extending too far beyond it. A few meters outside the hull—which he could now look through—the glowing curves dimmed and disappeared against the background of stars. The structure he could see was evidently part of some grander whole rather than an isolated, standalone component. It was as though the ship had somehow discharged the energy stored within this mysterious structure and caused the part touching it to glow.

As Tianming would find out later, at the moment Cheng Xin tossed away the trigger in her hand the Trisolaran Fleet had noticed, via gravitational-wave sensors, some barely detectable object a few million kilometers ahead of the fleet. The object moved along a complicated, chaotic course, as patternless as Brownian motion. The object's strange movements suggested that it was not a natural phenomenon. The Trisolaran Fleet Command, ever vigilant, placed every department on high alert. The Trisolaran crew members, however, were consumed with wild celebrations, and before they could deploy any defensive measures, the mysterious object changed course and rushed toward them at near lightspeed. It enveloped the several hundred ships of the fleet instantly.

Every ship of the fleet was now "wrapped" in similar eerie, glowing structures. The object adjusted its own speed and course to match the fleet's at the moment of interception so as to stay at relative rest.

However, the structure penetrated only into the ship Yun Tianming was on.

More precisely, it affected only Tianming.

At first, Tianming thought he was once again caught in some hallucinatory dream manufactured by the Trisolarans, but he knew that, given their cognitive habits, they were not capable of producing such an image. The aliens lacked artistic skills and imagination, and when they created dreams to torture or study him, they relied on elements taken from his memories and subconscious, and rarely inserted anything outside of his experience. This magnificent, beautiful three-dimensional figure was far beyond the aesthetic capabilities of the Trisolarans and exceeded human imagination. It couldn't be a dream.

But if it wasn't a dream, how could he see into every hidden corner of the ship? How could light rays blocked by opaque bulkheads enter his eyes? This was simply incompatible with the laws of physics. Tianming's brain churned chaotically as he tried to come up with an answer.

Because light's nature is infinite.

It was a voice—no, a *thought*—in his mind. Tianming knew that the thought didn't belong to him or to any Trisolaran. The aliens often communicated with him by directly injecting electrical signals into his brain, and he was familiar with that sensation. This thought was different. It seemed not to come from outside, but to emerge from the depth of his own mind.

At the same moment this thought came into his head, Tianming experienced a pang of unprecedented pain that took his breath away. It wasn't a physical sensation so much as a spiritual wound. A flood of other thoughts and emotions seemed to press against his subconscious, threatening to erupt into his consciousness and drown out what was left of his rationality: the birth of the universe, the light of heaven, the infinity of the cosmos, the profundity of space . . . unfamiliarity, mystery, terror, sorrow, joy . . .

Tianming was as frightened as Zeus was before Athena burst forth from his head. He held his head in pain, moaning uncontrollably. But he forced himself to focus, and used the Chan-meditation-like techniques he had developed over years of resisting Trisolaran mental torture to isolate himself from the surging torrent of random thoughts. The violent, chaotic thought stream solidified into ice, then melted into a vast, calm ocean.

"Who are you?" he asked, once he had recovered somewhat.

I'm the Spirit.

Treeshade in summer, shadows in moonlight, reflection in water, the self in the mirror . . .

Tianming felt another heavy blow against his mind. His consciousness teetered on the edge of an abyss. He struggled, and asked, "What . . . spirit?"

The Spirit of Light.

Light and shadow, brightness and darkness, a clarion call and perpetual silence, the deep and the firmament . . .

And the Spirit of God moved upon the face of the waters . . .

And God said, Let there be light: and there was light . . .

The light pierced the darkness, but the darkness did not know the light . . .

Still another torrent of thoughts buffeted the surface of Tianming's consciousness, barely held together by his will. Tianming's head felt as though it were about to split open. He finally understood the source of his pain. The voice did not converse with him in the usual sense; instead, it was arranging all his knowledge and memories to express concepts that he could not understand. Every moment brought him a nearly infinite amount of information, like that infinitely complicated glowing figure in which a grand meaning contained within it smaller understandings, and each smaller understanding was made up of even smaller significations. The various conceptual levels were connected to each other through refined, dense webs of logic, and not a single detail was extraneous. But his biological cognitive machinery was so limited that he could grasp only the most superficial layer and turn it into human linguistic symbols. The rest of the semantic structure inundated his mind, where memory and imagination stirred up a typhoon of emotions and ideas.

This was an experience the human mind was never meant to endure. Indeed, if he had not developed superhuman levels of self-control and psychological fortitude in his struggles against the Trisolarans, he would have long collapsed into madness.

"Are you a messenger of God?" Tianming asked, panting, his voice full of awe. Though he was not a Christian, he had gone to church a few times with his mother when he was a child. He remembered a minister who had told him, "If you pray, God will hear you. He will send angels to fill your heart. 'And there appeared unto them cloven tongues like as of fire, and it sat upon each of them . . .'"

Vengeance is mine; I will repay, saith the Lord.

And now, at the moment when the Trisolarans had betrayed humanity's kindness and love to invade their home, to eradicate them from the face of the Earth, it was time for the God of justice to appear. The bugs would get what they deserved.

And the next thought almost drove him to ecstasy:

From your vantage point, yes, I am the Spirit of the Master.

But then, Tianming's dream was shattered.

The Master is dead; I am only the dead Spirit.

Tianming was now growing somewhat used to this strenuous way of having a conversation. Gingerly, he asked, "Are you an extraterrestrial?"

Patiently, his interlocutor corrected him.

No, I'm the Spirit.

"What do you mean exactly by 'Spirit'?"

The answer this time was an incomprehensible concept that could not be translated into any fragment of language. Again, his mind was slammed by a tsunami of nearly paradoxical ideas: *an arid ocean, the end of the Earth, a war between dragons and giants, the treasure of the gods, songs hidden in stones . . .*

He screamed and fell to the ground. "Stop! Stop doing this to me. I can't bear it." Tianming didn't know if he was speaking or merely thinking.

This is the only way for us to communicate. In our universe, this is the simplest and most efficient means of exchanging information. But intelligence in this universe has devolved far too quickly, and you can receive ideabstractions only with great difficulty.

Tianming did not know what an "ideabstraction" was and didn't dare to ask. But he seized on the phrase "our universe" and asked, "Are you not from this universe then?"

Another incomprehensible ideabstraction struck him, and Tianming's head felt near explosion. Gasping, he wiped the sweat from his brow and said, despairingly, "I can't tolerate the ideabstractions. Why don't you go talk to *them*?"

By "them" he meant the Trisolarans, of course. Tianming had had enough. He had thought he could endure any kind of mental and physical torture, but he felt weaker than a baby against the power of ideabstractions. *Forget it. The Earth is gone. I don't care about universes or masters, or anything at all anymore. Let those heartless Trisolarans try making sense of fucking ideabstractions.*

I tried. But they are far weaker than you mentally and cannot even grasp a single ideabstraction.

"Why?"

They are bugs.

"Bugs" was how Tianming contemptuously thought of the Trisolarans, and the Spirit had borrowed the term and now endowed it with a very strange ideabstraction. Surprised, Tianming suddenly realized something. He looked around.

Under the influence of the strangely glowing structure, he could see into every nook and cranny of the ship. Yet something was missing.

He couldn't see any Trisolarans.

He couldn't see anything that might be a reasonable match for an intelligent extraterrestrial: not little green men, not walking lizards, not octopuses with eight clawed hands. Nothing.

Could this ship be without any Trisolarans? How was that possible?

Tianming noticed something about the design of the ship that he had not paid attention to before. There were no conduits or corridors similar to those found on a human spaceship. Other than the large compartment he was in, there were very few other cabins or open spaces. Most of the ship consisted of thin tubes and tiny cubbies, some the size of matchboxes, others as large as a drawer in a dresser. Each cubby contained numerous tiny apparatuses or devices glowing with an eerie light, each about the size of a grain of rice. Some of the grains squirmed and writhed on the floor . . .

They are bugs.

Tianming sucked in a breath. Everything finally made sense.

Those silvery "devices" were the Trisolarans, each not much bigger than an ant.

For centuries, the best human minds had dedicated their efforts to the study of the Trisolarans, and an area of intense focus in this research involved the physiology of the aliens. Although scientists on Earth could not gain access to any specimens, they were able to make some educated guesses based on what they knew of Trisolaris—an environment far more inhospitable to life than Earth's: the Trisolarans were capable of rapidly dehydrating and rehydrating; the Trisolarans could be arranged into a living formation computer; and so on. The consensus among human scholars was that Trisolarans were likely diminutive in size, perhaps no more than fifty centimeters in height. (Some scholars went as far as suggesting that they were about the size of rats.) In some science-fictional films depicting the Trisolaran invasion, the aliens were portrayed as large praying mantises with sharp mandibles and claws.

But no one had ever seriously suggested that Trisolarans were only a few millimeters in length. It seemed obvious that a creature about the size of an ant could not possibly evolve a complex brain or build an advanced civilization. In this matter, however, the human scholars committed a major error. Trisolaran cognition was very different from individual-based, human cognition. Because Trisolarans enjoyed a direct correspondence between thought and expression, their communication was highly efficient. They thus evolved a collective intelligence that was the foundation of the living-formation computer innovation. Although each individual Trisolaran could to some degree think independently, they primarily relied on exchanging information with each other to build up a large collective databank that was their primary source of intelligence. Moreover, after joining during mating, each set of Trisolaran parents split into multiple larvae who each possessed some memories inherited from the parents. This adaptation allowed young Trisolarans to acquire basic living skills in a very short period of time, because their relatively simple brains handled modular memory effectively.

But human scholars were not entirely wrong in their speculation. The adaptations that allowed the Trisolarans to survive extremes in planetary climate and build a lasting civilization also limited the size and development of individual Trisolaran brains. As a result, the Trisolarans lacked imagination and creativity, and relied primarily on proven techniques and collective wisdom from the past. Historically, the Trisolarans rarely experienced the kind of technology explosion common in human history. Even if they left their troubled home world and found a more hospitable environment, they would continue to be merely social insects, albeit insects with civilization and technology.

This was why the Trisolarans were intent on exterminating the humans even at the risk of triggering a gravitational-wave universal broadcast. They well knew that even if the two species broke through the dark forest state between them to coexist peacefully, humans would soon catch up to and then surpass them technologically. In addition, the Trisolarans experienced an atavistic terror of the gigantic humans, each of whom could flatten hundreds of Trisolarans with a single palm.

The relatively low intelligence level of individual Trisolarans had been masked from the humans by the unfamiliarity of their alien society. Humans simply could not imagine that a civilization far more advanced than theirs had been constructed by individuals who were much "stupider" than humans. This was the fundamental reason the Trisolarans had concealed from the humans their appearance, which they viewed as a weakness.

Now, however, the Spirit had revealed the truth with its mysterious light. The individual Trisolaran mind was too weak and barren to bear the power of ideabstractions, and the Trisolarans, panicked, couldn't engage in the kind of large-scale group communication that would have formed a collective intelligence.

Yun Tianming was in fact the only life who could converse with the Spirit.

"What are these . . . fibers?" Tianming pointed to the intricate, glowing structure all around him. One of his fingers accidently struck one of the fibers, and a colorful splash of light flickered around the site. Startled, Tianming examined his finger and saw that it was unharmed. The glowing fiber had simply passed through his finger and hand as though it wasn't made of matter at all.

This is my projection into this universe.

Tianming struggled to make sense of this. "You're saying that your body isn't in this universe? You *are* from another universe?"

I come from Eden. What you see is the projection of Eden.

"Eden? Like from the Bible? Is this a metaphor of some sort?"

I come from the Eden of this universe, the perfect world at the beginning.

A torrent of ideas followed "perfect world": the dazzling stars of galaxies; a placid lake; a classical garden arranged in perfect symmetry; the Venus de Milo; Mona Lisa's smile; Ingres's *The Source* . . . Then came scenes taken from his dreams: a heavenly kingdom found in a flower; a magnificent palace built over a rainbow . . . The sights piled one on top of the other, but each captured only a trace of perfection.

Finally, the Spirit gave up trying to convey the sense of a "perfect world" to him and left his mind with only a simple geometric figure: a crystalline sphere floating against a dark background, the perfect circle.

"Where is this world?" Tianming asked. Even with such an imperfect glance, he already sensed the indescribable beauty and grace of that world.

Destroyed.

The visions he had seen earlier returned, but now changed: dark clouds covered the stars; a storm wrinkled the lake; Venus's arms broke; Mona Lisa cried . . . blood and fire appeared; the demons of hell sacked the heavenly kingdom; darkness corroded the perfect silvery sphere from two sides until it was only a thin sheet, and then a line, and then just a pinprick of light.

Then the bright dot expanded rapidly and filled his consciousness before fading into darkness. But in this new night, millions of galaxies appeared: the Milky Way, the sun, the moon, the Earth . . . Tianming knew he was witnessing the birth of his world.

Tianming was too shocked to speak. The whole universe that he knew was but an insignificant fragment of the perfect world, the remnants of countless cycles of destruction.

Like Guan Yifan and Cheng Xin later, Tianming learned the deep secrets of the universe.

"Who destroyed that perfect world?" Tianming asked.

The Lurker.

"The Lurker?" Severe pain seized Tianming's head again. He understood that he was approaching the limits of understanding, but he refused to give up. "Why did it destroy Eden?"

I don't know. Only the Lurker knows.

"Why is it called the Lurker? Is it an individual or a civilization? Or something else? Doesn't every civilization conceal itself in the dark forest?"

At first, in the perfect world, there was no dark forest as you understand it. But rebellious intelligences brought forth the dark

forest . . . The perfect world collapsed, but the traitors escaped.
They are concealed in this universe.

The Spirit gave Tianming systematic and complete information,
but Tianming could only comprehend a minuscule portion of the
flood. The rest was beyond the limits of his mind.

"Wait!" said AA, who was having trouble breathing. "Are you telling
me that some piece of the civilization of a previous universe has survived into our universe?" Although she didn't know what Guan Yifan
had told Cheng Xin on the spaceship, she did remember the words of
the Ring: *The fish responsible for drying the sea are not here.*

She was beginning to understand what the Ring had meant.

"I don't know . . . or maybe I once did, but no longer remember."
Tianming said, dazed.

Tianming asked the Spirit, "Is there a way to end the dark forest and
rebuild the perfect world?" He seized upon this last hope as Earth's
salvation.

Yes.

"How?"

Destroy the Lurker, and I will be able to restore the perfect world.

"How do we do that?"

The Spirit was silent for a moment before answering.

I need you to become a Seeker . . .

Another tsunami of thoughts and images inundated him. He understood only the first half of what the Spirit said before the ideabstraction broke down his last mental defense. He was drowning in a sea of
ideas, grasping for anything to keep himself afloat. He struggled, but
no one came to save him. The Spirit insisted on injecting increasingly
more information into his head, and didn't seem to care as he sank
under the infinite storm of dreams and thoughts. A second before he

blacked out, something seemed to illuminate his mind. He thought he understood an important point, but it was too late. His brain activated the final defense of its own sanity, and he lost consciousness.

"And then?" AA asked. She had also been taken by the dream of restoring the perfect world. If the perfect world could be recovered, perhaps it was also possible to recover the Solar System and Earth, and the human world of the past . . .

Tianming shook his head. "Then nothing. By the time I recovered, the Spirit and its projection were both gone."

He looked around; everything had returned to normal. The Trisolaran ship was once again sailing through the darkness of space, with no trace of the Spirit anywhere to be found. According to the Trisolaran surveillance data that Tianming examined later, the glowing structure had vanished not long after he fell unconscious. Gravitational-wave sensors detected the structure moving away from the Trisolaran Fleet at near lightspeed along a strange course, and it was soon dozens of astronomical units away. Even Trisolaran technology could not follow it.

When the Trisolaran scientists analyzed the Spirit's movements, they discovered that if they eliminated the effects of the motion of the Milky Way Galaxy, the Local Group, and the Laniakea Supercluster, the Spirit's course was extremely simple. In other words, relative to the universe, or at least the immediate vicinity of the fleet, the Spirit likely was stationary in an absolute frame of reference. The near-lightspeed motion was the result of the universe moving, not the Spirit. It was only after the Spirit had discovered the Trisolaran Fleet that it had approached on its own to make contact.

What kind of unimaginable power could cause such a structure to remain still and resist the power of galaxies in motion?

Further research revealed that the Spirit itself was without mass. The mass effect detected by the gravitational-wave sensors was caused by a force field around it. The force field isolated the structure from the rest of the universe, but the isolated region was almost without volume. The immense glowing structure had been projected from a tiny point.

The Spirit was telling the truth: It was only a projection, without substance.

The Trisolarans understood that the Spirit was from a highly advanced civilization. That civilization seemed to bear them no ill will and had attempted to communicate with them, but no Trisolarans had been able to converse with its representative, the Spirit. More than two hundred individuals had gone insane trying, and had to be dehydrated and incinerated; their cognitive organs collapsed as soon as they received an ideabstraction, and their biology was such that they couldn't even protect themselves by blacking out.

Even Tianming seemed to lose his mind. It took more than a month for him to fully recover his faculties. But the Trisolarans had not given up on him in the interim. In surveillance recordings of the encounter, they saw Tianming muttering and looking thoughtful, which suggested that he had successfully carried on a conversation with the Spirit.

Patiently, they cared for Tianming, hoping to glean some advanced technology from his recollections of his conversation with the superior civilization. After he recovered, Tianming recalled the early part of his encounter with the Spirit, but despite his best efforts he couldn't remember what he had learned. Repeated interrogation, hypnosis, and dream analysis all yielded little of use. The Trisolarans scanned his brain in detail and found that a large region previously devoid of neural activity had been filled to the brim with information. But the Trisolarans could make no sense of the data stored there, and the region seemed to be completely isolated from the rest of his brain.

Only a dread of inescapable doom was left in Tianming's mind. Though he couldn't recall exactly what he was afraid of, the sense of foreboding persisted and often woke him at night.

As time passed, bits and pieces of the information hidden in

Tianming's subconscious surfaced. One day, when the Trisolarans described to Tianming the marvels of their new lightspeed spaceships, Tianming suddenly remembered the following fragment from his conversation with the Spirit:

The most primitive means for achieving security is . . . use the speed of light . . . turn yourself into a black hole . . .

Tianming had no idea what it meant to "turn yourself into a black hole" and no guess as to how that related to lightspeed ships; he only knew there was a connection. But after mulling over the matter for some time—or perhaps guided by some mysterious force—he finally understood the secret of black domains.

He proposed revealing a new way to escape from the dark forest state of the universe to the Trisolarans—he needed them to verify his theory—in exchange for their promise to cease the invasion of Earth.

"Impossible," the commander of the Trisolaran Fleet informed him. "We will not give up our grand invasion of the Solar System for some vague promise of a 'safety notice.' In any event, the Earth bugs have not initiated the universal broadcast and will never be able to do so. We don't need such a measure, at least not now."

"Then you'll never get any information out of me concerning that godlike civilization," said Tianming.

"Well, we do want what you have to tell us," said the Trisolaran commander. "But we won't buy it with the hard-won Earth. Perhaps we have something else you want." He showed Tianming some scenes transmitted by the sophons on Earth: the worldwide chaos after the droplet attacks; the anarchy that reigned everywhere; the millions of deaths caused by panicked stampedes, massacres, streaming refugees, famines . . .

One scene in particular caught Tianming's attention. In a suburb somewhere on the west coast of the United States, a young woman who resembled Cheng Xin was found in the midst of a group of refugees.

Someone shouted, "That's the bitch! That's the bitch who fucked up everything!" And then the mob surrounded her and began to punch and kick, tearing her clothes off . . .

A man by her side screamed and sobbed for the mob to stop. "Please! She's not Cheng Xin! We're Koreans!" But it was useless. Like a pack of wild beasts, the mob scratched and tore and bit and chomped until they literally gnawed chunks of flesh from her . . .

"That woman isn't Cheng Xin," the Trisolaran commander informed him. "Right now, she's under the protection of the United Nations. But we think the situation on Earth is going to deteriorate further, and perhaps she'll meet a fate even worse than the woman you just saw."

Tianming clenched his fists in rage. He had no choice.

"All right," he said through gritted teeth. "I will tell you about the safety notice, but only after you direct Sophon to form an Earth Security Force to maintain order and prevent needless deaths. They must also protect Cheng Xin and her friends."

And so the Trisolarans received the secret of the cosmic safety notice: reduction of the speed of light. Since they didn't know that the location of Trisolaris would soon be exposed to the universe, they didn't put much effort into constructing a black domain. Later, after the Trisolarans found out about the gravitational-wave broadcast from *Gravity*, they did try to create a black domain, but because the dark forest attack came so quickly, they couldn't get it ready in time.

The humans, who had plenty of time, also missed this chance.

Tianming dreamed that he had turned into the "Seeker" that the Spirit had described. He flew through the universe aimlessly, searching for the hidden "Lurker." He swept by millions of stars and through spiral arm after spiral arm, finding nothing. In the end, he arrived at the center of the Milky Way Galaxy, where the core was orders of magnitude brighter than any spiral arm, where millions of ancient stars orbited and twirled around one another, in a dazzling cosmic dance . . . and in the heart of the core was an invisible, monstrous black hole, whose existence was revealed by its massive accretion disk. Humanity's sun, if placed on this disk, would be nothing more than a speck of dust upon a vinyl record.

Tianming realized that the disk was so thin as to be two-dimensional. Like a record, it spun slowly around the black hole. He approached the disk to examine it in more detail and saw that it was inscribed with a massive picture that portrayed every stellar system in the universe in astounding detail. Coming closer, he could discern individual space-ships and odd-looking extraterrestrials. Every detail of every object was perfectly captured in this picture, though it was all lifeless. Tianming felt a powerful force tugging at him, trying to drag him into the pic-ture. He struggled to get away, but the irresistible force, like a magical spell, gradually pulled him down toward this two-dimensional plane.

He fought hard, and at last escaped the mysterious spell and departed the surface of the accretion disk. But immediately he fell into the fright-ening black hole, passed through the event horizon, and plunged into the lightless abyss . . . In the darkness he saw a ghostly fire, and by its light a warlock wearing a black cape and a pointy hat and grinning vi-ciously. He was busily painting on a large scroll, which he unfurled and pushed out of the black hole as he filled it with his work. The un-rolling sheet of paper joined the accretion disk, and he saw that the sun, the moon, and the Earth had all been painted into the picture. The warlock glanced at him, and instantly an image of Tianming appeared in the painting, including each strand of his hair, each wrin-kle in his skin, even the frightened expression in his eyes. He was then pulled into the image, merging with his own two-dimensional portrait . . .

Tianming screamed and woke from his nightmare.

Some have already been dimension-reduced; others are being dimension-reduced; still others will be dimension-reduced, until finally . . .

This is all part of their plan . . .

Snatches of his conversation with the Spirit peeked out of a hidden part of his mind, almost forgotten, and suddenly he understood the meaning of the dream.

"Dimensional strike!" AA's voice quavered. She recalled the terrible sight of the Solar System's collapse: flattened Neptune and Saturn like a pair of eyes; the space cities whose every detail had been preserved in two dimensions; snowflakes bigger than the moon . . . Tianming's absurd dream had become reality, and that reality was even more terrifying than the nightmare.

Tianming nodded, his expression grave.

"If your dream was really a message from the Spirit, then the effects of the two-dimensional foil will never end. Does that mean"—she shuddered in horror—"that the whole universe will eventually be only two dimensions?"

"Not only that." Tianming sighed. "The Spirit told me that our own three-dimensional space is the result of a dimensional strike. The original universe was of a higher dimension."

"So you're saying . . ." Although what Tianming was suggesting wasn't hard to understand, it was simply too incredible to accept. "The universe was originally four-dimensional? Those four-dimensional fragments were how things used to be?"

She recalled the words of the Ring:

When the sea is drying, the fish have to gather into a puddle. The puddle is also drying, and all the fish are going to disappear.

"Not four-dimensional, but ten-dimensional," Tianming said. "The four-dimensional universe is itself the result of many other dimensional strikes. The ten-dimensional universe was the perfect world that was the home of the Spirit. Pythagoras called ten the perfect number, and now I finally understand what he meant."

"Ten dimensions!" AA was only mildly surprised. For her, the difference between four dimensions and ten was just an abstract difference between two numbers.

"Human scientists had already discovered that fundamental particles have ten dimensions, though only three dimensions are fully extended, with the rest curled up within the quantum realm. Scientists had proposed many theories explaining this fact, but they never guessed that this was the result of intelligent life waging destructive warfare, which led to the collapse of the fundamental structure of the universe."

AA soon thought of a more practical question. "Do you think the Lurker was responsible for the dimensional strike against the Solar System?"

"I'm not sure." Tianming thought about this some more. "It's possible that other advanced civilizations can also produce dimension-reduction weapons for dark forest attacks. But I can guess that the goal of the Lurker is to reduce the dimensions of the cosmos."

"Why?" AA asked.

"I don't know." Tianming let out a long sigh. "That's probably the biggest mystery in the universe. Do you remember the sophon blind zones?"

艾 AA nodded. Blind zones were mysterious regions of space that caused the sophons to lose their power, and they could be found all over the universe. As an astronomer, she was very familiar with them.

"What do you think the universe would be like without such blind zones?"

AA shuddered. This hypothetical once had very practical implications. At the beginning of the Deterrence Era, scholars debated the question of whether the dark forest state applied across the whole universe. One influential group of scholars believed that any species that reached the technology level of the Trisolarans should possess the power to produce sophons or sophon-like communication techniques that relied on quantum entanglement. After billions of years, the most advanced civilizations should be able to send sophons to every corner of the universe, and with instant communication being available everywhere, the dark forest state should not persist. They believed that the threat of dark forest strikes that worried both humans and Trisolarans were only a phenomenon local to this part of the universe that had been improperly assumed to be universal.

The discovery of the blind zones negated their theory. A variety of evidence indicated that the blind zones were the result of artifice rather than nature. They darkened the universe and eliminated the hope of instant communication. Therefore, the dark forest state probably did persist everywhere.

The blind zones also posed challenges to dark forest theory. Imagine: If a civilization was powerful enough to establish blind zones across the universe, then such a civilization was also capable of influencing the whole universe. Such a civilization had no need to establish blind zones at all. It could simply use sophon-like technology to surveil and monitor the entire cosmos and slaughter any baby civilizations as they appeared, thereby achieving perfect security.

Unless it had some other goal in mind.

"Is it possible that . . . that the Lurker is responsible for setting up blind zones everywhere, thus ensuring the dark forest state persists in the universe?" AA voiced the most terrifying possibility of all.

"I have no idea," Tianming replied. "But it is possible. Without a universe-spanning, superadvanced civilization going around to set up these barriers, it's unlikely that the dark forest would still be with us. But if that was what really happened, it must have been an unimaginably evil civilization. Not only did it destroy Eden, but it also treated the whole universe as its plaything. Could Satan be real?"

They continued to discuss and debate clues regarding the identity of the Lurker without coming to any conclusions. It was possible that even more knowledge was buried in Tianming's mind, but even now, he could recall only a few fragments here and there. The deepest secrets of the universe were still hidden.

After a while, AA asked, "Did you make up that story about Princess Dewdrop and Prince Deep Water to warn humanity about dimensional strikes?"

"I didn't make up all of it. Like I said, some parts of that story came from my dream."

"Why didn't the Trisolarans suspect you? The metaphor in the fairy tale was so transparent."

"One of the biggest weaknesses of the Trisolarans is their lack of imagination," Tianming explained. "If they already knew about dimensional strikes, then they might have been able to see through my story. But they had no knowledge of it at all. If even humans couldn't solve my riddle, the Trisolarans had no hope at all. They had no experiences to draw on."

Tianming didn't tell the Trisolarans what he had figured out, because he couldn't see how the reality of the universe's loss of dimensions could contribute to solving the conflict between the Trisolarans and the humans. The Trisolarans had scanned this dream, but among numerous other strange dreams Tianming had had it didn't stand out. The Trisolarans couldn't figure out the true meaning of the dream, and Tianming wasn't going to help them.

Then, more than a year later, the Trisolaran Fleet finally received news of *Gravity*'s broadcast. The plan to invade Earth had to be abandoned because both the Earth's and Trisolaris's locations had been exposed. Though Tianming no longer had to bear the moral responsibility for the destruction of Earth by the Trisolaran invasion, he realized that he had been burdened with an even heavier duty: saving humanity from the dark forest strikes that would be launched by more advanced civilizations.

Although the Spirit had come from the ten-dimensional universe, it had extensive knowledge of the three-dimensional universe as well. It informed Tianming of seven possible types of dark forest attacks. The two-dimensional foil was one of the more advanced techniques. During the year after his encounter with the Spirit, Tianming was able to gradually recall the Spirit's teachings of all seven techniques. The Trisolarans made it a priority to obtain the valuable intelligence from Tianming to prepare defenses, and he shared six of the techniques with them. However, he kept dimensional strikes a secret from them, instinctively feeling that this was the technique most likely to be used against the Solar System. He also knew that if he revealed all that he knew to the Trisolarans, they weren't going to pass on the knowledge to the humans in the Solar System. Nor would they permit him to contact them.

In exchange for informing the Trisolarans of six dark forest attack techniques, Tianming extracted from them the precious opportunity to meet Cheng Xin through the sophons at a distance. During their meeting, he carefully mixed his dream with other elements and created three fairy tales for Cheng Xin. He constructed elaborate metaphors to conceal the intelligence concerning the black domain and curvature propulsion, but the rather naked description of dimensional strikes was beyond Trisolaran knowledge and understanding.

"But what if you had guessed wrong and advanced civilizations didn't launch a dimensional strike against the Earth but used one of the other techniques?" AA asked.

"It wouldn't have been a big deal. Lightspeed ships fast enough to escape a dimensional strike would have been sufficient to escape the other techniques. This was the safest way. I couldn't pack everything into my stories, and so I had to pick the most critical details."

"But there's another problem . . . During your meeting, you said that you and Cheng Xin knew each other from childhood and often told each other stories. But if the Trisolarans could look through your memories, wouldn't that lie have stood out?" For personal reasons, 艾 AA had long wanted to ask this question. But she hadn't dared to probe too deeply into Tianming's memories. Now she finally asked, but it wasn't for herself, it was for . . .

Tianming gazed up at the dark dome of the sky and thought of the past that already seemed to belong to another self, a self that had died long ago. Softly, he said, "That . . . wasn't entirely a lie. I did know a girl like that."

When Yun Tianming was a child, a girl briefly appeared in his life. A neighbor's niece, she was three years younger than he. One summer break, she came to his city to visit her aunt and got to know Tianming, who often recounted to her stories he had read in books: the Trojan War, King Solomon's treasures, the Knights of the Round Table, the Merchant of Venice, and so on. Most of these had come from the thick books his classics-worshiping parents had made him read.

The girl also told him many stories she had made up: the naughty prince, the clever princess, the happy pudgy pig, and so on. She was too young to create coherent plots, and some of these were barely stories at all. Tianming loved listening to her. He had no friends, and his parents refused to let him play with children whose families his parents thought "low class." Tianming's parents disliked his spending so much time with this girl, because he was in middle school and they wanted him to focus on his studies. However, by then his parents were in the midst of their own messy divorce and couldn't spare the energy to keep a close eye on him.

The girl stayed in Tianming's city for only a month. At the end of summer break, before she returned home, the two promised to see each other the next summer. However, not long after, Tianming's parents finalized their divorce, and he moved away with his father. He never saw the girl again. Even more socially isolated, he retreated into himself and sealed away those memories.

But the young girl left him a trace of warmth from his childhood, and the stories the girl told him were the prototypes for the fairy tales that he later told Cheng Xin.

"To kill Princess Dewdrop, Prince Evil used black magic. Many, many meteors fell from the sky . . . The little fairy descended to earth to protect her, and made a magic umbrella out of clouds to protect the princess from the falling rocks . . .

"Later, the little fairy, the princess, and the captain of the guards went to No-Worry Island, where they found Prince Tall Mountain. The prince had also learned magic, and he could make himself as big as a mountain or as tiny as a grain of sand . . .

"Prince Tall Mountain killed Prince Evil, and then the princess and the captain lived happily ever after. Prince Tall Mountain and the little fairy also left the kingdom and returned to No-Worry Island, where they married . . ."

Tianming could still vaguely recall the serious, childish face of the girl as she told him stories. He also remembered asking, "Why didn't Prince Tall Mountain marry Princess Dewdrop?"

"Ah, you weren't listening!" The girl pouted. "Prince Tall Mountain is Dewdrop's brother! That's why Prince Tall Mountain has to end up with the little fairy, and Princess Dewdrop has to end up with the captain . . ."

There was little resemblance between this young girl and Cheng Xin, but after meeting Cheng Xin, Tianming sometimes fantasized that they had known each other when they were very young and lost touch as they grew up. He projected the image of Cheng Xin into his childhood memories, and the girl he had known briefly one summer became the image of young Cheng Xin. The Trisolarans' understanding of his memories did not extend to differences this subtle. As Tianming deliberately confused his own memories, he persuaded the Trisolarans that he and Cheng Xin did know each other as children, and the Trisolarans didn't detect his misleading memory edits.

"What about that young girl?" AA asked, a tremor creeping into her voice. "Did you . . . did you ever see her again?"

"No. The world is so large; what are the chances of meeting her again? I can't even remember her name. I just know that everyone called her Weiwei . . . What's wrong, AA?" Tianming saw that her eyes were full of tears and her breath had quickened. Even the way she gazed at him was odd.

AA's smile was closer to a grimace. "You can't even recall her name? Let me help you there. Her name was Ai Xiaowei."

Tianming had once thought that after he'd found out the truth of the ten-dimensional universe, nothing else could ever shock him. He was wrong. We are moved most not by the grand mysteries of the universe, but by the emotional personal truths that define our individual pasts.

Tianming's mind went blank. He had never imagined that the young girl he once knew would have any connection to 艾 AA, who wasn't even born until more than two centuries after that long-ago summer.

But AA was right. That young girl was indeed named Ai Xiaowei. Tianming hadn't really forgotten her name; he simply hadn't wanted to recall the details. Subconsciously, he still preferred to maintain the absurd illusion that the girl had perhaps been the young Cheng Xin.

How does AA know this? Tianming stared at her and recalled the strange sense of familiarity that he always felt with her. This couldn't be just a lucky guess. Gradually, as he examined AA, he saw traces of Weiwei in her features. Back then, Weiwei had been only eleven, and even if 艾 AA was the same person as Ai Xiaowei—an impossibility— he would have had a hard time recognizing her.

It was inconceivable for AA to be from the Common Era. Although he had not researched AA's past in detail, he could tell that her habits, speech, and general demeanor were without a doubt the products of the world two hundred years after his own childhood. It was impossible to fake such characteristics. From what he knew of her—both by observing her through the sophons earlier and by spending every moment of every day with her for the past year—he was 100 percent certain on this point.

Unless she went into hibernation as an eleven-year-old? But that was . . . the 1990s, far too early for hibernation technology.

Countless theories pressed themselves against Tianming's awareness, but none of them seemed plausible. He had to ask her for the truth, but he found himself incapable of even forming a coherent sentence.

"How . . . you . . . what . . ."

"Stop asking questions," said AA, and gently placed a hand over his mouth. "Just listen, all right? There's something important that I've been meaning to tell you for a while, but I didn't know how to bring it up.

"You don't need to feel guilty about the destruction of humanity, my darling. The one who is responsible isn't you or Cheng Xin; it's . . . me."

"What are you talking about?!"

"I've played a far larger role in these events than you realize. But I have to start from the Common Era. There's one more person involved in the complicated relationship between you and Cheng Xin during the Common Era—she's the 'Lurker' in that story.

"Her name was Ai Xiaowei, or Weiwei, as everyone called her. She was a girl who loved fairy tales and who loved to fantasize. One summer break, she went to visit her aunt in another city. Her aunt lived in a tall building, one in a forest of other towers just like it. The first few days after her arrival, she still didn't know the neighborhood well. One day, she knocked on the door of an apartment she thought was her aunt's. When a strange boy a few years older opened the door, she realized that she had ended up in the wrong building. Terrified, she began to cry. The boy brought her into the living room and offered her some ice cream, which calmed her down."

As Tianming recalled the scene of meeting Weiwei for the first time, the corners of his mouth turned up in a smile. The intense curiosity to find out the truth gave way to the warmth of reminiscence.

"The boy offered to bring her home, but Weiwei couldn't tell him the exact address; she only knew that it was in a building nearby. They checked out corresponding apartments in other towers in the area, but either no one answered, or something else in the building told her that it wasn't the right one. Finally, having run out of ideas, the boy brought her to the garden at the foot of his building, hoping that her aunt would come looking for her.

"They waited for hours. To pass the time, the boy told Weiwei several stories. Weiwei also told him some stories she had made up. They were having a good time when Weiwei's aunt finally showed up to take her home."

AA paused and asked, "Tianming, do you remember the story that Weiwei didn't finish telling you?"

Tianming shook his head. He really couldn't recall such a detail.

"The story was called 'The Star-Giver.' In it, a young princess met a strange boy on a tour of the kingdom. The boy told the princess that he was going to give her a star, but she didn't believe him, and told the guards to drive him out of her sight.

"After a series of other plot twists, the princess's stepmother, the queen, wanted to kill her, and the princess escaped the palace. The queen chased after her at the head of an army. Just as the princess was about to give up all hope, a rope ladder dropped down from a star. The princess grabbed the ladder and climbed, higher and higher. The queen and her army also climbed up after her. Finally, a hand reached down from the star to pull the princess up—it was the strange boy. The two cut the rope ladder, and the queen and her army tumbled to their deaths.

"The princess and the boy lived happily ever after."

A long-buried memory gradually surfaced in Tianming's mind. He recalled this story and much more. During the thousands of subjective years of his long sleep in Trisolaran captivity, this crude, childish story had made its appearance in his dreams under various guises. He had thought it an echo of his gift of a star to Cheng Xin. However, it now seemed that the truth was perhaps the opposite: He had come up with the idea of giving Cheng Xin a star because subconsciously he remembered this story. It had changed the course of his life without his awareness.

"After that, Weiwei often went to look for you to play, and that summer break became one of her fondest memories. You probably remember that you and she had promised to meet the next summer, but the next year, when she returned to your city, you had already moved away. You lost touch after that."

AA was no longer her lighthearted, carefree self. Her voice was calm but laced with the chill of autumn. A breeze blew by them, as sorrowful and lonesome as a night breeze on Earth. Tianming felt his eyes grow moist.

"And so ended a childhood friendship. More than ten years passed, and Weiwei graduated from college and found a job. Coincidentally, she ended up in the same city as you. She hadn't seen you since the summer she was eleven. Occasionally, she thought about the boy she had known once and wondered how he was. What kind of work was he doing? Was he married? It was mere idle curiosity.

"But then, she and you met under completely unexpected circumstances."

"We met again?" Tianming was shocked into silence. He couldn't remember ever seeing the grown-up Ai Xiaowei. But as he stared at the sweet and sorrowful face before him, the vague sense of familiarity grew stronger. Finally, a hazy scene from deep in his memory came into focus.

"AA, I . . . I did see you! During the Common Era, I must have seen you somewhere!"

Tianming's thoughts were thrown into chaos as he struggled to search through his memories for the owner of that familiar face. High school, college, his company, the hospital . . . before leaving Earth, his life had been very simple, and he knew few women his age. But he couldn't remember anyone who looked like 艾 AA, though he was sure now he had seen her somewhere. Where?

Was she a student who had sat across the table from him at the library? Was she someone who had gotten on the elevator with him at work? Maybe a roommate that had shared an apartment? Faces flitted by his mind's eye, but none matched. He could recall only a fragment: a face that resembled AA's looking at him with a curious expression. But when was that? Where was it? Everything except that face had disappeared from his memories.

AA laughed self-mockingly. "I was hoping you would remember at least a little. It was an important event in your life, possibly the most important. On that day"—she pointed in the direction of the setting sun—"you bought this star."

That day!

The memory, long sealed away, came to life, as clear as though it were yesterday: He had gotten the text from Hu Wen, and then he asked Dr. Zhang for permission to leave the hospital. He took a taxi to the UNESCO Beijing office, walked into the headquarters for the Stars Our Destination Project, and met the director of the project as well as Dr. He . . . Wait, wasn't there someone else? Who? *Think!* He walked into the office, and the first person he saw was . . .

Oh, God, could it be?

Tianming sucked in a breath. He pointed at AA and stuttered, "You . . . you were the receptionist! But . . . but . . . but how?"

"That wasn't me." AA shook her head. "That was your childhood friend Ai Xiaowei, my . . . previous incarnation."

Tianming had no idea what AA meant by "previous incarnation." He thought back to that day: Yes, the receptionist was especially solicitous, bringing him tea and making sure he was comfortable, stopping from time to time to gaze at him, sometimes curiously and sometimes admiringly. He couldn't remember much else. Her extraordinary beauty should have left him with a deeper impression, but he was a dying man, his mood ashen, his mind on Cheng Xin. He had never thought of the receptionist after that, and he certainly couldn't have guessed that the woman had anything to do with 艾 AA.

"To you, she was only a stranger passing through your life, no different from the thousands who brush by you in the street every day. But that encounter with you changed her life.

"Xiaowei didn't recognize you at first. When you told her that you wanted to buy a star, her reaction was that you were some rich man's son who had run out of ways to spend money. Though superficially enthusiastic, she laughed at you behind your back. Later, when you explained to Dr. He that you were buying the star for a woman, she remembered the story she had told you. As she looked at you some more, she thought you looked familiar. But you refused to reveal your name. She only knew that you were buying the star for a woman named Cheng Xin. By the time she finally got up the courage to ask you if you were who she thought you were, Dr. He had already taken you away outside the city to look for the star you had bought.

"That was the last time she laid eyes on you.

"Later, Weiwei figured out your name based on the information you left in the files, and she knew she was right. She thought you had somehow gotten rich, and she didn't want to bother you. Then, the next day, Dr. He told her that he could tell you were suffering from some terminal illness, and probably didn't have too much time left. She felt such pity for you and wanted to find you. But other than your name, she didn't know anything about you.

"Finally, do you know what she did? She had the brilliant idea of getting on a website called 'Facelook' and searching for your name. Since your name was pretty rare, she managed to find your page."

"I don't think you mean 'Facelook,'" Tianming said. "I think it was 'Facebook.'"

"I think you're right. What kind of website was it?"

"It was a—" As Tianming struggled to explain the ancient technology, he also tried to remember when he had signed up for such a thing. He didn't remember doing much with it. It probably just contained some basic information about himself.

"I see," said AA. "I think you also linked yourself to a friend named Hu Wen? He seemed to be a good friend in college—"

"My only friend," Tianming interrupted.

"He was a clever businessman, and he had thousands of friends on

Facebook. After a few days, Weiwei finally managed to get in touch with Hu Wen and got your contact information. She rushed to the hospital but found out that Cheng Xin had already taken you away. The official explanation was that Cheng Xin had taken you to the United States for advanced treatment.

"Weiwei thought it was the most beautiful love story she had ever heard, but she didn't know the truth . . . Anyway, she was deeply moved by your hopeless romanticism. And, perhaps from that day, she . . . fell in love with you, and vowed to find you. She didn't know what she hoped to accomplish, only that she wanted to see you again. She couldn't have known that you had already been launched into deep space.

"The rest of her life was rather tragic. For the next three or four years, she searched for you. She quit her job and went to America to look for Cheng Xin. But by then Cheng Xin had gone into hibernation, and she made no progress. Finally, she heard a rumor that you had also entered hibernation to go to the future. Weiwei had no way to go to the future, so she had to give up.

"Later, she made a decent life for herself. She started an internet business and made some money. A man fell in love with her, and though he had little money, he was almost as romantic as you, which moved her. She became his lover and enjoyed a period of happiness. Soon, however, the man was diagnosed with a terminal illness, and she gave him all her money to find a cure. Unfortunately, that turned out to be just a scam, and the man disappeared with the funds. I imagine if he hadn't reminded her of you, she wouldn't have fallen for such a simple trick."

Tianming sighed, and AA's voice grew even more somber. "The worst is yet to come. Weiwei tried to recover, but she found out that the con man had given her HIV. After a few years of suffering, she died."

Tianming would never have imagined such a terrible end for his friend. He remembered again that happy woman and her sunny disposition as he opened the door to the office of the Stars Our Destination Project. How could he have known at that moment the fondness between them in their past or the unpredictable future that lay ahead?

"She knew that her life was ruined, but she refused to accept it. Absolutely refused." AA's eyes glistened with tears.

"When she died, she was just over thirty, childless. She sold what little property she had left to preserve some stem cells in a gene bank. She hoped that she could be cloned in the future and live a new life. At the time, many harbored similar hopes, and there must have been millions who could not afford to go to the future but who spent what money they had to leave their cells in gene banks across the world. Later, during the Great Ravine and the Crisis Era, no one cared about them, and no one bothered to clone them. Most of these cells were destroyed in the intervening years, and it was by pure luck that Ai Xiaowei's cells were preserved.

"Based on the contract she signed, her cells would only be preserved for two hundred years. If no one was interested in cloning her by then, the cells would be destroyed. Two hundred years later, in the middle of the Deterrence Era, humanity had returned to a stable track, and humanism and associated values were once again on the rise. Some people formed a genetic protection league and argued that the cells waiting to be cloned were all potential humans with the right to life, and they raised some money to clone us. Lacking funds to clone everyone, they were forced to clone only about one to two percent of the surviving cells. Maybe because I was pretty, I was picked. And so, two hundred years later, I carried on the dream of my previous incarnation—"

"Why do you keep on using that term?" Tianming asked.

"It's just a habit for us clones. If our donors were still alive at the time of our birth, we'd call them parents; but if our donors were dead, we'd call them previous incarnations. Maybe it's a way for all of us, orphans really, to find for ourselves some roots in time. My previous incarnation left me a long letter in which she told me her life story in detail. She also reminded me not to be foolish, and to live an easygoing life. This was how I became familiar with your story from the Common Era and how I knew about the star named DX3906. It was why I chose it as the topic for my dissertation." AA fell silent, as though she found it hard to broach the next topic.

Seven centuries' worth of fate's vicissitudes churned around them. What had seemed a coincidental meeting turned out to be a love sealed in a past life. At that moment, they each seemed to hear the heartbeats of the other.

To break the awkward mood, AA laughed carelessly. "Please don't misunderstand me, Tianming. 'Previous incarnation' is just a term we use, but I'm not Ai Xiaowei. I'm certainly not that foolish. I just want to let you know that you've never been alone. Even in the years when you felt most isolated, someone was always thinking of you. When your frozen brain was hurtling through the darkness of space, someone was searching for you back on Earth—" She stopped herself from uttering the sentence she really wanted to say next.

It wasn't Cheng Xin.

After a long silence, Tianming whispered, "I'm Jean-Christophe, and she's my Antoinette."

After a while, AA took a deep breath and continued to reveal her secrets.

"Actually, I was responsible for waking Cheng Xin. After I found out that Cheng Xin had gone into hibernation during the Common Era, I tried to look for her. The year of the Swordholder election, I finally located her record. She wasn't an important figure, and the government had no plans to wake her. But I wanted her to be revived so that I could meet your first love, a woman my previous incarnation never got to meet. That was also when I discovered the two planets orbiting DX3906—one of them the world we are standing on now. Since hundreds of extraterrestrial planets were discovered every year, most people paid no attention to such news. However, I sent the discovery to a reporter friend, who dug up the story of how Cheng Xin had been given a star nearly three centuries earlier. She wrote up the story with enough exaggerations to arouse the interest of the public and the government. As a result, I managed to get Cheng Xin awakened from hibernation. I made sure that I was assigned to help her so that I could get to know her better, and unexpectedly, we became friends . . . I never intended to generate so much public fervor as to make her the Swordholder."

Blood drained from Tianming's face. He never could have imagined that Cheng Xin's friend was responsible for her fate.

"I'm sorry, Tianming. I was just curious. I really didn't mean to . . ." AA's voice trailed off, her expression full of sorrow.

Tianming couldn't speak. He tried to imagine how everything would have been different if AA hadn't interfered or if she had awakened Cheng Xin a few years later.

Even if some other Cheng Xin–like candidate stood for election, maybe Thomas Wade's gamble would have paid off, and the Earth wouldn't have been destroyed? Then perhaps Cheng Xin could have lived out the rest of her life peacefully on Earth . . . or maybe . . .

"I've carried this secret with me for so many years. In a way, the one most responsible for the destruction of Earth wasn't Cheng Xin or you, but me. I tried to comfort Cheng Xin after the disaster, but a lot of things I said were for myself. If I hadn't been so curious, things would have been so different."

Tianming closed his eyes, looking somber as he tried to remember something. AA, her face pale, said, "You can blame me, but please don't blame Ai Xiaowei. She had nothing to do with any of this. She wanted to tell you—"

"No," Tianming interrupted her. "I won't blame you. I was just thinking now that if someone else had been the candidate for the Swordholder and Wade tried to kill them, I would have saved them, too.

"There is a cause for every effect, AA, but not all causes are responsible for all effects. To trace all causes and all effects is to end up in a twisted web with no end. No single person can make decisions independently; every choice is the result of changes and inputs from everyone else. Viewed from a higher vantage point, Cheng Xin was chosen by all of humanity to be the Swordholder, and her choice was humanity's choice, her values humanity's values. Viewed from specifics, Cheng Xin made her choice because you woke her; you woke her because of me; I was sent into space by Cheng Xin; Cheng Xin went into hibernation because of me . . . and the one who started it all was Wade, who wanted to kill Cheng Xin. It's a tangled mess.

"Stepping back even farther, Ye Wenjie, Luo Ji, and Zhang Beihai all could have made different choices in history and changed the course of humanity. Who knows what could have happened? But it's pointless to debate such hypotheticals, because we have to live with the facts: Humanity is gone . . . No, not quite. Based on what you've told me about Guan Yifan, it seems that the Galactic humans have already pioneered a new path. But the Earth and the Solar System are no more, and that is an unchangeable fact."

"True," said AA. "No one can change that."

"But that isn't everything!" Tianming grew excited. "Perhaps the Earth and the Solar System are only insignificant beginnings. A thousand years from now, ten thousand, or even longer, those who look back on the destruction of Earth may see it only as another fall of Constantinople. Do you know about what happened there?"

AA nodded, but then shook her head again. "I read about it in middle school textbooks, but I don't know any details."

"I knew only a rough outline at first," said Tianming. "But while on the Trisolaran Fleet, I had endless time to devote to reading and thinking about the fate of humanity, and I found history to be an unpredictable guide. More than twelve centuries ago, in the year 1453, Constantinople fell to the forces of the Ottoman Empire, thereby extinguishing the Eastern Roman Empire, which had lasted more than a thousand years. As the fortress of Europe fell, the entire continent trembled before the might of the Ottoman invaders.

"No one at the time could have thought that this tragedy would turn out to be the catalyst for the rebirth of Europe and the beginning of modern civilization. Many scholars from Constantinople fled to Western Europe, bringing with them the best that Hellenistic-Roman culture had to offer and facilitating the start of the Renaissance. Also, since the Ottoman Empire lay between Europe and Asia, European merchants had to find new ways to travel to India and China, thereby opening the Age of Exploration. Only a century later, Spanish, Portuguese, Dutch, and English explorers had already circumnavigated the globe, creating in the process a new civilization capable of wonders that would have been unimaginable to the Romans, let alone the denizens of the Middle Ages.

"With that history in mind, who can say that the destruction of the Solar System isn't the beginning of a far more brilliant and magnificent Galactic Age?"

AA's eyes also glowed with excitement as they enthusiastically debated the future of humanity. Maybe humans would hop from one planetary system to another, spreading colonies across the whole Milky Way and founding new republics, empires, and federations; or maybe they would build a superfleet containing billions and billions of ships and wander forever among the stars; maybe their civilization would advance to be nearly like gods, capable of reversing time and changing history . . .

In the end, Tianming returned to the present and laughed self-mockingly. "All our speculation is useless. We will never leave this black domain for the rest of our lives, and if there is going to be a Galactic Era, we will have turned to dust long before its advent.

"Still, I must thank you, AA." Tianming's gaze on her was full of love. "You liberated me from the shackles of the past. My love for Cheng Xin weighed me down, as did my guilt over humanity's destruction. But as long as we did what we believed was right, there's no reason to bind ourselves with the empty sentiments of duty. Not you, and not me. Let's seize the present and cherish the joys of the future, all right?"

AA laughed, though tears spilled from the corners of her eyes. They embraced, closer than they'd ever been before.

After a long time, AA gently whispered to Tianming, "At the end of Xiaowei's letter to me, she asked me to tell you something if I ever managed to see you."

A message that had traversed seven hundred years in the stream of time was about to be retrieved. Tianming's heart beat wildly.

"She said, 'I wish you a happy life.'"

Tianming said nothing, but AA felt something wet fall against her bare shoulders.

"We will lead a happy life," Tianming said.

Night didn't last long on Planet Blue. Rosy fingers appeared over the eastern horizon, and the long-suffering lovers who had only just truly fallen in love were bathed in a gentle, warm glow. All around them, the vegetation of Planet Blue stretched and faced east to begin its morning cantata: quaint and amiable, like a celebration of romance composed just for the two of them.

The pair of lovers, absorbed as they were by each other, did not notice a moving dot of light disappearing into the brightening sky along with the fading stars. On that ship traveling at the reduced speed of light in this black domain, only a second had passed. Cheng Xin and Guan Yifan had still not recovered from the terror and shock of the sudden expansion of the death lines. Yifan cradled Cheng Xin's head and their faces were pressed against each other. They were like that bottle the Tibetan boy tossed into the river, washed downstream by the heartless passage of time, not knowing where they would end up.

The two pairs of lovers, divided by the river of time, grew farther and farther apart. Perhaps they would never meet again.

Perhaps.

PART II

The Way of Tea

Another sunset.

The sun, half hidden behind the mountains, dimmed gradually. The cantata of Planet Blue's life continued as usual. Everything looked pretty much as it did that evening of conversation sixty-one Planet Blue years ago—about the same as forty Earth years.

Our protagonists, however, were no longer young.

Silver-haired 艾 AA, wrapped in a woven-grass mat and wearing a peaceful smile on her wrinkled face, lay unmoving in a long hole dug in the ground. She took up the left side of the hole, leaving the right side empty. Yun Tianming, his back bent with age, sat next to the grave, deep in thought.

This morning, his wife had finally shuffled off this mortal coil and entered the long sleep, and he was about to join her.

He recalled the first time he had seen her, so many years ago; he relived their first embrace, that night when they first revealed their hearts to each other, the years after filled with joy and labor; he recited the words they had carved into the cliffs last year: "We lived a happy life together."

He remembered a benediction from years earlier, so long ago that it seemed to come from the beginning of history: "I wish you a happy life."

Have I lived a happy life?

After a lonely childhood and youth, after the time of despair in the hospital, after an inhuman existence as a frozen brain plunging through the depths of space, he had endured decades of torture aboard the Trisolaran Fleet, a long nightmare that lasted tens of thousands of subjective years. Then came the even more excruciating experience of watching helplessly as his people were hunted to the verge of extinction. Finally, with the help of that magical ring, he left the Trisolarans and came to this star, where he and Cheng Xin had promised to meet.

But it was a different woman who greeted him. He learned of the complicated web fate had woven between them, fell in love with her, and then spent the second half of his life by her side.

Measured by material standards, the second half of his life wasn't happy, either. They spent the first two years of their time together on Planet Blue in relative ease, but in the third year, the magical ring vanished.

The "ring" wasn't solid; it was made of a glowing strand of insubstantial fiber. Like that mini-universe, the ring had been a gift from the Spirit.

Find the Lurker, and counter it . . . the ring will help you . . .

When he woke from a last nightmare involving the Spirit, he deciphered a few more of the ideabstractions planted in his mind by the Spirit. Perhaps triggered by his awakening mind, the magical ring suddenly appeared on his finger. Its silvery glow was like a memory of the Spirit itself.

He had spent several days figuring out how to operate the ring. It was controlled by his mind alone, and exhibited signs of being powered by incredible technologies. For example, the ring could open the entrance to the mini-universe; decipher and control the computer systems on the Trisolaran ship; modify the structure of the ship to endow it with unparalleled speed and other features; materialize any small objects he desired . . . In the end, he discovered only a tiny portion of its full capabilities. He knew that to unlock the full potential of the ring would require speaking to it in ideabstractions, an ability that he lacked.

That the Spirit had given him such a powerful tool was puzzling. Sure, the Spirit itself was probably just an artificial intelligence that needed his help to fight the mysterious Lurker. But why did the Spirit think he could shoulder such a burden? How could a single human being, not much more significant than a wisp of ionized gas in the grand universe, be expected to counter a devil that had destroyed god-like civilizations? It was absurd.

Slowly, more locked-away memories came back. Back then, as he lay half crazed, half comatose, he hadn't agreed to the Spirit's request. Even in his semiconscious state, he wasn't so deluded as to think he could war against such a powerful dark civilization. He recalled the conversation between them.

Why are you telling me these things? I have no wish to be a Seeker.

I'm running out of time. With each passing second, I grow weaker. This universe is too sparsely populated. After I leave you, I don't know when I'll meet another life suitable for the task.

I'm not suitable. It's an impossible task! I refuse.

I don't need your assent.

I don't understand . . .

You'll understand eventually.

He had never understood what the Spirit meant. Once, he had thought that the Spirit had seen something deep in his mind suggesting that he would eventually agree to this impossible mission. By the time he finally left the Trisolarans behind, crossing the galaxy in his lightspeed ship, he had been full of courage and idealism, vowing to destroy this evil cosmic Satan. But in the end, the black domain trapped him on this tiny planet, and he had lost all will to fight, hoping only to find some happiness in the rest of his life with his beloved.

Maybe his change of mind was the reason the magical ring had disappeared? Or maybe something in this black domain planetary system defused the ring's power? After all, $E=mc^2$. If the speed of light decayed to only a few kilometers per second, perhaps energy was also greatly reduced. Tianming was no theoretical physicist and couldn't work out the answer for himself. But in this world where light was incredibly slow, anything could happen. Even the all-knowing Spirit probably couldn't have predicted everything.

The same phenomenon that took away the ring's power was probably also responsible for draining all the power from his spaceship. After the disappearance of the ring, he and AA had no more access to advanced technology. For the last few decades, they had lived a pre-industrial, no, almost a Stone Age existence.

Their only way out would have been to enter the mini-universe, but they had sealed off that path themselves.

Many years later, when Cheng Xin landed on this planet, her guesses regarding the life of Tianming and AA were partially correct. At first, AA refused to enter the mini-universe. After hearing Tianming's story, the small universe seemed to her more like a tomb than a gift. She didn't want to cross an ocean of tens of billions of years to witness the end of the universe. She had the premonition that if they entered the mini-universe, Tianming would be obsessed with the Spirit's mission and go to the end of all that is known and unknown to fight against the Lurker and save this dimension-reduced cosmos. She refused to go in because she didn't wish to see the man she loved accept an impossible task and collapse under the weight of failure.

Tianming, of course, couldn't abandon her and enter the mini-universe by himself. And so they waited one day, then another.

Later, after the ring on Tianming's finger vanished, it was impossible for AA to enter the mini-universe at all. The ring was the only way for Tianming to alter the entrance restrictions, and only he and Cheng Xin were authorized. AA would forever be kept out.

He thought it might be possible for him to enter the mini-universe and alter the authorization from within, but he dared not leave AA for even one moment. He knew that time flowed inside the mini-universe independently of the grand universe, and even if he came back out as soon as he entered, millions of years might have already passed. Waiting by the entrance for him, AA would have long turned to dust.

He couldn't abandon her, and he feared being alone even more. The only choice was for them to grow old together on the planet.

In the third year of their time on Planet Blue, AA became pregnant. Without the protection of the magical ring, it was very difficult to ensure a healthy pregnancy. After two months, AA suffered a miscarriage; she lost so much blood that it was a miracle she survived. The experience injured her, and she couldn't get pregnant after that.

Tianming thought this was a blessing in disguise. If they had children, without access to advanced technology, it would have been difficult for them to thrive on this desolate planet. Moreover, they would have to resort to sibling incest to reproduce, and genetic defects would accumulate. He could just imagine how, after a few generations, their descendants would have lost all traces of civilization and lived a nasty, brutish life no different from beasts. He shuddered at the very prospect.

And since he knew that several hundred light-years away, Galactic humans—the fortunate descendants of the crew of *Gravity*—were continuing and extending human civilization in new colonies, he didn't feel that he had the duty of ensuring the survival of the species.

He and AA had loved each other and lived a life together. Was it a happy life?

Materially, they had lived like the most primitive tribes. Spiritually, their days had been filled with pain and terror: the terror of losing the other and having to go on, alone. When sleeping, they clutched each other; when awake, they never let the other out of sight. Even not seeing the other person for a few moments was a cause for panic; even the smallest cold in the other person felt like knives twisting in the heart. There was no seven-year itch in their marriage; each day, they gazed at each other's faces in tenderness, no matter how wrinkled their skin grew or how white their hair turned, because they knew that each look might be the last.

Yet the pain and terror were also mixed with indescribable tenderness and sweetness. There was no love in the universe, no romance in the galaxy, that could compare to theirs.

Yes, they had lived a happy life.

But the last day had come. This morning, after AA fell asleep in his lap, she did not wake up again. She died peacefully, with a smile softening her face. He didn't feel much sadness, knowing he was going to follow her soon.

There was nothing holding him to this world anymore. He should have died long ago—seven centuries earlier, to be exact, in that euthanasia room. He had been granted a reprieve of seven hundred years and lived a longer life than anyone, Cheng Xin excepted.

The only person who loves me in this world is dead. There's nothing for me here.

For a few moments he had the thought of entering the mini-universe to get a look at that mysterious shelter from the ravages of time. But an old man's fear seized him, and he was terrified at the thought of being parted from his wife in time and space, of dying alone at the end of the universe, not even having his wife's corpse to comfort him. He was an old, dying man, weak, powerless. There was nothing he could do in the mini-universe. He wanted to go in peace. Curiosity died in him; he already knew too much.

He knew what the end of the universe would look like. Millions of glowing galaxies would flatten into a magnificent scroll, which would roll up into an endless silvery thread, which would shrink into a bright dot, and then wink out. Even the darkness would then vanish. There was nothing after "the end," nothing.

He saw the future of the universe: There was no heat death, no big crunch, and certainly no new big bang. The universe would become nothing and disappear into the void. This was the truth about dimension reduction: The destruction of every dimension devoured an infinite amount of matter and energy, leading to nothingness.

Vanity of vanities; all is vanity.

He remembered a poem he read in college, a long time ago:

This is the way the world ends
Not with a bang but a whimper.

None of this had anything to do with him. In a few hours, he would join the meaninglessness that outlasts all, and no one would even be around to whimper for him.

Why worry about dusting
*When the mirror is nothing?**

To bury AA and himself, Tianming spent the whole afternoon digging a grave. He was too old for such hard labor, and he was soon drenched in sweat and panting heavily, and he had to take many breaks. He thought of simply falling down where he was, but the thought of dying without a grave still seemed wrong to his human habits, even if he was only benefiting the worms of Planet Blue.

The sun sank in the west, and the fiery glow faded. Finally, the light went out. It was time.

Holding a snipped lock of 艾 AA's hair in his left hand, Tianming crawled into the grave next to AA. With his right hand, he brushed the earth piled at the sides back into the grave to cover their lower bodies. Finally, with trembling hands, he took out a rusty piece of metal that he had taken from his rusty old spaceship.

He gazed up at the sky, where a few cold, bright stars winked from the gloom. None of them was the Sun, which had been extinguished more than three hundred years ago. As a young man, he had never thought the Sun would die before him.

But he also saw a twinkling, moving, silver speck, which he knew

---

Translator's Note: A koan by Master Huineng (638–713 CE), the Sixth and Last Patriarch of Chan Buddhism.

was Cheng Xin and Guan Yifan's ship. For the last few decades, he often saw the ship orbiting their planet at this black domain's reduced lightspeed. For them, these last few decades would be only a few minutes, or maybe even a few seconds.

One day, they'd land on Planet Blue, and maybe they'd discover the mini-universe. Would they enter and wait for the end of the universe?

Would they also become husband and wife and live out the rest of their lives like AA and he had?

No matter. By then even his bones would have turned to dust. He hoped that they would see the words AA and he had carved on the rocks.

It was time. With his last ounce of strength, he plunged the jagged piece of metal into his carotid artery and pulled it out. Blood burst from his body, carrying his life force into the soil of this planet.

They would become a part of this world forever.

Before losing consciousness, Tianming smiled at the sky. He gave his blessing to the woman he had once loved with all his heart and soul, a blessing she would never hear.

"I wish you a happy life."

The end.

Vanity of vanities; all is vanity.

In the beginning was the void, and he was one with the void. But in the void, a voice from a long-ago memory appeared, growing gradually clearer.

. . . flesh and blood cannot inherit the kingdom of God; neither doth corruption inherit incorruption. Behold, I shew you a mystery; We shall not all sleep, but we shall all be changed, in a moment, in the twinkling of an eye, at the last trump: for the trumpet shall sound, and the dead shall be raised incorruptible, and we shall be changed. For this corruptible must put on incorruption, and this mortal must put on immortality.

He seemed to be in the church that his mother took him to occasionally in his childhood. Somehow, he had fallen asleep during the minister's droning sermon. How long had he been asleep? Half an hour? Why didn't his mother wake him?

There was light. The shapeless void turned into substantive darkness, and then the light pierced the darkness and diluted it. His hazy, confused mind still churning, he felt light filter through his eyelids. Something was shining *at* him.

He opened his eyes. The traces of his dream faded away. He found himself in a hole in the ground, and underneath the eerie, dark sky, a few scattered rays of starlight landed in his eyes.

No, not starlight. The source of the light was right next to him.

He lifted his arm. On his left ring finger was a translucent, glowing band.

Within the ring were smaller rings, and so on without end. But he felt no weight, because the ring was only a projection, without substance.

Finally, he remembered. It was his magical ring, which had somehow returned.

He remembered everything. This wasn't his old church, but another planet, another time.

Light from the ring lit up half of his naked body. He felt that something was different, changed. He lifted up his head to look, and was stunned by what he saw.

Smooth skin, black hair, a muscular chest . . . and the feeling of inexhaustible strength. He looked and felt younger, healthier, more full of vim and vigor than he had ever felt in his life. He pulled his legs out from under the dirt covering them and found them bulging with muscles, like the legs found on Greek statues of Olympian athletes.

Amazed, he turned and saw the figure of the woman curled next to him. Silver-haired, half buried, skin so wrinkled that she resembled his grandmother. No one would believe she was his wife, and before he had fallen asleep, he had been just as aged and decrepit.

His hand shot up and felt the skin around his neck. It was perfectly smooth. No cuts; no scars.

Nothing at all.

He pressed his fingers against his neck, but he could not feel his arteries pulsing. Terrified, he moved his hand to his chest: no heartbeat.

He felt the impulse to gasp for breath, but he wasn't breathing at all. He put the back of his hand against his forehead, and it felt as cold as the rocks on this alien planet.

Jumping up, he jogged around the grave. Everything felt normal— in fact, his movements were so smooth, so energetic, that it felt strange. When he was a young man, his sickly body had never obeyed him so well.

He ran toward a nearby lake. As soon as his brain had issued the order, the muscles of his body coordinated themselves to carry it out with utter efficiency. He ran as gracefully as a cheetah, as steady as an arrow. His legs carried him over the blue grass faster than the best sprinters in the history of the human race. A few seconds was enough for him to cover several hundred meters.

By the gentle glow from the ring, he looked into the pale-yellow lake.

He was eighteen again.

No, even at eighteen he had not looked this handsome or strong. He was another Apollo, full of a divine glow that came from within.

After a few seconds of stunned silence, he began to laugh. He laughed so hard that he thought tears would flow from his eyes, but he had no more tears.

He should have known. After the Spirit had invested so much in him, it certainly wouldn't let him go so easily.

A delay of a few decades, a few centuries, even several millennia, was nothing to the Spirit. It had simply allowed him a brief respite to say good-bye to the world he was familiar with. Battles in the war he had been drafted into lasted billions of years; what was a human life span compared with that? It had patiently waited for him to die so that it could resculpt his body, so that the corruptible could be raised incorruptible, so that he could better serve its purpose.

He was immortal.

He recalled the mission assigned him by the Spirit, and he was happy to obey. There was no more doubt, fear, or hesitation. He was willing to devote the rest of his—however much time he had in this form—to this seemingly impossible enterprise.

He understood that this willingness wasn't voluntary. He had been branded with some kind of inescapable mental seal by the Spirit. He could only obey, and do so happily.

Yet, other than that, he hadn't lost his individuality or sense of self. He was still Yun Tianming. Only now did he understand what the Spirit meant when it had told him:

I don't need your assent.

It truly didn't need his assent; it had simply manufactured his assent.

Truth after truth awakened in his mind; he understood the causes of every step that led him here, but he was powerless to resist. He knew that he would become a loyal slave of the Spirit; he would dedicate himself to the realization of its breathtaking goal.

He stood up and dashed over the blue plain like a breeze, finding himself moments later standing next to a rocky outcropping carved with words. "We lived a happy life." AA and he had worked hard last year to carve the words as a message for Guan Yifan and Cheng Xin, when they would return millions of years in the future.

The past had been nothing but a brief prelude; his life was only starting. Compared with what was to come, the last few decades and even the ten thousand years he spent dreaming were but a momentary flash.

There was a faintly glowing frame about the height of a human next to the rocky outcropping. The frame was empty, but he knew that a new world lay inside. As soon as he entered, he would leave Planet Blue behind forever.

How many worlds had he left? The Earth of the Common Era, the countless worlds he had dreamed, the Trisolaran Fleet . . . what was one more to the list?

At last, time had begun, again.

In the silent night, he hesitated before the door. Remembering something, he turned around and ran back to the grave to stare at the aged body within. He wanted to cry but his new body was incapable of tears. Determinedly, he pushed the rest of the soil piled next to the grave back into the hole, covering up the face of his wife forever.

After the hole was filled in, he placed a ring of rocks around the site so as to mark it, though he knew that he was unlikely to ever return. He was about to go to another—universe.

AA, I'm going to leave now. But know that you'll be with me forever.

He stood before the grave for a long time, until the eastern sky glowed again with the promise of a new day, and then returned to the glowing frame.

This time, without hesitation, he stepped through and disappeared into the emptiness within.

And so Yun Tianming entered Universe 647, his universe, for the first time.

Outside time, our universe

In this universe, the heavens had not yet divided from the earth, and all was primordial chaos. Light wasn't yet distinct from darkness, and even time had not yet begun to flow.

Tianming stood at the other shore of the universe, gazing back at the "door" he had come through, but found to his surprise that the door had already vanished. He was wrapped up in a pale mist, suspended in midair, as though inside some unformed virtual reality. There was no depth in any direction, and he doubted if he still was made of matter.

But soon, a voice came to him—out of the void or out of his mind, he couldn't tell. "Seeker Yun Tianming, welcome to Universe 647. I am its manager." The voice was placid and neutral, devoid of any identifying characteristics. He couldn't even tell if it was male or female.

Universe 647. Tianming smiled wryly. He couldn't have been the only one selected by the Spirit. After so many billions of years, after so many dimensions, the Spirit must have touched hundreds of thousands of civilizations. Even if many, like the Trisolarans, were incapable of communicating through ideabstractions, surely many others were like him, and probably even exceeded him in capability. The Spirit must have given them the same mission.

What about the 646 universes before his? They must have all failed, or at least there was no sign that they would succeed yet.

The voice continued, "I have retrieved and reviewed your basic personal information. As the highest authority in this universe, you may determine all its basic parameters."

"Basic parameters?" Tianming asked, his voice stiff. He was no longer used to communicating with anyone other than his wife.

"Such as number of dimensions, physical constants, distribution of matter, proportion of basic elements, and so on. But please note that the mini-universe has a limited energy reserve, and once the basic parameters are set, they cannot be altered. If you decide to set the number of dimensions to be less than three, your body will be immediately reduced in dimension in the tide of creation. Although your body has been restructured, such reduction will still lead to instant death. If you decide to set the number of dimensions to six or greater, the geometry of the resulting universe will be smaller than the space needed by your body, and you will be instantly crushed into high-dimensional fragments. I suggest you choose from three, four, or five." The explaining voice was patient.

What incredible power is this?! Tianming understood now that the Spirit, which claimed to have ten dimensions, probably also existed in a mini-universe isolated from the grand universe, only projecting itself into the three-dimensional universe. This was also probably its secret for not being reduced in dimension as the grand universe changed, and also the source for its ability to remain absolutely still while everything else moved.

A ten-dimensional universe outside the universe! What kind of existence is that?

Tianming thought over his choices, and said, "I prefer a three-dimensional universe, with gravity set to one G . . . Oh, could I create life?"

"You can re-create any life-form in my databank. I can construct an ecosystem for you, but it will be subject to the limitations of the basic parameters of the universe."

"Perfect. I'd like a sky, earth, a sun, houses and some fields . . . and some trees. Just like a rural farm on Earth. Do you know what I mean?"

"Yes," said the manager.

He felt the sensation of weight, and his feet touched solid ground. The sky was overhead, and the sun generously showered the earth with golden light. A cluster of white houses stood not too far away, and a copse of trees swayed in the breeze next to them. The quivering leaves sheltered the houses in shade.

"That was quick!"

"This is the normal speed of the universe," came the answer. It would be a long while before Tianming understood the real meaning behind those words.

He gazed into the distance and saw himself on the horizon. He looked to the left, right, behind—his image could be seen in each direction, extending in columns into infinity.

"This universe is rather small in size. You can view it as a cube with each edge being one kilometer in length. The universe is completely self-contained and topologically a 3-sphere—in other words, no matter in which direction you head, you'll return to the starting point after one thousand meters."

"This really is a universe!" Tianming said in admiration.

"Of course. Also, in order to facilitate communication, I can appear to you in human form. You can now determine my basic parameters, such as figure, voice, personality, form of address, and so on."

"How do I do that?" Tianming had never been big on designing avatars in video games, and he dreaded the task.

"Just think about who you want me to be, and I'll be them."

"Oh, that's easy." Tianming relaxed. "After so many years, I'll finally get to see another human being."

He thought over the possibilities. He wasn't willing to endow this alien manager with the form of Cheng Xin or AA, but he didn't know other people well. Still, there was one "person" he was very familiar with, who had in fact been born from his mind in the first place. And that "person" was as alien as this manager.

"How about Ran Asa—no, Sophon?"

"Are you sure?"

"Um . . . let me think about this—"

"There's no need," interrupted the manager. "I've already examined your mental activities, and I know you will be sure."

Before he could protest, the door to one of the white houses opened and out stepped a feminine figure. Long hair draped over her shoulders, and her every movement was charged with allure. She was indeed the robot, both murderous and beautiful, Sophon.

Sophon crossed the field gracefully and bowed deeply before him. It was a while before Tianming could take his eyes away.

"Why . . . why aren't you dressed?"

"You tell me!" Sophon winked at him. "You didn't give me the parameters!"

Tianming sat in the living room, gazing around curiously. Sophon, who was now dressed in a gorgeous kimono, knelt on a tatami mat opposite him and carefully manipulated the implements of the tea ceremony. For a moment, Tianming experienced the illusion that he was back in the Deterrence Era at the tea ceremony where Cheng Xin had met Sophon for the first time; he had of course admired Sophon's performance from afar back then.

"Since your body is still new, you can't exchange ideabstractions with me directly. We're limited to human language for now, for which I apologize," said Sophon.

"You're not the real Sophon," Tianming muttered, getting back to the present.

"You already know that," Sophon said. Her smile was as mysterious as the Mona Lisa's.

"But you really do look just like her."

"That's to be expected. The intelligent module—that's your ring—contains all the data from the Trisolaran Fleet. When the Master encountered the fleet for the first time, it scanned the ships and gathered all the data in their computers, including the parameters for Sophon. Other than the fact that I'm far more intelligent and have a different basic design, I am physically an exact copy of Sophon. Are you satisfied?" Sophon grinned.

Tianming thought of something. "Does that mean you have all information concerning Earth as well?"

"Of course. That's trivial for the Master. For example, we have the complete genetic code of the seeds you brought with you to the Trisolaran Fleet." Sophon extended a finger and pointed at a corner of the room, where he saw a bag of seeds. Now he understood how this mini-universe could duplicate an Earth farm so accurately. The greenery he saw wasn't an illusion or a model, but real trees and crops re-created based on the genetic information of Earth flora.

Tianming was delighted by this surprise. He knew how advanced the Trisolaran system for sharing information was, and that meant that the mini-universe now contained all information known to Earth and Trisolaris. If Cheng Xin and Guan Yifan came in here and saw all this, surely they'd also be overjoyed . . .

But what did they have to do with him? He was only a tool now, nothing more.

"This 'Master' you speak of . . . is it the Spirit?"

"Yes, the Spirit is the spirit of the Master, but for us, it's the same thing as the Master."

"Okay. So what is your relationship to the Master or the Spirit?"

"I am nothing more than a program created by the Master, and you are my master." Sophon was finished with the tea ceremony and presented a cup to him with both hands. "This is why I can speak to you using your language, but the Master can only communicate with you through ideabstractions."

"Those ideabstractions! I almost died."

"That's not surprising. Most intelligent life-forms are incapable of receiving ideabstractions, because their mental capacities are limited and cannot be uplifted. The use of ideabstractions serves as a threshold for selecting Seekers."

"Seekers?"

"They're charged by the Master to find the Lurker."

"I see. How many Seekers are there?"

"There used to be many, but few are left now. You're likely the very last one. Universe 647 is the very last mini-universe that can be given to an intelligent life-form. You're very lucky."

"Why did the Master give me this universe?" Tianming accepted the teacup.

"To free you from the constraint of the speed of light so that you can traverse every corner of the grand universe in your search for the Lurker."

Tianming had expected this; he knew that the Master wasn't going to just give him a personal paradise and allow him to live the rest of his life in peace. Still, he was shocked by the extent of the Master's power.

"What about time? Could I travel to the past of the grand universe?" Tianming asked with barely suppressed excitement. If it was possible to travel to any point in time, including the past, then how many mistakes could be fixed, and how much of life could be relived!

"The mini-universe follows its own timeline, completely independent of the flow of time in the grand universe. But the moment you entered the mini-universe, an absolute reference point in the grand universe's time was established. We can't reach any point before the absolute reference point, but we can go to any point in the grand universe's time after the absolute point. However, I suggest that you don't go to any point too far in the future. If the grand universe at that point has entered the two-dimensionalized era, you will be flattened as soon as you enter the grand universe and thus be annihilated."

"What happened to the other six hundred and forty-six mini-universes?" Tianming stared at the tea leaves unfurling in his cup, still unable to believe that he was discussing the profoundest questions of the universe with an algorithm in the midst of a tea ceremony.

Sophon smiled. "I'm sorry, but I don't know the answer. It's impossible for an observer inside one mini-universe to know the exact conditions inside a different mini-universe. I do, however, know that most of the Seekers inside the other six hundred and forty-six mini-universes have returned to the grand universe to carry out the mission the Master assigned them. Unfortunately, most of them have perished, and none have succeeded."

"Then some Seekers have survived?"

"Most of the mini-universes came from epochs in the grand universe's past when it possessed more dimensions. Thus, their inhabitants could no longer function in the grand universe after it was reduced to three dimensions. Only nineteen mini-universes have been active in the grand universe since it was reduced to three dimensions, and of those, only a few are still operational. I don't know what has become of them."

"Are there any other humans who have become Seekers?" Tianming asked, hoping that he would have at least one other member of his species as a companion.

"As far as I know, no. But a Seeker on the verge of death could pass on their mission to any other sentient being, and so theoretically, other humans could have become Seekers. Of course, the probability of such a thing is virtually nil."

Disappointed, Tianming took a sip of tea. "So why was I picked?"

"You were indeed not the Master's first choice. However, the Master was running out of time and getting weaker by the day. Three is the lowest number of dimensions the universe could possess for the Master's projection to exert an effect. Once the universe is reduced to two dimensions, though the Master can still project itself into it, such a projection will be without intelligence and incapable of stopping the Lurker. The universe will be doomed."

"Ah, so I guess the Master is not omnipotent after all."

Sophon ignored his mocking tone. "The Master's powers are sufficient to remake the universe. But . . . the Master is only a surviving consciousness from the perfect ten-dimensional universe. After the destruction of that perfect universe, the Master survived in a mini-universe and repeatedly projected itself into the reduced-dimension universe to seek out other consciousnesses and converse with them in ideabstractions. Without finding a suitable candidate to carry out the key steps of its plan, the Master's powers cannot be expressed to their fullest extent."

"Did you just say that the Master is in a mini-universe? What really is a mini-universe?"

"A fragment of the ten-dimensional universe. All mini-universes are fragments of the original, perfect universe."

"How is that possible?" Tianming was astonished.

"The origin of the mini-universes isn't a mystery. Fundamentally, they are simply small collections of matter. But to partition the material of each mini-universe from the rest of the grand universe requires extremely large amounts of energy—a mini-bang, if you will—as well as the complete unfurling of every dimension in matter. Only when the universe was ten-dimensional were there sufficient power and dimensions to create mini-universes and give them existence independent of the grand universe. After the collapse of that Eden, no civilization in theory should be able to create mini-universes."

Tianming took another sip of tea and nodded thoughtfully. Something as incredible as mini-universes couldn't be common. If any civilization could create them after developing to a certain stage, then the grand universe would have long since been partitioned entirely into such mini-universes by now.

"Is the goal of the Master to re-create the perfect ten-dimensional universe?"

"You already know the answer to that." Sophon bowed slightly. Tianming could tell what she didn't say, but implied: *Aren't you also devoted to the achievement of this sublime goal?*

"True. But I don't know enough. In order for me to serve the Master well, you must tell me everything. Why do I need to find the Lurker? How does that help with the recovery of the ten-dimensional universe?"

Sophon straightened up and her mien turned serious. "The Lurker is the Master's only enemy and the reason your services are needed. The Master isn't worried about any of the other innumerable civilizations and intelligences in the universe. As soon as the Master wills it, it can initiate the process of dimension reversal. But the Lurker is of great concern to the Master. The Lurker, being also from the ten-dimensional universe, is the only one with the power to thwart the Master, and is also the only one capable of preventing the dimension reversal."

"What's dimension reversal?" asked Tianming.

"At the macro level, the grand universe right now is in a three-dimensional state. Higher dimensions still exist, but are imprisoned within the quantum realm as a result of the fundamental structure of matter in the three-dimensional universe. Dimension reversal is a process that takes advantage of vacuum decay to split existing matter at the most basic level so that fundamental particles could follow their natural state and reassemble in higher dimensions, thereby re-creating the ten-dimensional universe." Sophon gently lifted the lid to the tea bowl and covered it again, as though she were discussing a simple task.

But Tianming understood the implication of those words. From the vantage point of his low-dimensional existence, dimension reversal would destroy everything. Other than fundamental particles, nothing would survive the process. He was utterly awestruck by the Master's power.

Sophon sensed his unease. "The Master will only be eliminating the degradation of Nature by artifice, returning it to its natural state."

"Would dimension reversal restore . . . the flattened Solar System and Earth?" Tianming asked.

"I'm sorry, but that's not possible." Sophon smiled and gently shook her head, like a teacher facing a particularly slow student. "The three-dimensional Solar System is itself the result of degradation. Dimension reversal would restore the world to its original state. It won't be three-dimensional or four-dimensional, but ten-dimensional."

Tianming's last ray of hope extinguished. "If the Master possesses such power, why hasn't the Master started the process?"

"It's not that simple. The Lurker has established a special kind of barrier throughout the universe. If the Master is careless and initiates dimension reversal while these barriers are in place, the Master's location would be revealed."

"Special barriers . . ." A light went on in Tianming's head. "Wait! Do you mean . . . the sophon blind zones?"

"That's right." Sophon nodded. "Humans have long speculated about the nature of sophon blind zones, but most of your theories are far off the mark. In fact, the blind zones were not set up expressly for the purpose of inducing the so-called dark forest state, although that ended up being a minor side effect. The real purpose of the blind zones is to detect the superstring waves emitted by the Master's energy reactions. As soon as the Master initiates dimension reversal, the Lurker would be able to locate the Master and destroy it."

Tianming was speechless. He couldn't accept the fact that the dark forest state, which had destroyed both the Earth and Trisolaris, and governed the behaviors of countless other civilizations in the universe, was nothing more than a minor "side effect" of minefields laid by two vast forces at war.

"But I thought the Master is concealed within a mini-universe. How could the Lurker attack it?" Tianming asked.

Sophon patiently explained. "All the universes—the grand one as well as all the mini ones—are located on the supermembrane—" She saw Tianming's puzzled look. "Sorry. The supermembrane is the ultimate foundation for the cosmos, and I can't give you an in-depth explanation right now. A mini-universe must be located close to the grand universe on the supermembrane because otherwise it would be impossible for one to project onto the other and form a connection. Thus, the most highly advanced civilizations in the grand universe are capable of striking at mini-universes over the supermembrane if they can locate them."

"How . . . do the attacks work?"

"Mainly by taking advantage of differences in universal potential energy. The details are probably beyond you at this point, but occasionally the mass of selected galaxies is converted to pure energy and then directed onto the supermembrane." Sophon sipped at her tea nonchalantly, as though she were explaining something as trivial as "You have to wait until the water is boiling before adding tea leaves."

"How is that possible? That would involve hundreds of billions of stars over tens of thousands of light-years and billions of civilizations! You must be speaking hypothetically."

"Not at all. Exploratory strikes of the kind I spoke of have occurred many, many times. The Lurker is capable of altering the gravitation configuration within a galaxy and, by manipulating Cherkoff forces, cause all the stars to rapidly fall into the center of the galaxy, where the Steffankin effect results in a supermassive black hole that is capable of deforming space to penetrate the barriers between universes. The energy is then directed against the supermembrane for the transuniversal strike. These types of attacks have led to heavy losses for us. The Master once possessed twelve copies. Before the grand universe degraded to three dimensions, the Lurker was able to destroy seven of those copies, and then, during the early days of the three-dimensional universe, four more were destroyed. Only a single copy is left now."

"Are you telling me that the Lurker has already converted four galaxies in the three-dimensional universe into pure energy?" Tianming was shocked.

Sophon smiled, as though taking pity on his lack of imagination. "Not four, but hundreds of thousands. It isn't easy for a transuniversal strike to hit the target, and the energy from most of these galactic conversions was wasted. Actually, long ago, scientists on Earth discovered the remnants of galaxies that were subjected to this treatment and the accompanying secondary radiation."

"What? I've never heard of such a thing!"

"You have. Way back in the Common Era, human scientists discovered some unusual astronomical structures. They looked like stars, but they emitted more energy than entire galaxies and were orders of magnitude brighter than galaxies. Scientists were puzzled by them and dubbed them 'quasars.'"

"Wh—" Tianming forgot that he had a mouthful of tea and spat it all over Sophon's face. "I'm sorry! But you're telling me that the quasars are all . . ." Tianming was utterly amazed by the nature of the conflict he had been drafted into. The flattening of the Solar System had once seemed impossibly wondrous to him, but compared with the struggle between these two ancient titans, it seemed no more than a war between ants.

Sophon cleaned her face with a napkin, and then added, "Quasars are nothing. There are more wonders than you can imagine. Humans had long been puzzled by many oddly shaped galaxies and could offer no explanation for their structure. These irregular galaxies are all the remnants of the Lurker's energy-extraction efforts dating back to the early days of the three-dimensional universe."

Tianming contemplated this new information silently for a few moments. "All right . . . but if the Lurker is so powerful, why does it need to conceal itself?"

"It is still situated within the grand universe. From its ten-dimensional mini-universe, the Master is capable of performing a dimension reversal on any single spot in the grand universe as soon as it has the coordinates; of course, such a 'spot' could be as large as thousands of light-years across. There is absolutely no defense against such a transuniversal attack in the grand universe. Without concealing itself, the Lurker would have been eliminated long ago by the Master.

"In reality, during the early days of the three-dimensional universe, the Master did succeed in destroying the Lurker's control center by initiating dimension reversal. But the Master didn't realize that the Lurker had a backup control center, and the Lurker took advantage of the lapse to destroy multiple copies of the Master and halted the dimension-reversal process. This early war resulted in the basic topography of the three-dimensional universe; regions where dimension reversal had occurred became empty 'holes' a hundred million to three hundred million light-years across. In these holes, besides spatial dimensions that had been twisted beyond recognition, all the matter had been turned into dark matter. The regions of the universe unaffected by the halted dimension reversal formed a lattice packed with galaxies."

One after another, the solutions to cosmological puzzles that had once plagued human scientists were revealed. The truth made Tianming tremble, but he was now only a pawn that had advanced into enemy territory in this cosmic Great Game. He had no choice but to press ahead.

"Let me summarize the situation," Tianming said. "The Master lives somewhere on the supermembrane beyond the grand universe. If the Lurker found out the coordinates of the Master, the Lurker would be able to destroy it. Similarly, the Lurker is concealed in the depths of the grand universe. If the Master discovered its location, it would also be able to eliminate the Lurker. Am I right?"

"Yes," said Sophon.

"However, if either side made a mistake and launched an ill-aimed strike, the error would reveal the attacker's location to the other side, thereby leading to its own destruction. And thus we have a stalemate."

"Exactly," said Sophon. "So the dark forest state does exist, though not at the level of billions of civilizations who are strangers to one another, but at the level of two opponents who are intimately familiar with each other."

"So . . . what can I do then?" Tianming gave a wry smile. *What can an ant accomplish in a battle between two armies?*

Sophon's response came quickly. "You must find the Lurker before the universe decays into two dimensions. The Master can only project itself into the grand universe from time to time like a ghost. It also cannot create more than nine projections, because otherwise the Lurker would be able to calculate the precise location of the Master's mini-universe on the supermembrane from the coordinates of the various projections. Thus, the Master needs intelligent beings like you to become Seekers and help us."

Sophon's voice now grew more enthusiastic. "This is no easy mission, but you will have at least tens of billions of years to accomplish it. Besides, the Master has endowed you with this incorruptible body and given you that ring you're wearing. As long as you have that ring, you can return to this mini-universe at any time."

"All right. What other clues do you have concerning the Lurker?"

"Not much. Right now, we just suspect that a mysterious group called the 'Zero-Homers' might have something to do with the Lurker."

Tianming frowned. "The Zero-Homers?"

"That's what they call themselves. They've been very influential during the last few hundred million years. Maybe they're a civilization, or maybe they're formed from multiple civilizations. The Master doesn't know much about them other than that they wish to reset the universe and return it to the Edenic Age."

"Um . . . isn't that the same thing the Master wants?"

"But their approaches are polar opposites. The Zero-Homers believe that in order to restore the universe to ten dimensions, it must first be reduced to zero dimensions, at which point it would cycle back to ten dimensions. This is utter nonsense. Zero dimensions means absolute death, where no civilization can survive. Either these individuals are idiots who know nothing about the principles of dimension recovery, or they are manipulated by the Lurker from behind the scenes. Or maybe both."

"Where are they?"

"We don't know where the Zero-Homers are from. During the last few hundred million years, they constructed bases in multiple galaxies. The closest base is found in the Milky Way Galaxy's Wild Duck Cluster—also known to you as Messier 11, or NGC 6705—and the farthest one is about seven billion light-years away. But as far as this mini-universe is concerned, all these bases are equally close. I suggest that you go to the Wild Duck Cluster first. The Zero-Homers there have been very active in the Milky Way recently. At the cosmic scale, you are practically from the same neighborhood. I'm sure you'd be able to communicate more easily."

"Practically the same neighborhood? Surely you jest—wait! I remember now. Aren't these the same bastards who generated those death lines on Planet Gray around DX3906?"

"I don't have anything about that in my databank," said Sophon. "But if you're talking about death lines . . . yes, that does seem likely."

"Perfect! I'd love to settle a score with them." The memory of how the Zero-Homers had been responsible for trapping him on Planet Blue for decades enraged him, but soon his anger dissipated. "The Wild Duck Cluster is huge. Once I get there, what am I supposed to do?"

"Another Seeker is already there. Perhaps it will help you."

Tianming's eyes brightened at the good news. "How do I find it?"

"The Master needs your help for that. According to the Master, Mini-Universe 589's Seeker was there and left some signs, but then it disappeared and ceased all communications with the mini-universe. This is an extremely unusual event. The Master wants you to go find the Seeker, who may possess information that we need."

"What kind of . . . entity is the Seeker from Mini-Universe 589?"

"I'm not sure," admitted Sophon. "It's extremely energy-intensive to transmit information across the supermembrane, and so I have only the most crucial bits. Mini-Universe 589 is one of the few mini-universes still active, and the Master had handed it out when the grand universe was still four-dimensional. The Seeker in possession of the mini-universe was probably an intelligent creature from the four-dimensional universe that had then been reduced to three dimensions, or maybe it was a successor to the original Seeker. It should also have a ring like yours. Once you arrive at the Wild Duck Cluster, you can read the message the Seeker left, or you can try to initiate contact through the ring. But the specifics have to wait until you get there. When do you want to leave?"

"Wait! Let's talk about going there in a minute. I still have another question," said Tianming. "Why did this war start? Why did the Lurker destroy that perfect ten-dimensional universe?"

"Not even the Master knows," said Sophon. "But I can transmit the ideabstractions about that time to you. Perhaps you can figure out the answer yourself."

Tianming stiffened. Sophon hurried to reassure him. "Don't worry! Your body and brain have been modified by the Master to be capable of receiving basic ideabstractions. They won't hurt you."

Compelled by curiosity, Tianming gritted his teeth and nodded. Sophon smiled, stood up to walk in front of Tianming, bowed, and said, "Get ready." Then she held him by the shoulders and gazed into his eyes.

Tianming gazed back into her eyes, which seemed like two bottomless whirlpools that pulled him in. In a moment, he was overwhelmed by an endless ocean of images and concepts.

Receiving an ideabstraction must rank among the most wonderful experiences in the universe. To Tianming, the storm of information was like a tempest-tossed sea that threatened to drown him. But unlike his previous encounters, a force soon lifted him above the ocean of information and then bathed his mental landscape in bright sunlight. Suddenly, everything became clear. All ideas, forms, and images were endowed with a unifying meaning. Connected to each other, combined into basic units of logic and grammar, and then layered upon one another, the ideabstraction elements assembled into a whole that encompassed millions of concepts at once. This was an understanding that surpassed any of his past experiences, when he had glimpsed but the barest outlines. This time, he understood everything from top to bottom, inside out.

He saw the origin of the universe: From a single dot, an infinity of matter and energy emerged. No, at this moment, matter *was* energy, and there was no distinction between the two. In a flash, the ten-dimensional universe appeared. Tianming finally saw perfection itself.

Words were inadequate. Light could travel from one end of the universe to the other without the passage of time. There were no limits on speed. From every corner of the ten-dimensional universe, billions of life-forms appeared. Because of the infinite velocity of light, life throughout the universe conversed, forming a unified whole. Intelligence evolved, followed by civilization, science, culture, art, and all advanced to perfection in an instant.

Only now did Tianming understand what Sophon had meant by "This is the normal speed of the universe," back at the beginning of their conversation.

Sophon's voice reverberated in this marvelous universe, providing additional gloss for the ideabstractions. "The ten-dimensional universe was a world of light. The entire universe was constructed upon energy exchange between photons. All particles and antiparticles were formed from photons, and their mutual annihilation resulted in yet more photons. Thus, everything occurred at the speed of light, which was infinite. Even more marvelously, because particles and antiparticles balanced each other out, the total energy level of the universe was zero. This was an incredible state of symmetry, and the foundation of the emergence of intelligence in the ten-dimensional universe."

Matter, life, sentience, civilization . . . in this Edenic universe, everything was part of the same whole. All matter possessed life, and all life possessed sentience, and all sentience existed in a state of harmonious civilization. Unlike the three-dimensional universe, in which lonely stars hung in the vast emptiness of space, the entire universe was a living being. All life was but a part of this one grand Life, and all intelligence but a component of the highest Intelligence. The dark forest state was an impossibility for this transcendent being of unified matter and spirit.

Tianming felt awe at the root of his soul. This was the original form of the Master. The ten-dimensional universe was itself alive.

Sophon offered more explanations. "The Master is not an individual like a human being; rather, it is the sum of an infinite number of self-aware consciousnesses. Every consciousness shares the awareness of every other consciousness as well as the presence of the universe itself, and yet each possesses an independent will. This is a state of existence simply unimaginable by humans: individual presence absolutely, seamlessly harmonized with the universe, akin to the geometric construction of the Spirit you saw."

Finally, Tianming understood the Master's yearning and craving to recover that perfect Edenic Age. How could anyone who had experienced the vibrancy of that world tolerate the emptiness and crudeness of the three-dimensional universe? He found it even more incomprehensible that the Lurker would wish to destroy such a beautiful world in harmony. How vicious and crazed was such evil!

Then he witnessed the moment of destruction.

In a particular corner of this world, the gentle light of life suddenly went out, leaving behind a tiny patch of darkness, as though a single drop of ink had marred a fresh sheet of white paper. The darkness, at first insignificant, did not remain confined, but began to spread at light-speed. Since the speed of light was infinite, the darkness also spread at infinite speed. The entire ten-dimensional universe plunged into darkness.

Although the destruction took place within an infinitesimal slice of time, the events comprising it took place in a specific, clear order. Through the ideabstractions, Tianming was able to decipher the details. It was a transformation impossible to describe with languages devised within the three-dimensional universe. An analogy, however inadequate, would be a picture that had been built from countless domino tiles standing on their ends; all the tiles had fallen, but the "flattened" picture remained discernible.

The universe had collapsed from ten dimensions to nine. A traitorous child of the Edenic Age had committed matricide against the source of its life.

"Of the infinite number of consciousnesses that collectively formed the Master, a single consciousness suddenly launched a rebellion, leading to the dimension reduction of the universe." Sophon's voice was tinged with rage. "Caught off guard, the Master could neither stop the revolt nor understand it. If a child still within the womb decided to attack the mother from within, how could the mother have been prepared for it? And that was how the Lurker succeeded."

But just before the process of dimension reduction completed, what was left of the ten-dimensional universe fought back with all remaining strength. Where darkness met light, blindingly bright rays flashed; if one were to compare the glow of the Milky Way to this incandescence, it would be like comparing a candle to the full power of the sun. In this final apocalyptic battle for the fate of the ten-dimensional universe, Tianming received an ideabstraction emitted by the Lurker, a war cry of despair:

This universe is too small. I need a grander universe!

Tianming could not understand what this meant. How could a nine-dimensional universe be bigger than a ten-dimensional universe?

Then he saw some fragments separate from the collapsing ten-dimensional universe amid the fiery light of the final battle, and vanish. He knew that he was observing the Master and its mini-universes.

"The Master tried to halt the dimension reduction, but it was too late. It could only break off some pieces of the grand universe and turn them into independent mini-universes so as to preserve a ray of hope. Fortunately, each fragment also contained a copy of all the Master's information."

Tianming understood now that the Master was the soul of the ten-dimensional universe, or, perhaps more accurately, the last fragment of that soul. This was why it was so dedicated to the goal of dimension reversal: Recovering that lost paradise would also allow it to recover itself.

The nine-dimensional universe then appeared among the ideabstractions. It was a broken version of the ten-dimensional universe, like a cracked egg. As in the Chinese myth in which various parts of the god Pangu's body turned into the sun, the moon, the mountains, and the rivers after his death, the nine-dimensional universe was formed from the dead body of the ten-dimensional universe. Though it was now but a lifeless corpse, it remained the battlefield over which countless lives fought. Yes, a battlefield. This universe was a city in ruins, torn by war and confusion.

"The history of the nine-dimensional universe was a continuation of the ten-dimensional universe. Unlike dimension reduction for lower-dimension universes, the unified life of the ten-dimensional universe did not die after being reduced to nine dimensions; rather, the consciousnesses split and became divided from one another, turning into countless parallel civilizations. Most of them, however, kept the memory and civilization inherited from the ten-dimensional universe, and a large number of them came together to try to revive the ten-dimensional universe. But some of them were deceived and seduced by the Lurker and joined the enemy camp."

Deceived? How? Tianming could not understand it.

As Tianming continued to interpret the ideabstractions, he saw that in the nine-dimensional universe, although light was still traveling at an incredible speed, capable of almost traversing the universe from one end to the other within one second, lightspeed was no longer infinite. Wars could no longer be completed instantaneously, but had to be resolved over a complicated series of steps. Attempts at dimension reversal and dimension reduction often occurred at the same time, leading to fantastic bursts of light. Finally, after a bright flash that was impossible to describe, all light vanished from the universe.

"During this period, the mutual annihilation of particles and antiparticles theorized by your cosmologists occurred. Due to the breakdown of the universe's basic symmetry and the reduction in the speed of light, all antiparticles and virtually all particles were annihilated, leaving behind only about one-billionth of the particles, which formed today's universe. The energy released by the mutual annihilation of particles and antiparticles then caused the universe's rapid expansion."

"But why were there more particles than antiparticles?" Tianming asked. He remembered that this was a tough puzzle for cosmologists.

"The dimension reduction destroyed the balance in the universe. As one of the dimensions vanished, a large number of antiparticles decayed into neutrinos, which led to the strange phenomenon of what you call parity violation," said Sophon.

As the particles and antiparticles annihilated each other, another shocking dimension reduction occurred. Darkness descended, and, as millions of civilizations cried out in despair, the universe, like a deflating balloon, lost another dimension. Soon, the nine-dimensional universe was replaced by the eight-dimensional universe.

The eight-dimensional universe was strange; the entire universe was a gigantic hyperspherical solid, crisscrossed by billions upon billions of tunnels and caves (all eight-dimensional, of course). To employ an inadequate three-dimensional image: It resembled a piece of Swiss cheese. In the caves of the eight-dimensional universe, civilization after civilization, having survived dimension reduction, revived, and they began to struggle against each other. Although the speed of light in this universe was even slower, war still proceeded rapidly. Within but a brief moment, walls as thick as ten thousand light-years were drilled through, and caves as large as several galaxies were filled in. Of course, these were just estimates in Tianming's mind; it was really not possible to measure size in eight dimensions using comparisons and units drawn from three dimensions.

The war caused the universe to collapse further, into seven dimensions, resulting in a world far simpler in structure than before. A six-dimensional "plane" divided the universe into two halves: One half was solid, and the other half empty space. All the civilizations in the universe were spread over this six-dimensional plane billions of light-years across, but the plane was itself billions of times more complex than the three-dimensional universe. Like the predecessor universes, the seven-dimensional universe was caught in the warfare between the various civilizations from the moment of its birth. Of these civilizations, few were survivors from the Edenic Age of ten dimensions. New, native civilizations were dominant. The dark forest state became the norm, and civilizations fought mercilessly. Dimension weapons were widely employed in every corner of the universe, leading to yet another dimension reduction.

"The nine-, eight-, and seven-dimensional universes were all continuations of the ten-dimensional universe," Sophon said. "The two warring camps fought through these three successive ages, but with each reduction in dimension, the side of the Master weakened further. Of course, the Lurker's side also weakened, but overall, the situation favored beings in that camp. The goal of the Lurker was to reduce dimensions, and the Lurker and its followers were prepared for it. Even if the use of dimension weapons reduced their dimensions, it simply pushed the war into the next universe."

In the six-dimensional universe, it was almost impossible to see any traces of the original, ancient civilizations. This universe had a particularly odd structure: a vast energy sea on which an archipelago of billions of islands made of dark matter floated—six-dimensional islands and a six-dimensional sea. Each island was tens of thousands of light-years across, and while the interior of any of them could be considered a separate universe, the islands were also millions of light-years apart. The energy sea and the dark matter islands all evolved a multitude of different civilizations, and the heroic and magnificent battles between them were far more astonishing than any fantasy or science fiction. The fire phoenix that rose from the energy sea, the shade dragon that circled the islands, the flower kingdoms that danced on the winds . . . the victories achieved by these civilizations were as awe-inspiring as the power of the gods, and their eventual destruction was as pitiable as the swan's final song.

Dimension reduction, reduction, still more reduction.

The five- and four-dimensional universes were very similar to the current three-dimensional universe in most ways, other than the difference of having extra dimensions. The basic structure of each was a vast, dark space in which faint energy flames formed systems based on mutual gravitational attraction. The speed of light and other limits suffered further reductions. By now, the time required to go from one end of the universe to the other was no longer measured by seconds or minutes, or even days and months, but tens of millions of years. The vast gulfs between worlds caused civilizations to be permanently divided from each other, and the triumph of the dark forest state, the gift of the Lurker, was complete. Every mature civilization concealed itself in the darkness, ready to launch a fatal strike against any prey that revealed itself, though each also lived under the perpetual terror of becoming prey to a stronger hunter.

Universes were born and died; civilizations rose and fell like the tides. After eons measured only by the grains of sand on the shore of the Ganges, a bug named Yun Tianming watched it all.

Finally, Tianming looked away from Sophon's eyes. Though his modified body tolerated the buffeting ideabstractions far better than in the past, he still felt so weak that he could barely speak. It wasn't so much exhaustion of the flesh as of the mind.

"I don't understand. Why did the Lurker say 'This universe is too small'?" Tianming muttered.

Sophon shook her head in puzzlement. "Not even the Master understands that. But you don't need to understand it to complete your mission. The Lurker cannot be . . . reasoned with."

Tianming nodded. Someone who would destroy the perfection of the ten-dimensional universe could not be subject to reason.

Tianming walked outside the house. The door of the mini-universe—a rectangle outlined by faint lines—appeared in the distance. He walked toward it, with Sophon following silently. When he arrived at the door, Tianming turned to Sophon. "How much time has passed in the grand universe?"

"Time in this mini-universe is independent of the passage of time in the grand universe. In some sense, you can think of time in the grand universe as being paused at the moment you entered here. We could also adjust the ratio between the two timelines as you like. But as I mentioned, don't head for the distant future in the grand universe. By then, the universe may already have been reduced to two dimensions. We already don't have much time left."

"How much time do we have?"

"No more than fifteen billion years."

Tianming smiled wryly. It was absurd to hear fifteen billion years described as "not much time." Just a day earlier, he had thought the seven centuries he had skipped across was everything.

He had once lived a nightmare that lasted thousands of years; compared with what was to come, though, that was nothing. He was facing a nightmare that might last billions of years, from which he would never awake.

His resolve slackened in the face of such an unimaginable future in the vast darkness between the stars. There was someone he wanted to see. He had not wanted to show his frail, dying self to that woman, who was likely still full of the promise of youth, but the situation was now different.

"Could I wait a bit? I would like to wait until . . . they come here."

Sophon of course knew who he meant by "they."

"That wouldn't be a problem," she said, "as long as you don't wait more than a hundred million years. If you like, you could live here for many years before leaving. Or you could adjust the flow of time so that you get to see them sooner."

Tianming's sense of joy didn't last long. He had, after all, spent a whole lifetime with another woman. To see Cheng Xin after his wife's death, and after Cheng Xin and Guan Yifan had probably fallen in love, seemed inappropriate. He would feel like a third wheel.

Is Cheng Xin the person I truly love? Or 艾 AA? Or even Ai Xiaowei, who died long ago?

Tianming shook his head in bafflement. None of these questions would have been relevant had it not been for those death lines, which interrupted the happy life he could have led with Cheng Xin. Sloweddown light and eons separated them. They stood at the source and mouth of time's river, gazing, searching, seeking, but would never see each other. If only they had lived in the ten-dimensional universe, where the speed of light was infinite—

Wait!

A barely formed thought emerged in Tianming's mind, soon coming into focus: a key point whose familiarity had caused him to ignore its significance until now.

"How long has the three-dimensional universe existed?" He gazed at Sophon intently.

"About thirteen billion, eight hundred and ninety-four million years," said Sophon.

"How long did the four-dimensional universe exist?"

"About one million years."

"What about the five-dimensional universe?"

"One hundred thirty-one years."

"And the six-dimensional universe?"

"Nine days and eleven hours."

"Seven-dimensional?"

"Two minutes and three seconds."

"Eight-dimensional?"

"Twelve milliseconds."

"Nine-dimensional?"

"Thirty-one nanoseconds."

Tianming suppressed his rising excitement, and asked the final question: "What about the ten-dimensional universe?"

Unexpectedly, Sophon was silent for a moment before she said, "Forever. There was no time in the ten-dimensional universe."

"Of course," Tianming murmured. "Infinite speed, infinite efficiency, everything completed from the start, finished in an instant without the passage of any time . . . It was a universe without time.

"No time, no motion, to change, to process . . . the start was also the end! An instant was eternity! There were no real, vibrant lives, only stacks of frozen pictures. This was a world . . . of death."

"I don't understand," said Sophon. "I don't understand what you're saying at all. A perfect world has no need for time. Time consists of . . . nothing more than annoying delays."

"You think that way because you serve the Master," Tianming said. "Just like him, time is your blind spot. You don't live within time, and thus you can never see time itself. Let me tell you a myth of Earth."

"I know all the myths from Earth," said Sophon, clearly unimpressed.

"I doubt you truly understand them all, however. Otherwise you would have understood the motivation of the Lurker. In Greek mythology, this is how the world began:

"Ouranos, the god of the sky, mated with Gaia, the goddess of the earth, and gave birth to many gods. But Ouranos loathed these children, and pushed them back into Gaia's womb with his phallus. Heaven and earth were thus joined together and could not be separated. Later, Gaia, pained by Ouranos's oppressive embrace, called on her children to slay their father. In the end, her son Chronos cut off Ouranos's penis, thus separating father from mother, dividing sky from earth, and allowed the gods to be born. Life then came into the universe."

"That is a primitive, vulgar story recorded in Hesiod's *Theogony*," Sophon said, her lips curled in disgust. "What does it have to do with the ten-dimensional universe?"

"Since you're well versed in all the tales of Earth civilization, you ought to know that 'chronos' means time. The myth is a metaphor; time is the beginning of everything. The Lurker needed time. A universe without time would be too small no matter what. The Lurker could not stand it and had to reduce the dimensions of the universe. With each lost dimension, time stretched out tens of thousands of times. The Lurker wasn't crazy, and it wasn't even evil. It simply wants one thing: time.

"For the Lurker, the lost dimensions were amply compensated for by the gain in time. It, or at least a part of it, was transferred into time. This was the net benefit of dimension reduction: Without the degradation in dimensions there would have been no time."

Sophon looked thoughtful. "I've never thought of it that way. But we did discover early on that time itself seemed to be a compensatory effect of the diminished speed of light."

"Just as Chronos split the heavens from earth, time divided the universe, and destroyed the eternal, changeless being that was the ten-dimensional universe. After that, all civilizations had to exist within the limits of time and space. The universe became the infinite unknown. With time came hope, anticipation, surprise, remembrance, oblivion . . . and above all, freedom."

"These are meaningless," said Sophon drily. "Eternity is the only existence."

"That wasn't how the Lurker felt. It was suffocating under the ten-dimensional universe, with its perfect symmetry and eternal immutability. As the dimensions collapsed, more and more consciousnesses, separated from the unity of the Edenic Age, came to believe in the Lurker's cause and joined its legion. Risking annihilation, they wanted to join time and to call for yet more time. This was the reason the Master failed, don't you see?

"They need time. Other than the Master, all living beings need time."

"But I know that time is also the source for most of humanity's tragedies," Sophon countered. "For example, without time, you and Cheng Xin would still be together."

Tianming gave a sorrowful smile. "But without time, there wouldn't have been any happiness for us. I would be without that summer of telling Weiwei stories, without that hour spent with Cheng Xin by the lake, without the thousand years spent in magnificent dreams, without the four decades when 艾 AA and I lived as husband and wife. Without time, perhaps I wouldn't even have consciousness."

"Mere hypotheticals," said Sophon. "Even if you're right, the Lurker already had time in the nine-dimensional universe. Why did it continue the degradation?"

"I can only guess," said Tianming. His rebirth had made his mind particularly acute and clear. "The Lurker created time through dimension reduction, but it was also overwhelmed by time. Once it had opened the magic box, it could no longer stop. In time, there was birth but also death. Of course it wouldn't be satisfied by a few milliseconds, days, years. It didn't want to die in time, but to last forever, and so it had to reduce dimensions again and again. It did so both to avoid the Seekers and to gain more time. Later, when other civilizations appeared, they also joined this game. The universe turned into the dark forest, and dimensional strikes were but one of the weapons. Every civilization, in order to last longer, chose to reduce the universe's dimensions.

"As the game continued, each successor universe lasted ten thousand times longer than the last one, at the price of yet another precious dimension. By the time we reach the zero-dimensional universe, it would be an emptiness possessing nothing but time."

Tianming shuddered. Such a universe was another universe dominated by death. The dark forest was bracketed by the perfect beauty of death and the emptiness of death. True life could only exist in the cruel and severe dark forest; death was the required condition for life.

"That is why the Master must stop it!" Sophon brought the conversation back on track. "The Lurker is insane. It wants to sacrifice the entire universe on the altar of time. If the universe is reduced to zero dimensions, nothing can be done. By then there will be no life or intelligence. And even if anything *could* exist in such a universe, it would be stuck in infinite time. Even a billion billion years would be but a second in this interminable prison sentence."

"But the Master lives outside of the universe," said Tianming. "Why doesn't it initiate dimension reversal when the universe is in zero dimensions? By then I'm sure even the Lurker will have been destroyed in that world, and nothing will be able to stop the Master."

"You're wrong. Since there are no dimensions in such a world, it will be independent of the supermembrane. The Master will not be able to find it. When such a thing happens to a universe, it is said to have evaporated, which happens on the supermembrane from time to time. I bet the evaporated universes were ruined by the time-worshipers in those universes. That is why you must help us and stop the Lurker in the three-dimensional universe."

Tianming shook his head. "I must have a reason. I can't see why I should fight to stop one kind of death only to replace it with another."

"You shouldn't need a reason. I know that the Master has already imbued you with its will. You only have to carry out this will." Sophon sounded a bit puzzled.

"That's right. You have this mental seal." Tianming's face twisted in pain as he held his head, struggling to think. Sophon understood that it was because the Master's will was forcing him to comply and did not disturb the man, waiting for him to surrender. But in a few seconds, Tianming lifted his face. "The Master's mental seal cannot control me. From this moment on, I am free."

Sophon almost jumped out of her skin from shock. She looked at

Tianming warily. "How . . . is that possible? No intelligence has ever been able to escape the Master's mental shaping. What happened?"

"Let me tell you what happened. The Master's ability to impose its will is based on an appeal to reason and requires an absolutely flawless conceptual foundation. But if the premises contain a fatal error, then the power of the Master's seal vanishes. The Master is perfect and rarely makes an error, and that is why it has such faith in this technique for control. But it did commit a fatal error in this case. Because it doesn't understand the meaning of time, it doesn't understand the fundamental flaw in the ten-dimensional universe, which is not a perfect world at all. The Master ordered me to recover the perfect world, but now that I know such a world does not exist, the Master's order has lost its meaning. I have already dissolved its directive in my mind, and from now on, I will not need to obey any person or power."

Sophon remained silent, though she was looking at Tianming with a strange expression. Tianming backed up a step, concerned that she was going to retaliate against him.

But after a while, Sophon smiled helplessly. "Don't worry. I won't do anything to harm you. The Master never imagined you would disobey, and so my only programming is to obey all your orders. You're very special. Of the six hundred and forty-seven individual intelligences who have been gifted mini-universes, you are far from the most intelligent. Yet you're the only one who has been able to resist the authority of the Master. It's incredible."

"I have the Trisolarans to thank for that," said Tianming. "The decades of torture they subjected my brain to taught me much. Even under the seemingly irresistible pressure of the Master's flood of ide-abstractions, I was able to preserve a small black box in my mind for reflection. Otherwise my self would have long since been overwhelmed by it, and I would have become its tool."

"Since I'm faced with such an unprecedented situation, I have to compute whether we can give you a reason to help us."

Sophon closed her eyes and seemed to meditate. Tianming stared at the projection of the two of them on the horizon, waiting quietly. Sunlight bathed the two strange figures, one male and one female. Finally, Sophon's eyelids snapped open, revealing two bright orbs. "I can indeed give you a reason."

Tianming looked at her suspiciously, and Sophon grinned at him. "A little earlier you asked whether dimension reversal could recover the Solar System and the Earth, remember?"

"Yes, and you said it was impossible."

"That was only half the answer. The complete answer is this: To recover only the Solar System and the Earth is impossible, but if we recover everything, we will certainly be able to recover your star system, your home world."

Tianming's eyes brightened. "What do you mean by 'everything'?"

Sophon spoke slowly and deliberately. "Dimension reversal will allow each particle to follow its nature and return to its original state, release all dimensions that are currently curled up within the quantum realm, and rebuild the ten-dimensional universe. Even the Master cannot arbitrarily decide the form of the world after dimension reversal. The only choice is to absolutely, completely, comprehensively recover the original state, without deviating one iota."

Tianming felt that he still wasn't understanding her.

Sophon elaborated. "Even the timeless ten-dimensional universe follows the laws of nature and is consistent with the demands of cause and effect. If everything is returned to its original state, then everything will evolve thence along the same tracks as before."

"Oh!" Tianming suddenly understood. "Are you saying—"

"Yes, the ten-dimensional living consciousness will be formed in an instant, and simultaneously, the Lurker will rebel. The universe will again descend into nine dimensions as before, and then, as the war rages on, into eight, seven, six . . . until it turns into your universe.

"Your Milky Way will again coalesce, and your sun will again appear in a corner of the galaxy. The Earth and the other planets will reappear, bathed by the same sunlight. On Earth, the first life will again form in the primitive sea on a day identical to the one four billion years ago. The long process of evolution will lead to multicellular organisms. The first amphibians will climb onto land. Reptiles will spread over the whole planet, and then an asteroid will kill off the dinosaurs. An undistinguished monkey will climb down from the trees, create civilizations, states, religions, science . . . and your homeland will, like other nations, be reborn. Ancient emperors will again reign over all-under-heaven, and war and rebellions will follow. The poets will again recite their famous lines, and the scientists will struggle over the same puzzles. Ye Wenjie will again invite the Trisolarans to invade; Luo Ji will again deduce the laws of the dark forest; Cheng Xin will again become the Swordholder . . . and just as before, you will be reborn on the same second of the same minute of the same hour of the same day. Everything will . . . happen again."

"Happen . . . again," Tianming murmured. He was utterly amazed by this simple but incredible idea.

"Yes, everything will repeat itself, including the tiniest details. When you see Cheng Xin or Ai Xiaowei again, they'll be wearing the same clothes, and speak to you with the exact same words. When you converse with Cheng Xin by the lake, the same breeze will caress your hair, and the same misty rain will fall around you. On the day you're scheduled for your euthanasia, Cheng Xin will stop the procedure at the same moment, not one second earlier or later. You will dream the same dreams, and then rescue Cheng Xin from the same shot fired by Wade. You will meet the Master's spirit, and once again come to Planet Blue, fall in love with 艾 AA. Even your kisses will be in the same poses . . . Finally, twenty or a hundred billion years later—who knows how long it has been—you will stand here again facing me, having this very conversation. Of course, neither you nor I will remember any of this."

"That's . . . that's—"

"That's the result of my computations."

"What is the point of repeating everything exactly?"

"The point? I can't answer that. But since every iteration is exactly the same as the iteration before, we can deduce that if the first time has meaning, then each subsequent repetition will also have meaning."

"Then is the goal of the Master to let the history of the universe repeat endlessly? The ten-dimensional universe will last but an instant, to be followed by ten billion years of dimension reduction? And then everything will reset, so that the destruction can play out all over again?"

"You forget that time does not exist for the Master. The eternal ten-dimensional universe is no different from its eternal recurrence. Once is the same as forever."

Tianming laughed hysterically. "I once thought the Lurker was without reason, but the Master is even more so. The end of the universe is not nothingness, but a film playing on eternal loop."

Abruptly, he stopped laughing, as another terrifying possibility occurred to him. "If everything will repeat in the exact same way, then it must also have happened already, perhaps even countless times. We are probably only the latest incarnations of an endless, identical sequence of Sophons and Tianmings."

He stared at the projections of him and Sophon on the horizon; that distant Tianming was also staring at another projection of himself on his horizon; and that invisible Tianming must also be staring at an even farther Tianming . . . ad infinitum. Every image was in fact himself.

"It's very possible," said Sophon calmly.

"Do you . . . does even the Master not know?"

"Remember that after dimension reversal, even the Master must start all over without any memories of the last universe."

"Fine. Are you telling me that the chance to repeat everything again exactly the same way is the reason for me to help you?"

"That's right."

"Then my answer is simple: No. Absolutely not. A long time ago, I saw an idiotic series of anime episodes called 'Endless Eight,' in which the content of every single episode was almost exactly the same. A young girl—about as crazy as the Master, I'd say—took over the world and made everyone repeat the same sequence of actions without the memory of having done them. The same plot points looped over and over, recurring thousands of times, until the series showed virtually the same story eight times. I was so mad that I wanted to smash my computer. Do you think I'm interested in making this universe as dumb as that cartoon?"

"You're only talking about superficial similarities," Sophon said, completely ignoring Tianming's outrage. "If this universe is a cartoon, there is no audience who want to smash the computer—well, at least you and I aren't the audience. Like the characters in that anime, you won't have any memory of things repeating. Even if you repeat the same actions and words, each iteration will feel to you unique and completely fresh. Remember what I said: If the first time has meaning, then each subsequent repetition will also have meaning."

Gradually, Tianming calmed down and chewed over Sophon's words. He admitted to himself that she had a point.

The intolerable rage brought on by seeing the same thing happen over and over was an effect of memory. Without memory, there would be no repetition. Look at bacteria, bugs, and most lower organisms: Generation after generation, they live the same lives as their ancestors, repeating everything virtually unchanged. But life isn't meaningless for them. If a man lived a life of joy, why would he refuse to live it exactly the same one more time? He would be born again, learn to walk again, learn to talk again, go to school again, kiss his beloved again . . . it would *not* be meaningless.

What about him, though? He had once thought his own life worthless, had thought himself responsible for unforgivable crimes, had wanted to commit suicide time after time . . . but after everything he had been through, did he still think his own life was wasted? Would he really not want to live one more time? Would he not want to see the nervous Ai Xiaowei knock on his door? Would he not want to sit by the lake with Cheng Xin, stealing glances at her eyes? Would he not want to buy a DVD featuring Ran Asakawa for the first time, his heart leaping with excitement? Would he not want to experience the happy, long dream again? Would he not want to kiss 艾 AA's lips on that memorable evening on Planet Blue?

Of course he would! Like the Master, even if he had to wait millions of years, even if he had to suffer countless setbacks and unimaginable pain, so long as he could lose himself in those magical moments again, he was willing to go through the cycle twice, thrice, a thousand thousand times.

And he knew that life on Earth and human civilization, born in original sin and infinite suffering, would make the exact same choice as he.

"You're right," Tianming said in the end. "You've given me a good reason, a fucking good reason."

Tianming left his mini-universe and returned to the grand universe. He was on his way to find the unknown Seeker, traversing the billion-light-year dark forest like a ghost, visiting innumerable civilizations intent on concealing themselves, all in service of his impossible mission—to find the most deeply hidden Lurker among the hidden civilizations.

Before he left, he instructed Sophon to add Guan Yifan to the list of those allowed to enter the mini-universe. He knew that Guan Yifan and Cheng Xin were eventually going to come to the mini-universe, and he told Sophon not to tell them that he had been there already. He wanted her to act like the real Sophon and did not want to mar their happiness with his own shadow.

"Render unto Caesar the things that are Caesar's, and unto God the things that are God's." So let Guan Yifan and Cheng Xin have the joy that belongs to them, and let Yun Tianming have . . . nothing.

Still, he handed the lock of AA's hair to Sophon before he left. "If I return here before the end of the grand universe, will you be able to clone her? I don't want to have to wait for the life span of the universe to see her again."

"That's a simple technical problem. I can clone her right now."

"No, please wait until my return. A clone will not be the same as her . . . previous incarnation. I don't know how to face this brand-new AA—" Somehow, he felt that this woman whose fate had already been entwined with his through two lifetimes would still return to him in the future in some way. The universe was grand, but life was grander. Perhaps they would see each other again . . .

"Oh, why can't you come with me?" Tianming asked. He knew nothing about his new duties, and if Sophon could come with him, it would certainly make everything easier.

"Fundamentally, I'm just the management system for this mini-universe. If I leave, the mini-universe will collapse," said Sophon. "But if you can find the Seeker in Universe 589, it should be able to help you."

Tianming nodded. With a last glance at this paradise that he was not fated to enjoy, he turned and left. His figure disappeared through the rectangular outline and appeared among the stars of a bright cluster about six thousand light-years away.

He no longer needed a spaceship, because he was a spacecraft himself. Apart from superficial appearance, his body no longer had any similarity with biological humans. Indeed, other than the fact that he still possessed human memories and thoughts, he was practically the same as Sophon: a robot constructed out of pure energy. Like a biological human, he was also made from cells. But each cell in his body was a nanomachine more complicated than any known computer. His body was even capable of curvature propulsion and traversed the vast universe at the rate of 300,000 kilometers per second.

After a break that wasn't a break at all, a signal appeared. But it wasn't Tianming.

Sophon opened her eyes. She knew instantly that 18.9 million years had elapsed in the grand universe.

Tianming hadn't returned, but two others with the right authorization had.

Although Sophon had no time sense, she understood what 18.9 million years meant to humans.

Perhaps Tianming had long since turned to fragments and dust, and would never return. After all, no matter how much his body had been enhanced and reconfigured, it was no match for black holes, quasars, and neutron stars. Or perhaps he was still trudging through some distant world, seeking the faintest traces of the Lurker; or perhaps he was simply taking his pleasure in some corner of the universe, his mission long forgotten . . .

As a robot bound to her programming, Sophon was not disappointed, worried, scared, or even curious, and she certainly wouldn't feel sorrow for a Yun Tianming that had perhaps long since disintegrated. All these emotions were irrelevant for her. She was simply going to follow Tianming's instructions and carry out her duties.

She left the house, walked over the fields, and came to the tree under which not long—that is, 18.9 million years—ago she had seen Yun Tianming, and bowed deeply to the curious man and woman she found there.

"The universe is grand, but life is grander. Fate has indeed directed us to meet again."

PART III

Sky Calyx

Singer was not expecting the King's summons.

After a career of billions of time grains, he had become an elder on one of the seeds. But from the vantage point of the supreme King, he, as a fourth-degree indurate, was but one among hundreds of thousands of low-ranked elders, distinguished only by the fact that he enjoyed singing more than others did. He had no idea why the King wanted to see him. Could it be that the King cared that he . . . was about to die?

Around him, countless worlds within a distance of ten million structures had already been colonized by the descendants of those early Star-Pluckers. Who knew how they managed to breed so fast—faster even than the disgusting matrix insects. The arrogant little Star-Pluckers were almost flaunting their coordinates now. However, other low-entropy entities no longer dared to cleanse them. They had apparently achieved the capability to defend against mass dots and deflect dual-vector foils. And if more powerful weapons were used against them, they might be able to trace the attack and locate the homeworld, even if they couldn't defend against the weapons. Singer had personally witnessed several cleansing species destroyed in this way.

Because of these Star-Pluckers, an ancient proverb had been changed.

Once, everyone whispered, "Hide yourself well; cleanse well," but now the saying was, "Hide yourself well; don't cleanse at all."

But Singer didn't believe that he would be discovered by the Star-Pluckers. The seed trekked among the worlds at the absolute-limit speed, like a spirit heralding death. From time to time, the seed launched a light-deflector or an inversion ring at a world inhabited by the Star-Pluckers. They were still helpless against such violent tools.

However, cleansing the Star-Plucker worlds one after another did not bring Singer much joy. He had seen many low-entropy entity species flare into prominence in history, and all of them had been extinguished within a few hundred million time grains, their destruction as inevitable as the fall into the star abyss. The Star-Pluckers would be no exception.

Everything dies; only the homeworld endures.

This was the fundamental truth about the world. There was a time when the fringeworld had thought itself strong enough to contest the homeworld and launched an assault, but the homeworld had destroyed it in an instant, eliminating all traces of the fringeworld from the universe.

It was said that the homeworld was built by the Creator himself and possessed the power of the ancient gods, sufficient to destroy the universe. At one time, this was treated as a mere myth. But after the destruction of the fringeworld, everyone came to understand that the legend was literally true. The homeworld possessed the terrifying power to convert the matter in a spiraling branch of a river of stars into a fireworks display.

There was no need to fear a few Star-Pluckers. None at all.

Over time, he had cleansed the Star-Pluckers from more than four hundred worlds. He knew that in this star-cloud, all the other low-entropy entities had died or entombed themselves in silence. He was the only cleanser working on exterminating the Star-Pluckers. Sometimes he felt proud of his achievement, which reminded him of an ancient song:

I am the last cleanser to sweep the cosmic battlefield.
One by one, I heap bodies at the feet of my beloved.
When all the worlds have been cleansed,
I won't have to hide my love,
And she will emerge from her nuptial cocoon as my bride.

Incredibly, the Star-Pluckers did manage to locate his seed and launched a swarm of interstellar worms at it. The interstellar worms shot a constraint ring at the seed in an attempt to immobilize it. Such primitive tools! The seed easily broke the ring, but the swarm shot another. The insane Star-Pluckers managed to toss out tens of thousands of constraint rings, equivalent to the energy of hundreds of stars.

So you want to play! He thought. *Fine, we'll play.*

The seed tore through the constraint rings as easily as ripping the vulnerable skin of light pixies.

He had planned to rid the seed of all constraint rings before exterminating the detestable interstellar worms. But the swarm, apparently terrified, had scattered at the absolute-limit speed before he was completely free. Cowards!

The victorious Singer was about to leave this region of space when the alarm began to sound. The main core on the seed had detected an unsealed dual-vector foil that was rapidly flattening the space around him.

Singer immediately directed the seed to flee, but it was too late. Only then did he realize that the Star-Pluckers had tricked him. The constraint rings had distracted him, and their massive energy release had concealed the reaction signature of the dual-vector foil. The dual-vector foil was now too close for his seed to escape by accelerating to absolute-limit speed.

Crafty little beasts, Singer thought, *do you really think you can defeat me so easily?*

Singer directed the main core to counterseal the dual-vector foil. In principle, this wasn't a difficult task. But the primitive dual-vector foil produced by the Star-Pluckers was so irregular and crude, and had already unfurled over such a large region of space, that the main core had to be pushed to its limit to generate a force field powerful enough to contain it. The seed had no energy to spare for propulsion; the moment the seed tried to leave, the dual-vector foil would break out and reduce this region of space to two dimensions.

Singer's seed was stuck.

Although the seed held the foil at bay temporarily, the power source of the seed wasn't limitless. Every passing moment drained an enormous amount of energy. By the main core's calculations, it could sustain the current output for only a tenth of a time grain. Singer could already see his ultimate fate: flattened by the dual-vector foil into a form without thickness, vanishing into nothingness, leaving not even a single musical note behind.

He was slightly annoyed that the homeworld had not actively taken the step of reducing itself to two dimensions earlier; if it had, he would have been safe from this strike. But then he calmed himself. He was already aged, and wouldn't have survived long as a two-dimensional being anyway. Rather than living out his remaining time grains within the tight confines of two dimensions, it was better to die in the familiar universe of three dimensions.

At least he had time to sing a song he enjoyed.

Singer adjusted the oscillation organ and found the score for a few ancient songs. But just as he was about to sing, the King summoned him.

The King didn't bother announcing herself through the main core; she activated the big eye and surveyed the whole seed, including Singer. This was the King's prerogative—she had the authority to enter any and all big eyes and watch what was happening on all the seeds—but there were more seeds than matrix insect eggs on the beach, and Singer had never imagined that the King would be interested in his insignificant seed, forty billion structures away from her. That his existence was about to be snuffed out meant nothing to the King, separated from him by thousands of star-clouds. He mattered less to her than a speck of dust on the shrine of the Thousand-Dimension Palace—at least she could see the speck of dust with the naked eye.

Using the big eye required great caution. It was the only tool that could bypass the constraints of the absolute-limit speed and connect any two spots instantaneously. Although other low-entropy entities constructed tools similar to the big eye, those tools could not pierce the veils of oblivion as the big eye could. It was a gift from the ancient gods. But according to the wisdom contained in traditional songs, the magic could not be used too often. Otherwise, the Exiled God of Death, who wished for the universe's destruction, might discover the users.

A long-distance big eye summons was used only between the royal family and important ministers, or when an important criminal was put on trial.

He belonged to neither category.

But the King contacted him anyway. She loomed in the big eye, and Singer was overwhelmed by her magnificence. He prostrated himself on the floor, not daring to insult her even with his gaze. Almost by instinct, he murmured the formulaic terms of worshipful praise.

This was only the second time in his life that he had seen the King.

When he was still a child on the homeworld, there was a time when the King's carriage passed over the sky. He had been sitting on the canopy of a stone tree then and managed to catch sight of the King from a distance. What a lovely visage she had—too beautiful to even look at directly. She was more beautiful than any other pliant he had ever seen. But she was the King, eternally youthful, impossible to compare against any other pliant. In his heart, there was none of the carnal desire between indurates and pliants, only a pure spiritual love like the admiration of the abyss whale for the star-clouds. Like poets of antiquity, he learned to sublimate his passion for the King into beautiful but sad songs.

The King had no idea who he was on that day, of course, and never even glanced at him. After the passage of all those intervening time grains, he was now an ancient indurate on the verge of death, and she still looked exactly the same as she had on that day, and she would live on forever.

"Are you Elder Singer?" the King asked, her voice cold and elegant. What a joy it would be to hear the King sing! Singer tried to suppress this thought as soon as he had it. He did not dare let the King sense this disrespectful idea in his organ of cogitation.

"I am indeed the unworthy individual you name," Singer said, his body trembling.

"Come to the Thousand-Dimension Palace. I wish to question you."

"I obey." Singer was surprised by the summons, but he didn't question her. Quickly, he turned on the electric field feeler and attempted a long-distance connection. The homeworld's frequency was already open, and the connection was made without issue. Singer turned off most of his sensors, and a marvelous feeling overwhelmed him. It was as though he were gliding on the wings of an indescribably wonderful melody.

The long-forgotten gravity of the homeworld woke him out of his reverie, and he found himself in a vessel body. The vessel body was young, and he could feel the surging strength in it. Steeling his courage, he looked around. Through the big eye, his organ of cogitation had managed to traverse a distance of forty billion structures to be telepresent in the Thousand-Dimension Palace under the star abyss. It was just as if he had returned to the homeworld himself. He marveled at the sights around him—a wonderland that he had never had the fortune to visit when he had lived on the homeworld.

But soon he realized something was wrong. The palace was no longer the embodiment of perfect beauty. Although he had never been here before, he was sure it had not always looked like this. Ruin was all around. The stone trees that made up the walls and columns of the palace had wilted, and the ground was covered by a layer of crimson leaves, some of which still wriggled. The great hall was half collapsed, and even the altar in the distance was damaged beyond recognition. The photon murals on the walls were covered by messes of string worms. Through the broken walls he could see that the rest of the capital was also in ruins. Carcasses of gargantuan earth-bearing turtles lay all over the place, and only one or two remained standing in the far distance.

Singer gazed up. The sky was dominated by the darkness of the star abyss. The magnificent, incandescent living sea that had once surrounded the abyss was mostly gone, and of the hundred-plus flying cities, only a few remained. A balance bird cried plaintively as it beat its wounded wings with all its strength, but still it fell from the sky. The air of death was everywhere.

Finally, he looked in the direction of the King. The King's spotless body was still sheathed in holy fire, but the flames were very weak, far dimmer than the blinding light that had once outshone the star-clouds. The King's face, though still incomparably beautiful, was filled with sorrow. She was no longer the supreme, inviolate symbol of authority; indeed, she looked just like an ordinary, despairing pliant.

His organ of cogitation began to shake violently. The King and the homeworld, like his seed, were about to die. How was this possible? The homeworld was eternal, and the King deathless!

Then he heard the King's voice. "I'm sorry that you're about to die, Elder."

"It is my honor to die for you, my king. Everything dies, but my king lives in eternity." Though it was but a formulaic phrase, Singer injected it with sincere passion.

"I'm grateful for your loyal service. But . . . I'm about to die as well." The King's voice was serene.

"Impossible!" Although he had guessed at the truth, he still couldn't accept the terrible news from the King's own lips.

"A mysterious low-entropy entity has come," said the King. "My palace has been wrecked; my city has been destroyed; my people have been slaughtered; and my world is in ashes. Though the entity is temporarily gone, it may return at any moment. I and the homeworld . . . we're about to die."

Singer trembled. The impending destruction of the homeworld filled him with rage and despair, but he had no idea why the King chose him to share this news with. The King's next words satisfied his curiosity, but also shocked him to his core.

"Since all this may have something to do with you, I need to access your memories."

"I don't understand," said Singer. Without bothering to explain, the King extended a fiery feeler and stuck it into his organ of cogitation. Singer was stunned. He had not known that it was possible to conduct direct access of the organ of cogitation through the big eye and across forty billion structures.

The King touched him, and he shuddered with delight as she riffled through his organ of cogitation. Despite a long time spent sifting through his mind, she seemed unable to find what she needed. Finally, the King retracted the fiery feeler, disappointed. "I don't see any data about the mysterious low-entropy entity."

"I've never heard of that mysterious low-entropy entity, and it's no surprise that I don't have any data on it." Singer was still baffled.

The King sighed. She extended a fiery feeler to point into the sky, and said, "We suspect that the mysterious low-entropy entity is one of the Star-Pluckers from your patch of star-cloud. Since you were the first to discover this species, I summoned you to see if I can find any clues about it."

"Impossible!" Singer said. "Although the Star-Pluckers have developed quickly, they barely dominate that half patch of their star-cloud. Even now, they haven't been able to leave the star-cloud they call the Path of White Nourishing Liquid. How could they possibly have crossed forty billion structures to attack the homeworld? Even if they came, given their primitive technology they wouldn't even be able to kill a single earth-bearing turtle."

"Not 'they,' but 'it,'" said the King. "The mysterious low-entropy entity is a single individual. We have never encountered such a terrible being on any of the countless worlds we know of. But based on reports from witnesses, we managed to match the description of the mysterious stranger to an entry in the universal core; it is very close to the Star-Pluckers you had cleansed."

"That must be a mere coincidence. The universe has trillions of species of low-entropy entities. It's no surprise that a few of them will resemble each other."

"Perhaps. But I still want to hear your thoughts on the Star-Pluckers. Perhaps it would be helpful to us."

"The Star-Pluckers? I guess they're a bit strange. After I cleansed the home system of the Star-Pluckers, I didn't give them much thought. But later, after a species of low-entropy entities began to spread all over my patch of star-cloud, I wanted to find out more about their origin. One time, I managed to capture one of their interstellar worms and discovered that they were the descendants of the original Star-Pluckers. During a war between the Star-Pluckers and a neighboring system, some individual Star-Pluckers fled their home. All this happened before I cleansed their home system, and so these new Star-Pluckers were not survivors of my initial effort." Singer laid out his explanation with care. Although he was certain the King had already found out everything he knew when she riffled through his memories, he still wanted to clarify any potential confusion. As someone on the verge of death, he wasn't very concerned about being punished, but he didn't want his beloved King to think he was somehow incompetent.

"Don't worry, Elder Singer. You followed established protocols for cleansing, and no one is going to blame you for what happened. It's possible that the mysterious low-entropy entity really has nothing to do with the Star-Pluckers." The King fell silent after these words.

Singer knew that according to courtly protocols, the King's silence indicated that the meeting was over. Although the King hadn't explicitly dismissed him, he should bid his farewell and depart from the vessel body to return to the sinking seed at the other end of the universe. But he wanted to make his time by the side of the King last as long as possible, so after hesitating for a moment, he didn't move.

"Why don't you tell me your opinion of the Star-Pluckers?" the King asked. "I noticed that they had almost taken over a whole star-cloud, a rare accomplishment among low-entropy entities."

"Of course. These lowly beings are cunning, evil, but also full of tenderness. They are xenophobic, arrogant, but also full of anxiety. They view the entire star-cloud as under their dominion, but they've also invented various religions to worship it, calling it their mother. Actually, in some ways, I think they . . . they . . ."

"Don't worry. I'm interested in anything you have to say."

"All right, but please forgive me for any offense. I think they are . . . similar to us in some ways." As soon as the words were out, Singer regretted them. How could he compare the despicable Star-Pluckers to the noble Abyss-Gazers? And in front of the King, too!

But the King seemed to approve of the comparison. "I think you're right, Elder Singer. We call ourselves descendants of the gods, but our nature isn't too different from those base low-entropy entities."

While Singer thought over the King's words, she went on talking. She seemed to be conversing with him, but also to be speaking to herself. "There have long been legends about the havoc wreaked by such mysterious low-entropy entities. Some say that it's a single individual; others say that there are in fact two separate individuals, or perhaps two branches from the same root. We have never paid much attention to such stories. However, a million time grains ago, the Zero-Homers vanished; four hundred thousand time grains ago, the Cogitators disappeared; three hundred and fifty thousand time grains ago, the world of the Danger-Disposers was snuffed out. It was said that the same mysterious force eliminated all of them, perhaps even the same low-entropy entity."

Singer knew very little about the vanished species of low-entropy entities mentioned by the King, except that they were among the oldest civilizations in the universe. They had long advanced beyond the rules for lesser species, and did not conceal themselves. Other than a few idiots who didn't know better, no cleanser dared touch them—not unless they wished to be cleansed themselves. What kind of terrible power could cleanse these civilizations one after the other? If those civilizations had already been eliminated, it was not so strange that it was now the equally ancient homeworld's turn.

"Other than the destructive assault, what else did the low-entropy entity do to the homeworld?" Singer asked. He was really too low-ranked to ask the King such questions, and he was prepared to be reprimanded by the King and to be summarily dismissed from her presence.

But the King answered his query. "That is exactly what I'm worried about the most. The low-entropy entity looked through the databank in our universal core, seeking information about a . . . hidden species."

"But my king! Practically every species in the universe conceals itself. The hiding gene is a part of the nature of all low-entropy entities. Other than a few ancient species and a few foolish newborn species, everyone works hard to conceal themselves," Singer said.

"No, I do not think the mysterious stranger was in search of a common species; rather, it was in search of the Creator's issue. It probably has something to do with the war among the gods in the distant past. Rumors are now rampant on the homeworld that the mysterious low-entropy entity is an envoy from the Exiled God of Death, here to destroy the world on behalf of its master. The ministers have denied the rumors through official channels, but I . . . I don't know." The King's voice quivered like a frightened spirit fish.

Singer understood now why the King was telling him all these secrets. The King at this moment was no different from any commoner. She needed someone to listen to her, but her terror and worry could not be revealed to those serving her by her side. Singer, an ordinary elder about to die billions of structures away, made the perfect audience. The King could reveal her vulnerability to him without concern that he would add to the rumors.

Singer gazed at the King's slightly wan face. The King was simultaneously galaxies away and close enough to touch. He was joyous but also heartbroken.

> *My king is the Creator's most noble daughter,*
> *Here to guard the world on behalf of her father.*
> *The unlit star abyss lies prostrate at her feet,*
> *While the eternal holy flame bathes her in light.*

Singer recalled the ancient songs as well as the creation myths that had been passed down for billions of time grains.

The first god was the God of Death, and death ruled the original universe. Later, the God of Death's eldest son rebelled against his mother, finally exiling the elder god to bring life to the universe and to create a new universe, thus becoming the Creator. But soon, the Exiled God of Death struck back, and so the Creator and the God of Death fought a war that shook the very foundation of the cosmos, ending with the God of Death being exiled once more. But the Creator departed as well, leaving behind the Abyss-Gazers—the descendants of the Creator, and Singer's people.

This was no mere myth. The King was herself the best proof. She had lived from the distant age of gods until now, and she was different from every other Abyss-Gazer. The historians of the homeworld had combed through the few surviving documents from that ancient age to reconstruct the origin of their species.

The Abyss-Gazers had been born in a cloud floating on the living sea surrounding the star abyss. When they had first developed their civilization, they, like the Star-Pluckers, did not know the rules of survival and did not conceal their coordinates. As a result, they were almost cleansed by others, but a superadvanced civilization came to their aid and taught them advanced technology, even creating the homeworld as their permanent shelter. This superadvanced civilization was the Creator, and the ancient myths were largely derived from their contact.

It was possible that the King was originally a member of the Creator civilization.

The historians could not figure out why this ancient civilization would break the rules of survival and help the Abyss-Gazers, even restructuring their civilization. The details of the contact between the Abyss-Gazers and the Creator were lost to time. The Abyss-Gazers could only speculate that the Creator was one of those rare civilizations that embodied universal love and mercy. Of course, this theory had its flaws as well. In their myths, in order to give the Abyss-Gazers security, the Creator had helped them exterminate hundreds of nearby civilizations.

Perhaps only the King knew the truth. She was the only one who had lived through the age of myths and survived until today, and she was the only one who had witnessed the journey of the Abyss-Gazers from mere worms in that cloud on the living sea to one of the most powerful species in the universe. One of her titles was "Daughter of the Creator." The King did not stop people from speculating, but neither did she answer their queries. Indeed, apart from her involvement in decisions that affected the survival of the species, she did not participate in politics at all. It was the Council of Elders that made most policy. Most of the time, the King was worshiped only as a figurehead. But everyone believed that she held the great power passed on from that ancient Creator civilization. She was the perpetual guardian of the Abyss-Gazers and the homeworld, and had rescued her people from multiple crises.

Singer recalled the storied glory of the King when she had ridden forth at the head of the homeworld's army to pacify the fringeworld's rebellion. There was a song about it:

Daughter of the Creator, King of Hosts!
The star-cloud is her battle cape;
Long membrane waves are her feelers.
Like superstrings, she plucks all creation.

She kneads the cosmos into dark matter,
And tosses it into the eternal shadow of the abyss.

But the King in front of him wasn't so terrifying. The curious Singer asked, "Forgive my presumptuousness, my king, but the Creator's issue that this mysterious low-entropy entity is in search of . . . isn't that us?"

The King shuddered, but the flaring light around her indicated anxiety rather than rage. She had apparently been thinking the same thing.

"I don't know," said the King. "Perhaps the low-entropy entity is something we cannot understand at all."

Singer had to think for a moment to understand the King's meaning. He felt shaken to the root of his soul. "If the low-entropy entity really is an envoy from the Exiled God of Death—"

"Then it is looking for us," said the King.

Singer could think of nothing to say.

"I don't know why I'm telling you this, Elder Singer," said the King. "But it doesn't matter. The secret will die with you. I've kept this secret for one billion and three hundred million time grains. I don't want to keep it any longer."

Singer saw that the protective holy flames around the King had grown even weaker. This meant that her life force was weakening. She was growing to be more like just a common pliant.

A pliant he could love . . .

Singer suppressed the disrespectful thought and listened to the King's story.

"The war between the Exiled God of Death and the Creator wasn't a myth; rather, it was true history that happened before the birth of our people. The star abyss itself was the remnant of a great battle. In order to escape slaughter at the hand of the Exiled God of Death, the Creator hid in the living sea near the star abyss. But the Creator was too weak and could only live for a few million more time grains, which was why he created the Abyss-Gazers. We're not the descendants of the Creator, but his creation. As soon as we had evolved primitive intelligence, the Creator taught us civilization and technology, and made me King. And after that, the Creator died.

"I am not the daughter of a god, and I did not come back to life after three days. Like you, Singer, I was once just an ordinary individual, a pliant like any other. But the Creator picked me and gave me an incorruptible body and an indomitable spirit. I had only one mission: protecting the homeworld. The homeworld is a gigantic machine made by the Creator, which disguises incredible mechanisms and power capable of surveilling and detecting the Exiled God of Death's attempts at wreaking vengeance in the universe. As soon as it detects the Exiled God of Death casting the ultimate spell, the machine will be able to trace the god's death palace. At that time, the entire star abyss and the twenty star-clouds around it will be converted into pure energy and projected beyond our universe to destroy the exiled god's death palace."

"Heavens!" exclaimed Singer. "I had no idea that the homeworld possessed such powerful technology." Singer well knew what it meant to convert the star-clouds into energy. It would be enough to destroy everything between the homeworld and his seed, even if a distance of forty billion structures separated them.

"This isn't technology developed by our own species, but an automatic mechanism constructed by the Creator himself. If the exiled god casts her ultimate death spell, everything will be triggered automatically without any action from us. Our only purpose is to protect the homeworld. That was why the Creator endowed us with enough power to dominate the universe. The ancient myths emphasize this point repeatedly."

"But . . . doesn't such an arrangement draw attention to the homeworld?" asked a puzzled Singer.

"The universe is full of life and civilization. The Abyss-Gazers are but one of innumerable civilizations, and no one would have paid any attention to us absent our error of expanding too quickly. For the last few hundred million time grains, we called ourselves the Creator's people, and we expanded everywhere, cleansing all civilizations that stood in our way until our feelers extended to half a universe away, justifying our actions under the guise of better concealing the homeworld. In doing so, we failed to hide ourselves well. I also forgot my own mission. After putting down the rebellion from the fringeworld, I arrogantly believed that the Creator would forever protect us. This is why we have been divinely punished."

Singer didn't know what to say. In the end, he simply said, "But that mysterious low-entropy entity must still not know the secret you're keeping."

"It was able to find those myths and songs of antiquity," the King said, her voice full of sorrow. "If it truly is an envoy from the exiled god, it shouldn't be difficult for it to decipher the truth behind the myths. Even if it doesn't know the true purpose of the Abyss-Gazers, it won't let us go. Many are saying that the low-entropy entity has already left, but I know that's not true. The havoc wreaked by the first assault was simply to allow it to get our data. The real attack hasn't come yet. It's just a matter of time."

And time was running out, as the next time strand approached.

Suddenly, Singer experienced an odd sensation—as though something invisible and insubstantial had permeated his body. An Abyss-Gazer's instinct told him that it was no illusion, but a real change in the physical environment, though he couldn't tell what the change was. He saw the King struggling to stand up, but abruptly the wall behind her collapsed. The bright figure of the King vanished; she was buried under a pile of rubble. Singer cried out in alarm, "No—"

Struggling, he tried to crawl toward the King, but a massive stone tree fell in front of him, separating him from her. Sounds of alarm rang out all around, indicating that disaster had struck the whole city. Abruptly, Singer felt his body become weightless and float off, but the next moment it fell back heavily against the ground. He heard pitiable cries fill the air, and the whole palace grounds tilted, causing his vessel body to roll into a corner. Pain racked him as he came to understand that the earth-bearing turtle that carried the Thousand-Dimension Palace on its back had died.

Like many other low-entropy entities on the homeworld, earth-bearing turtles were both living beings and intelligent machines. The gigantic creatures were basic units in the structures of homeworld cities. In the distant past, the Abyss-Gazers had ridden them and wandered all over the homeworld in search of suitable places to settle. Today, their movements were controlled by the universal core, and they would never fall without warning. Although the Thousand-Dimension Palace appeared as a classical building constructed out of stone trees, it had been thoroughly modified by the universal core so that every load-bearing joint was constantly monitored. It was inconceivable for living walls to collapse or column trees to suddenly topple—and if such an accident did happen, protective force fields would immediately engage and contain the damage. But after the last assault, the intelligent systems had been knocked out of commission. The homeworld, which had been protected in the hothouse of superadvanced technology for hundreds of millions of time grains, was now forced to endure the pain of earthquakes like the worlds inhabited by primitive species.

An earthquake! Impossible! There had never been an earthquake on the homeworld, because it didn't have tectonic plates or a liquid mantle. Singer now knew that the homeworld was a massive machine left by the Creator. Could its interior have suffered catastrophic damage?

Singer felt himself pressed against the ground by some heavy force and could not get up. Even the basic motions necessary to sustain life felt extremely difficult. He could sense his own life field issuing the highest alert for danger. Just then, a balance bird gave out a grievous cry and fell out of the sky, landing next to him, unable to move its wings. Before he could react, a swarm of matrix insects fell and skittered over the ground. They struggled to open their wings and buzzed, but couldn't take off. Singer lifted his gaze to the sky; every flying creature was falling, like a rain of stars.

Singer could leave his vessel body at any time and return to the Star-Pluckers' star-cloud, forty billion structures away, where none of these forces ravaging the homeworld would be able to injure him. But he didn't want to leave, because—the King was here. He struggled to look in her direction, but the fallen stone tree was in the way.

A silver streak flashed. An out-of-control seed swept out of the sky, falling straight at him. Singer thought the seed was going to crash into the altar, but the seed exploded overhead in a burst of blinding white light. The fiery, expanding wreckage, like a blooming dragon-eater flower, threatened to swallow him. But then the conflagration vanished—the Thousand-Dimension Palace's protective field was still in operation. Singer tried to calm his terrified organ of cogitation, but he was surrounded by the barrage of collapsing buildings and the screams of dying Abyss-Gazers.

An invisible enemy was attacking. Singer didn't know what weapon he was using or where the enemy was. It was an apocalyptic scene. For some reason, he thought of the Star-Pluckers. Many time grains ago, when their world sank into the trap of the dual-vector foil, did they also feel as helpless and terrorized?

The same fate had now befallen the homeworld—

Rubble scattered everywhere as a bright colorful beam of light shot heavenward, and the figure of the King rose into the air like an immortal goddess. Gently, she landed next to the Singer. "Are you all right?"

A column of holy fire shot out of her and struck Singer. It wrapped around his body, and he felt the oppressive weight sloughing off. He stood up effortlessly.

"Antigravity," she said, smiling at him. Once again Singer felt full of strength and joy. The King had not fallen; she was still fighting. There was hope for the homeworld.

"My king, what happened? Have the world engines been engaged? Are we leaving the shore of the star abyss?" Singer asked. Now that he had had a chance to calm down, he finally figured out why he had been unable to get up from the ground, why the palace walls and the stone trees had toppled, and why the flying beasts and insects had fallen down—it was because the homeworld's engines had been activated to accelerate somewhere. It was said that the homeworld had the power to accelerate to the absolute-limit speed within a short period of time. Typically the world would never accelerate without giving some warning or taking protective measures, but this was a crisis . . . Still, if the homeworld was about to change course, why had the King seemed not to know about it?

The King's feelers flickered in denial. "I don't think that's possible. We can't depart the star abyss, otherwise the countermeasures against the Exiled God of Death would be rendered ineffective. This was the most important directive from the Creator. Could the Council of Elders have decided to do this? But they don't have the authority to turn on the world engines. Unless—"

Singer thought of another possibility: An extremely massive object had suddenly appeared on the other side of the homeworld, and the homeworld was falling into its gravity well. The world engines would be activated in such an emergency to ensure that the homeworld didn't deviate from its orbit. This would also be manifested in a sudden increase in gravity on the surface of the homeworld.

But what could such an object be? A sun? A massive planet? Singer could not imagine what force would be capable of suddenly moving a gigantic heavenly body behind the homeworld, past the layers of advance-warning systems around the homeworld that extended several structures into space. Just imagining the homeworld sinking into the fiery flames of a sun made Singer's body stiffen with terror.

"There's no need to be afraid." The King sensed the agitation in his organ of cogitation and tried to comfort him. "Even if the sudden increase in gravity came from a giant sun nearby, the homeworld's automatic protection systems would be able to snuff it out like a chemical flame within a single time strand."

The King turned to the altar and asked, "Universal core, what is this new gravity source?"

A bright, simulated sphere of flames appeared above the altar. "I have not detected any new gravity source."

The King and Singer stared at each other. The King said, "Impossible! The gravity on the homeworld has increased by at least a factor of ten. Have the world engines been activated?"

"No. You're the only one with the authority to start the world engines, my king."

"Then . . . what is happening?"

"I apologize," said the universal core. "These conditions are unprecedented. I am currently trying to gather the data from two million four hundred thousand monitoring points on the homeworld and around it. I hope to have the results of my analysis soon."

The wait that followed was almost maddening. At last, the flames of the universal core jumped, indicating that it had the results.

"My king, preliminary analysis indicates that we are the target of a physical law alteration strike. The epicenter is at star abyss coordinate □142. 522▽624.713◇64.214, and the affected region is a sphere 1.43 structures in diameter centered around that point. Within the targeted region, all gravitons have been stimulated by unknown high-energy particles to increase their rate of rotation, resulting in the local gravitational constant changing from 31.772 to 381.213, about a twelvefold increase."

A *fundamental physical constant has been altered?* At first, Singer wasn't sure what this meant, but it at least seemed to be better than having a massive heavenly body suddenly materialize behind the homeworld or being the victim of a dimension-reduction attack. As long as they had the protection of antigravity, it shouldn't be a big deal.

But Singer was surprised by the odd expression in the King's presentation-pose: It looked simultaneously like shock and like tranquility, as though inescapable despair had paradoxically given her peace. Singer knew something was wrong. Gingerly, he asked, "My king—what does this mean—"

The King remained mute.

Singer repeated his question.

The King extended her feelers helplessly and pointed at the sky. Singer looked up. All the flying creatures and flying machines had fallen. There was nothing up there except the star abyss.

But the star abyss! Oh, Creator!

Singer understood. Simple physics equations dictated that the gravitational constant was directly proportional to the collapse radius of the star abyss. If the gravitational constant increased twelve times, then the star abyss's collapse radius would also grow by a factor of twelve, which would now extend beyond the orbit of the homeworld.

The homeworld is going to fall into the star abyss.

No, not "going to fall," but "has already fallen."

The homeworld was already within the collapse radius of the star abyss. It was going to sink rapidly and inexorably into the bottom of absolute darkness.

The homeworld had 120,000 space engines. With all of them in operation, the homeworld could approach the absolute-limit speed within a very brief period of time, sufficient to escape any conventional attack. But this was of no use now. Even if they achieved absolute-limit speed right away, they wouldn't be able to escape the star abyss. The collapse radius marked the boundary within which even long and short membranes, which traveled at the absolute-limit speed, could not escape.

The homeworld had been swallowed by the star abyss.

This was the true assault by the mysterious low-entropy entity. It gave the homeworld no opportunity to resist.

The King and Singer entwined their feelers, comforting each other. In this instant, they were no longer ruler and subject divided by an unbridgeable gulf in rank, no longer strangers separated by billions of structures in distance, but only an ordinary indurate and an ordinary pliant facing desperate straits together.

In the dark space far above the Thousand-Dimension Palace, a door limned by a faint rectangular glow opened.

The angel who brought death upon the homeworld appeared in the door. He was drifting in space, as though unaffected by gravity. Silently, expressionlessly, he watched the homeworld below him turn into a hellscape of flames.

He was not proud of what he had done, but neither did he experience any guilt. An envoy from this world had once destroyed his homeworld, and now he had destroyed it in return. This was fair. It wasn't vengeance; it was—fate.

Life required death, and destruction gave rise to rebirth. Everything was going to recur along the same paths. Billions and billions of years later, this world would reappear once more and repeat its long and glorious history: prosperity and dream, love and conspiracy, democracy and science, war and death . . .

The same as what had already happened.

The same as every other world.

The same.

That same moment, 2.5 structures away

There was a tiny, inconspicuous patch of interstellar dust floating beyond the border of the star abyss world, not too far from the thousands of interstellar routes filled with traffic of the Abyss-Gazers, who considered the dust cloud a useless wasteland. There were bits of dark matter hidden within the dust, but the quantity was minuscule. No one thought there was anything worth digging for in the dust patch, and if they did try to dig, they'd find nothing.

The homeworld's space engines rumbled to life. The ground shook as the world struggled above the abyss like a curvature fish flapping in a too-shallow puddle, striving to gain a few more moments against its inevitable doom.

But the universal core had already computed the precise moment of the homeworld's destruction. "The space engines have sufficient power to maintain state for another 18.53 time nodes. The homeworld will then begin to accelerate toward the abyss and in another 22.12 nodes reach the fragmentation limit and be torn apart by tidal forces."

In other words, if the local gravitational constant wasn't restored within approximately forty time nodes, the homeworld would be annihilated. The King and Singer both understood that their terrifying enemy had probably accounted for every eventuality and given them no chance of escaping this trap, but they still had to try.

The universal core reported to the King that the surface of the homeworld had descended into complete chaos, and representatives from the Council of Elders, the Executive Council, the Military Council, and the Assembly, as well as officials of every rank, were clamoring for an audience with her. The King denied all requests and wearily said to the universal core, "I have little desire to spend my last few hours in the company of politicians. Besides, what is there to talk about?"

"But it is your duty to comfort and encourage your subjects."

"I have performed my duty for 1.3 billion time grains. I think I have earned the right to rest in the fraction of a grain left. In fact, why don't you rest as well?"

"I will carry out your order instantly," said the universal core.

The universal core vanished, and tranquility returned to the Thousand-Dimension Palace. But the screams and howls of the people continued to filter into the palace from the distant ruins of the city. Impatiently, the King waved her hands, and the gesture seemed to activate some kind of noise-cancellation mechanism, as the pitiable cries of the people faded.

Singer gazed at the King, terrified. He wasn't scared of death, but of

However, there was indeed *something* deep within the dark m
in the dust—

The reminder stimulus activated. One dot, two dots, then
third dot.

That meant a level-three alarm. Something *big* had happened

A long-dormant cognition field awakened. It took a long time
fore the cognition field understood what had happened. It turned
second cognition field.

"2012, wake up! Come see this!"

"Listen, 2046, how many times have I told you? Unless it's *that th*
don't wake me up!"

"You idiot! I'm telling you *that thing* has happened! The thing w
been waiting for for thirty thousand grand years!"

The cognition field let out a sensing filament. The information
turned was so incredible that the cognition field had to reconfirm
result. It was true!

The sensing fields, the cognition fields, the energy fields
everything was coming back to life. Excitement flashed through
the dust cloud.

"My dear, now we are going to get the show of countless lifetim

That same moment, within the collapse radius of the star abyss

The King did not give in to despair. She let go of Singer's feelers
issued an order to the universal core. "All space engines to maximu
Head away from the star abyss. It is possible that our enemy's powe
limited and this state of increased gravitational constant will not
long. We still have a chance."

"We lost 55,144 engines during the initial assault," reported the u
versal core. "Insufficient power."

With a bitter smile, the King quoted an ancient proverb: "A dead l
ance bird is easy to cure."

"I will carry out your order instantly," said the universal core.

the possibility that the King might force him to leave so that she could face death alone.

The King remembered his presence. Turning to him, she said, "The homeworld is about to be destroyed. You should go. At least you're still safe." Indeed, as soon as he left the vessel body Singer would return to the star-cloud forty billion structures away. Even if the homeworld collapsed into a singularity, it wouldn't affect him.

Singer shook his head. "It's all the same. I was about to be two-dimensionalized by those bugs. I'd rather die here than far away at the edge of the known universe. I feel fortunate, as a subject, that I get to welcome my death by the side of my sovereign. Please grant me the honor of staying with you, my king."

The King nodded and smiled at him. "It's good to have you as my companion."

Singer was filled with such overwhelming joy that his voice-making organ stammered, unable to produce a suitable response. The King asked, "Do you know why I'm letting you stay?"

Singer's presentation-pose showed ignorance. The King chuckled. "Because I saw in your organ of cogitation that you like singing old songs, isn't that right?"

"Forgive me," said an embarrassed Singer. "It's a silly habit."

"Not at all. I like it. Some of the songs you like were passed down from the era of my birth. Few people alive now know how to sing them. Could you sing one of them for me?"

"I'm afraid that . . . my rough oscillation organ would be an insult to your heavenly ears."

"Please don't be self-conscious. I like the music made by an indurate voice. Most indurates don't like to sing, but that makes you special."

"All . . . right. I will do my best. Which song would you like to hear?"

"You pick."

Singer pondered for a while, and then selected the song he was most familiar with out of his organ of recall:

I see my love;
I fly next to her;
I present her with my gift,
A small piece of solidified time.
Lovely markings are carved into time
As soft to the touch as the mud in shallow sea.

Slowly, Singer's voice faded, and then stopped. The King's intense gaze seemed odd to him. "What's wrong, my king? Did I . . . sing it wrong?"

"No, you didn't sing it wrong at all. It's just that . . . I wrote the words of this song."

"You are the author?" Singer was astonished.

"No, the song came from the Creator's revelation," said the King. "The Creator implanted the ideas for the song into my organ of cogitation in the form of extremely complex, profound idea-figures. I just recorded the most accessible parts with our written language. Superficially, what I wrote down is just a love song, but I'm certain that the revelation contains important messages, though I don't know how to decode them. What do you think?"

"I don't know either," confessed Singer. "I've always been baffled by 'solidified time,' for example. I thought at first maybe it was a kenning popular in ancient times but whose meaning has become obscured down the ages."

"No," the King said with absolutely certainty. "This was not some ancient metaphor whose tenor has been lost. 'Solidifed time' came directly from the Creator's oracle—there's no mistake. Keep on singing, Elder. Perhaps we can discover some significance together."

Singer continued.

She paints herself with time,
And pulls me to fly together to the edge of existence
In a spiritual flight.

The stars appear as ghosts in our sight;
We appear as ghosts in the stars' sight.

  . . .

When Singer used to sing this song, his organ of cogitation had always been filled with a sense of sweet sorrow. But now that he knew that the words of the song represented a mystery dictated by the Creator, Singer was hearing them in an entirely new light; every word seemed to be the locus of countless competing esoteric interpretations.

Solidified time; spiritual flight; stars appear as ghosts . . .

Singer's organ of cogitation trembled. "My king, if this poem really represents the Creator's truth, then I think it's possible that—no, forget it. It's too absurd."

"Tell me your theory, Elder. What can be more absurd than what is already happening to us?"

"All right." Singer tried to sort out his thoughts. "I think it's possible to read the poem as an extended metaphor. 'I' refers to the Creator; 'my love' refers to our universe; 'solidified time' is the gift the Creator gave us. The Creator solidified time, gave it shape, and endowed the universe with it."

The King's seven eyes grew very wide, indicating that she was concentrating. After some time, she looked up into the sky. "Did you hear that, universal core? What do you think? Can time be solidified?"

The universal core came back to life immediately. "Since this is a metaphor, it can be interpreted in many ways. But if we restrict the domain to physics, time's solidification can be read as a description of the dimensionalization of time. In other words, it was the process by which time became . . . time."

"Isn't time fundamentally a dimension?" asked the King.

"No. Time itself is not a dimension, but a form of energy distribution. Scientists had long since realized that the dimensionalization of time is a compensation for the universe's dimensional differential."

"What's dimensional differential?"

"The only balanced state for the universe is in ten dimensions. When the number of dimensions has been reduced below that, the curling up of certain dimensions into the quantum realm ruptures the balance between matter and energy and leads to the mutual annihilation of particles and antiparticles. The disturbance in the total energy in the universes leads to the separation of energy and gravity, which must be balanced by the transformation of time."

Singer did not seem convinced by this explanation, and the King looked just as baffled. The universal core went on.

"Scientists believe that the universe's initial state is ten-dimensional, but it is in the process of collapsing into ever fewer dimensions. Each collapse leads to a dramatic imbalance between matter and energy, leading to space constantly expanding in the remaining dimensions. Since energy is unevenly distributed in the expanded universe, the high-entropy universe becomes low-entropy, which leads to directed transformation going from a low-entropy state back to a high-entropy state. This is the meaning of time."

"Are you saying that there was no time in the ten-dimensional universe?" Singer asked.

"That is not an easy question to answer. The ten-dimensional universe was changeless, and so it could be described as lasting but an instant or for eternity. All we can say is that it had no time as we understand the concept."

As Singer thought over the universal core's ideas, his organ of cogitation flashed with bursts of light. Then he cried out to the universal core, "Then the Creator made time! And it gave time to us! Am I right?"

"This is a guess without any scientific basis," said the universal core drily. "I can offer no useful response."

"But then the explanation is obvious. The purpose of time is to bring us to the edge of existence, which is just another way to describe the unceasing process of dimension reduction in the universe. This is the meaning behind the 'spiritual flight'!" Singer was excited that the lyrics that had resisted his understanding for so long yielded such profound meanings.

"What about the two lines about ghosts and stars?" asked the King. Since the universal core was no expert at literary interpretation, it remained silent.

"It seems to be a description of space flight, but something about it doesn't feel quite—" Singer hesitated, but then his organ of cogitation flashed again. "The ghost imagery suggests something that is visible but insubstantial. Everything in the universe is subject to the absolute-limit speed. To fly from any star-cloud to any other star-cloud requires at least hundreds of millions of time grains, and even flying from one star to another often takes more time than is allotted to one life. For most low-entropy entities I've encountered, the stars are untouchable ghosts, and the intelligent species themselves, carefully hidden from the stars, are also ghosts to the inhabitants of other worlds. Everything is divided from everything else by vast gulfs of time and space. If you think about it, out of the billions and billions of worlds in each star-cloud, most will live and die in obscurity without our knowledge at all, and most of them will never know anything about us, either. We and the rest of the universe are mired in time."

"But the condition you describe is a consequence of the absolute-limit speed and has nothing to do with time," said the King. "Indeed, the situation may be said to be the result of there being too little time in the universe." Singer thought this made sense and wondered if his own speculation had veered too far off the right path.

"I'm not so sure about that, my king," said the universal core. "Theory suggests that the absolute-limit speed and time are intimately connected. With the loss of each dimension by the universe, due to the expansion of space-time, the absolute-limit speed seems to go down by an order of magnitude or two while time simultaneously increases by multiple orders of magnitude. Although Elder Singer's explanation is not subject to proof, it is at least self-consistent."

The King and Singer gazed at each other in wonder. Somehow, the grand mystery of the stars had been unveiled before them.

The Creator gave the universe time. Time not only brought change and progress, but also gave low-entropy entities existence. Time and the absolute-limit speed are two sides of the same blade that divided the universe, isolating most species of low-entropy entities and their civilizations in tiny corners of the vast cosmos. It was impossible for most to understand the true mystery of the world, and the madness of preemptive slaughter for the sake of survival became the norm.

But in some sense, the condition in the universe was a kind of mercy. The darkness of space was a cloak for the protection of the weak. It meant that it was possible for those we loved to conceal and hide, rather than to lie exposed to the enemies' strikes.

Time was the Creator's greatest gift. Time gave rise to life and everything that accompanied it. Time frustrated the ambition of tyrants who wished to conquer the universe and ground them into dust, and gave countless embryonic civilizations the space necessary to evolve and flourish. The only things sacrificed on the altar of time were dimensions—and the Exiled God of Death.

(If Guan Yifan, who was at this moment enjoying a bucolic life with Cheng Xin in the mini-universe Yun Tianming left for them, could hear this song and understand its meaning, he would have understood that what he termed "the universe's three and three hundred thousand syndrome" was in fact a blessing for the cosmos.)

"Universal core, why couldn't you have decoded the important hidden message in this song earlier?" The King's voice was tinged with anger.

"I haven't decoded anything," the universal core said patiently. "I'm simply providing some scientific support for the interpretation offered by Elder Singer. You know very well that scientists have no interest in such ancient songs, and would never have connected the songs with any scientific mystery."

"Oh, but if we had understood the songs much earlier, then

perhaps . . . perhaps . . ." The King could not continue. Dejected, she shrugged her feelers. "Forget it. Even if we had known the meaning earlier, we couldn't have done anything with the information. We could not have stopped the angel of death."

"No!" Singer said. "Even if the answer to the riddle of the song can't help us escape our fate now, it still tells us something significant."

"And what's that?"

"My king, time is the Creator's gift. Time made our rich and varied existence and society possible, but we had to pay a price for this gift: to be bound up in time. We had to submit to death and destruction. From the coddled interior of an eternal existence, we were pulled to the edge, where we must live and die in time. We are neither of existence nor of nonexistence, but always in a state of growth and change, ending with death."

The King smiled painfully. "I think you're right. There was a time when I thought the Creator had given me eternal life, but only now do I understand that the purpose of my life is to witness the destruction of the homeworld. The Creator must have known this day would come because he understood that everything must die in the universe. Look, even the Creator has drowned in the river of time. Why should we be so troubled by our impending death then? Elder Singer, why not sing some more old songs, and see if they also contain answers left by the Creator?"

They went through more than a dozen songs passed down from the age of the Creator, and two more songs seemed to contain the same information as the song they had just deciphered. From a few other songs, they managed to recover metaphors describing the ten-dimensional universe as a pool of stagnant water, portrayals of the tragic warfare raging across the universe as it lost dimension after dimension, and reflections on the divergent civilizations of the Creator and the Abyss-Gazers. The rest of the songs no doubt held important information as well, but no matter how much they tried, the King and Singer could not decipher them and had to give up in the end.

"How much time is left, universal core?" the King asked as she lifted her feelers.

"11.32 time nodes."

The King laughed. "So soon? Ever since the Creator made my body incorruptible, I've never felt time pass so quickly."

"As fast as the blooming of star-dust flowers—" Singer sang, a line from an old song.

"And love's half-life," the King sang, the next line.

Singer was about to say something when the King turned to the universal core and spoke first. "It's time. We should abandon all pointless fantasies. Universal core, please connect me to all reachable big eyes, I will now speak to my subjects on all awayworlds and seeds."

Singer realized that somehow, strength and determination had returned to the King.

The big eye's ability to bridge vast distances instantaneously wasn't affected by the change in the star abyss's collapse radius—otherwise Singer couldn't have maintained his telepresence in the vessel body. Nonetheless, the universal core issued a warning to the King. "This requires complex multistate tele-entanglement. Given that we have over a hundred thousand awayworlds and thirty million seeds, that means more than two hundred million big eyes need to be connected. This will present an immense drain on our energy, and the universal core may stop working at any time."

"I must carry out my duty," said the King calmly. "As must you."

"I will carry out your order instantly."

The universal core flashed through a constantly shifting spectrum of colors as it operated at maximum capacity. A few moments later, the King walked onto the half-collapsed altar. Holy fire in twelve colors sheathed her unsullied form, lifting her high into the air. Singer gazed up at the rising figure of the King and saw a silvery sphere appear around her. This meant that the big eyes were in operation. A three-dimensional projection of the King was instantaneously being broadcast to every corner of the universe where Abyss-Gazers lived. At this moment, the inhabitants of the awayworlds did not yet know what had happened.

"My noble Abyss-Gazers." The King's greeting was without any trace of fear or despair, but also without any melodrama. It was strong and calm. Only Singer understood the torrents of emotion under her tranquil exterior.

"I am your King, and this will be the last time I speak to you. The apocalypse predicted by our ancient epics has come true: We have been struck by an unknown physical law alteration strike. The local gravitational constant near the star abyss has been increased twelvefold, which means that the homeworld and I are now falling into the star abyss and cannot escape. We will be destroyed in little more than ten time nodes."

Although Singer could not see what was happening on the other worlds, he could imagine that on thousands of prosperous, peaceful worlds, countless compatriots were seized by extreme terror and pain. The emotion organs were on the verge of collapse as the Abyss-Gazers were lost in helpless confusion.

But the next pronouncement from the King shocked them even more.

"Do not lament us, my fellow Abyss-Gazers. The destruction of the homeworld is insignificant compared with what is about to happen next: The life of the whole universe is at an end."

In the darkness among the stars, the angel of death quietly observed this farewell speech, as though nothing in the cosmos could break his calm demeanor. Still, his eyes flashed at these words from the King.

The riddle has been answered; the Lurker has revealed itself.

But the angel of death did not know that behind him, not too far away, two more mysterious observers were also following the proceedings avidly.

"For eons," the King continued, "I have protected the universe's greatest secret alone. But it is now time to reveal everything. Abyss-Gazers, you have the right to know. The universe has the right to know.

"You all know the legend from ancient times. The God of Death had once reigned over primeval chaos, and the Creator rebelled and exiled his mother and created the world of forms. I tell you now that the legend was true. From the age of gods, the war between the God of Death and the Creator has never stopped. In that war, our universe collapsed by stages from ten dimensions to three. Each time, the Creator stopped the God of Death's attempt to destroy the universe, but was also weakened in the process.

"In the early days of the three-dimensional universe, the Creator and the God of Death engaged in what they thought of as a final contest. The God of Death was defeated once more and escaped out of the universe, leaving behind only a single avatar. But the Creator didn't win either; he died soon after. Our universe thus lost its sole protector and lay exposed to the gaze of the Exiled God of Death.

"Fortunately, the Creator made our world before his death. He left us his final directive and a countermeasure against the God of Death. We, the Abyss-Gazers, are his heirs, protecting the universe in the Creator's stead. That's right, we can trace our lineage to the beginning of time; we're the children of the gods.

"The homeworld is the countermeasure left by the Creator. As long as the homeworld exists, if the Exiled God of Death tries to release the death spell, her death palace will be destroyed, and the exiled god herself will be erased from existence. Because of the homeworld, the universe has been safe for more than a billion time grains.

"The only power in the universe capable of destroying the homeworld is the Exiled God of Death. She knows of the existence of the homeworld, but she doesn't know the location. For hundreds of millions of time grains, she sent numerous envoys across the universe in search of the homeworld. All of them have failed until this last one, who has found us and breached our databank. And so we shall die.

"I do not despair over our loss, my fellow Abyss-Gazers, and neither should you. This is a war where mere mortals dare to challenge a god.

That supreme power and intelligence, originating in the ten-dimensional universe, is capable of collapsing the universe as well as reexpanding it. How can we be expected to contest such power? More important, we have maintained our civilization for more than 1.3 billion time grains and defended the homeworld throughout that time, protecting the whole universe. Any species should be proud of such an achievement.

"More than 1.3 billion time grains ago, the Creator left me a message. However, I didn't understand its meaning until now. I hope to share the message with you now, in my final moments: The Creator brought forth time and gave the universe life. From that moment on, everything in the universe was doomed to be lost in the vastness of space-time and, with time's passage, corrupted. We are no exceptions. Even if our lives were extended for a hundred billion more time grains, we'd still have to face death one day.

"With our death, the universe will not last much longer on a cosmic scale. My people, you will likely spend the remainder of your lifetimes in peace, and perhaps so will your children. Tens of thousands of time grains may still lie ahead of you. I wish you all to remember that time is a precious gift from the Creator. Don't waste it! Everything ultimately will return to nothingness, but you must enjoy every time grain, every time node, every time strand—that is the true meaning of life.

"The Creator endowed civilization with time, but we gave time the gift of civilization."

The King still wanted to speak a few more words, but the universal core reminded her that the homeworld's energy supply was nearing exhaustion. She was running out of time. She ended her speech with a common phrase that brought heartbreak and anguish to all low-entropy entities, all civilized species, and all mortals and gods in the cosmos: "Farewell then, for the last time."

The King's image disappeared from big eyes across the universe. All Abyss-Gazers everywhere sank into sorrow, terror, and despair.

In the darkness on the other side of the homeworld, the angel of death shook his head and sighed.

"2046, she's really something, isn't she?" one of the two observers in the dark matter exclaimed.

"Indeed . . . I've always admired and loved her," the other said after a beat.

Their energy supplies depleted, the world engines shut off. The lights over the homeworld dimmed. Like a will-o'-the-wisp, the homeworld drifted toward the ocean of darkness.

Inside the Thousand-Dimension Palace, the silvery sphere vanished like a popped bubble. Like a periodic swan, the King gracefully landed. Singer and the King gazed at each other with their multiple pairs of eyes. It was so quiet that even the whispers of the stardust blossoms could be heard.

"Thank you, Elder Singer," said the King.

Singer looked confused, and so the King explained. "I'm grateful for your interpretation of the ancient songs. You have released me from the heaviest burden of guilt in the universe. For 1.3 billion time grains I've dreaded the arrival of this moment, but now that it's here, I'm not afraid at all.

"Three hundred million time grains ago, during the terrible war between the homeworld and the fringeworld, I made the difficult decision of rejecting the plan to two-dimensionalize. At the time, many protested my choice, and the voices of opposition didn't subside until the defeat of the fringeworld. One of the reasons behind my choice was our civilization's mission: to defend and preserve the homeworld. Two-dimensionalization would have destroyed the homeworld, and I could not take such a step. This was why my heart was in ashes when the gravitational strike from the angel of death occurred. Had we entered two dimensions, perhaps none of this would have happened. I thought it was my fault.

"But your explanation made me realize that the Creator did not make us so that we could merely survive forever, but so that we could enjoy each time node and face death with tranquility. As long as we keep that in mind, it doesn't matter if we live for a single time grain or ten billion."

"No, it is I who should thank you!" said an excited Singer. "I'm utterly disgusted by the idea of living in two dimensions. The very thought of living a single day in a flat world makes me suffocate. Even a prisoner gets to have a space to live in, but we would have been imprisoned in an infinitely thin plane. We would have forgotten even the existence of another dimension. What a tragedy!"

"Do you really think so?" The King was moved by Singer's display of emotion. "I felt the same way, but the other elders and the generals did not understand me. I should have made you prime minister."

"It's not too late. I could be recorded in history as the last prime minister of our people."

"Oh, but that's impossible. The appointment would require the consent of the Council of Elders and the Assembly, and there's no time for that now. I suppose you'll have to settle for being recorded as the last power-hungry indurate who plotted to seize the office of the prime minister."

They laughed together—though laughter for the Abyss-Gazers consisted only of body movements expressing joy, a harmonious dance of swaying feelers. After a while, the King said, "Singer, let's sing that old song together one more time, shall we?"

Singer noticed that the King was calling his name without the title of "Elder."

"Let's do it, my king—"

"Oh, stop that. I have carried out my last duty as the king. Call me by my name . . . Red."

"All right, Red." Singer did not feel odd calling his sovereign by her name. After all, before death, everyone and everything was equal.

And so, together in harmony, they sang that song from time

immemorial, a song that perhaps had been devised by the Creator from countless universes before this one, from the time before the cosmos had time.

> *I see my love;*
> *I fly next to her;*
> *I present her with my gift,*
> *A small piece of solidified time.*
> *Lovely markings are carved into time*
> *As soft to the touch as the mud in shallow sea.*
> *She paints herself with time,*
> *And pulls me to fly together to the edge of existence*
> *In a spiritual flight.*
> *The stars appear as ghosts in our sight;*
> *We appear as ghosts in the stars' sight.*
>
> . . .

Singer heard the King's voice, cool yet passionate, like a burning comet, like a frozen solar corona, as distant as a river of stars, as melancholy as a cooling star-fog, as moving as the love that he had never had . . .

Singing for the Abyss-Gazers consisted of the oscillation of a particular kind of electromagnetic wave, which the Abyss-Gazers called primitive membrane. They could "hear" with their eyes the actual waveforms that made up their song. Singer saw that the King's warbling voice was transforming the light in the space around her into a shimmering lake of mercury, and the notes fell into the lake like drizzling raindrops, producing overlapping concentric ripples. The ripples from the King's song collided with the ripples from his, and the notes reinforced each other, merged into each other . . .

Maybe these are the "lovely markings . . . carved into time"? thought Singer.

And maybe they're on the "spiritual flight" now, the flight to the edge of existence, to the star abyss . . .

The moment of destruction was at hand.

As tidal forces overwhelmed the structural integrity of the home-world, a massive interior explosion broke it apart. Suspended in midair and protected by the last remnants of the holy flames, the King and Singer watched helplessly as long cracks and fissures ripped through the land beneath them, merged into massive canyons, and then cleft the ground shell of the world to reveal the massive, intricate interior machinery.

The mysterious, gigantic mechanisms unveiled to their eyes were incomprehensible, unimaginable, but also now meaningless. The countermeasure mechanism had been destroyed, and there was now no force in the universe that could resist the return of the Exiled God of Death. A storm caused by the air escaping the interior of the world seized Singer and the King and lifted them high into the sky, from where the stunned pair watched the apocalyptic scene playing out far beneath them.

"Singer, I'm afraid." The King pressed herself against Singer, and unveiled her organ of cogitation to him. They now communicated by passing thoughts directly to each other.

What do you think is inside the star abyss? Is it a dark hellscape where all matter is compressed to a density impossible to imagine?

No, maybe we'll find a warp point inside, leading to another space-time, another universe.

Do you really believe that? We will head to another universe?

No one has ever gone to that universe, and so I don't know. But there is an ancient song that I remember:

"Outside this universe, there are nine other universes.
*This life is at an end, but no one knows about the life to come."**

*Translator's Note: A reader familiar with the work of the Tang Dynasty poet Li Shangyin (813–858 CE) will probably recognize this song as paraphrased from a line in Li's "Ma Wei," a poem that meditates on the love between Emperor Xuanzong and his consort Yang Guifei.

It's lovely, but I've never heard this song before.

It's not a song from the traditions of our people. I discovered it in the databanks of the Star-Pluckers. It's about a king of the Star-Pluckers and his yearning for his dead lover.

Their king also loved someone?

That's right. Their king was just like an ordinary individual. He lived, he died, he loved, he raged . . .

As they conversed, Singer sank into the King's organ of cogitation and lost himself in the intoxicating embrace of another, unfamiliar but also welcoming consciousness. The King pressed herself into Singer's organ of cogitation, and felt the presence of her own thoughts in the thoughts of the other . . . The organs of cogitation entwined themselves, and as the pair trembled, they completed the oldest ritual of expressing love among the Abyss-Gazers and became one.

A part of Singer's consciousness reminded him that back in the star-cloud where his true body was located, his seed had used up its last bit of power. The dual-vector foil launched by the descendants of the Star-Pluckers was dragging his body into the expanding plane of death. His death in that world was probably going to come even faster than his death in this one.

That's all right, he thought. And he extended all his feelers to embrace even more tightly the King, who was immersed in the joy of a love that had arrived too late.

At that moment, the angel of death still observed everything calmly.

If he wished, he could rescue that dying world as easily as extending his hand. All he had to do was to pull an invisible string, and the local gravitational constant would return to normal. And if he pulled it again, it would become even smaller, asymptotically approaching zero . . . and then the star abyss would be nothing more than an insignificant hard ball of matter, devoid of fatal attraction. The people from the homeworld could even land on it and jump around.

All he had to do was to extend his hand.

Finally, the angel of death made up his mind and extended his left hand, as though grasping for something invisible. A small ball of flame appeared in his palm, which quickly extinguished and turned into something substantial.

A tiny, transparent glass tumbler, filled with a strange green liquid.

The angel of death admired the glass in his hand. He had re-created the temperature, pressure, gravity, and other conditions of his homeland. He drained the glass in a single gulp and sighed satisfyingly. Then he extended his hand again.

"Give me another Green Tempest," he muttered.

No matter what, this was a day worth celebrating.

Another glass filled with Green Tempest appeared. But as the angel of death reached for it, another hand, feminine in appearance, grabbed it first.

"*Hic mihi.*" The voice was clear and smooth. A figure emerged from the floating rectangular outline behind him. Limned by the faint light from the door, the figure appeared to be a woman with blond hair and Caucasian features. She was dressed in silver, and her blue eyes flashed with strength and confidence.

"*Sis,*" said the angel of death, the Latin pronounced as gracefully as his wave at the drink.

They continued their conversation in Latin.

"You've found them?" asked the woman.

"Looks like it."

"Shall we inform the Master?" She raised a hand, and a ring glinted brightly on her finger.

After a beat, the angel of death nodded.

That same moment, 2.5 structures away

"Turn on the cosmic surveillance system," said 2012. "The fourth lure has been destroyed. The Prime Mother may make her move soon."

"I can't believe it," 2046 said. "After thirty thousand grand years, the day we've been waiting for is finally here!"

"I still remember what it was like when we first started feeding those little lizards. They've turned out to be rather gentle and obedient, haven't they?" He sensed a subtle shift in the cognition field of his companion. "What's wrong? Why are you upset?"

"Didn't you see? My little pet Red is dead! For the past thirty thousand grand years, my only entertainment has been observing her running around: riding a flying cart to survey her domain one moment, and getting suited up in armor to go to war the next. What a cute creature! And now she's gone, crushed in the star abyss."

"I do feel bad about that. But at least she made the most of her death by telling the whole universe that she was our heir and descendant. That was some speech she gave there at the end!"

"Of course it was a good speech. Do you know how hard I worked way back then to implant the order deep in her mind? I had to be incredibly careful so that she wouldn't detect it; else it wouldn't have worked so well."

"You are certainly clever."

"I didn't come up with the idea myself. It's all part of the Great Mind's plan."

At the mention of the Great Mind, both observers' cognition fields flattened to be more serious. After a moment, 2046 said, "Is it time to awaken the Great Mind?"

"Do you want to be eaten by him right away? Forget it. Let's wait until the last possible moment before waking him."

"Fine. I prefer to stay independent for a little while longer, too. It won't be long anyway."

But as time passed, nothing happened. Only the three-dimensional numbers on the display field flickered rapidly, shifting through a series of odd geometric shapes.

After a while, 2012 asked, "Do you think those Seekers saw the speech by little Red?"

"If you saw it, then of course they saw it," said 2046.

"So I'm guessing that they've received our message?"

"Of course."

"And they've probably passed the message on to the Prime Mother?"

"Very likely so."

"Then why hasn't the Prime Mother attacked?"

"Be patient! You're talking about dimension reversal. To restart the whole universe is not as simple as exploding a couple of galaxies."

"What's the difference? You know as well as I do that the old witch doesn't require any time to think. If she wants to act, she will act immediately."

"Maybe she's waiting . . ."

"For what?"

"To see whether this is a trap."

"Are you suggesting that the Great Mind's plan might have a flaw?" 2046 was growing agitated.

"No. But who knows if you executed it perfectly?" 2012 countered.

"That's ridiculous," said an angry 2046. "I implemented the Great Mind's foolproof plan of four sequential lures with impeccable precision. That was how we managed to lead the Seekers down the path we wanted them to follow. The Zero-Homers at the beginning were the most obvious targets, but if they were the main lure, the Seekers would have been suspicious of their easy success. That was why we had them find clues from the Zero-Homers that led to the Cogitators. We planted two sets of clues with the Cogitators: one set leading to those rather insane Danger-Disposers, and the other leading to the Star Abyss Lizards. Sure, the Danger-Disposers looked like the bigger threat, since everyone knew that vacuum decay was part of dimension reversal, and so the Seekers had to go check out the Danger-Disposers first. But then they discovered that the Danger-Disposers were not the real targets, though their creation myth also came from the Star Abyss Lizards. With both investigative paths converging, they had to come to the conclusion that the lizards were the true target they sought.

"They then dug out the 'proof' from the lizards' databank, and that speech from the Lizard King provided additional confirmation. They knew that they had found the Lurker! We even provided an explanation for why it was so easy to destroy the Lurker—it had died, and the lizards were just servants it had left behind. Everything happened exactly according to plan, which shows that there's no flaw with either the plan or the execution."

2012 had no response to this, but he wasn't willing to concede just yet. "The Seekers are all very suspicious. There's still a chance they think all of this is a trap."

"Maybe. The universe is full of oddball low-entropy entities. But I don't think the Prime Mother will doubt her success here. She's too arrogant! Just listen to what she calls herself: 'Master.' What is she master of? And she calls us the 'Lurker'! Does she really think all we want to do is to hide, holed up in some obscure corner of the universe? She sends waves of Seekers to find us because she thinks as soon as we've been discovered, we'd be helpless. But she never even considered the possibility that we would do the exact opposite: let her find us, let her think we're exterminated, let her celebrate her victory, let her initiate dimension reversal—Oh, I really want to see her stupefied cognition field when she finds out the truth!"

"That would be a hilarious sight," said 2012. "It's too bad that a supermembrane flash attack will destroy the whole mini-universe. The old witch will be gone in an instant, leaving us nothing to see."

"Anyway, there's nothing to do now except to wait," said 2046.

One grand hour passed. The displays of the cosmic surveillance system continued to show nothing but noise.

Two grand hours passed. Still nothing.

Three grand hours passed. 2012 could take it no more. "Something is wrong! Maybe the Seekers did detect something."

"Impossible! We left no clues! The only supersensing system is located inside the lizards' homeworld, and it would have been destroyed along with that planet. I assure you that though the Seekers are para-noid, they'll make their move in the end. Now that there aren't any more clues, they're not going to examine all the galaxies in the universe one by one. I'm sure they'll swallow the bait."

"I just hope they hurry up!"

Grand hour after grand hour passed, and still nothing happened. The two numeric entities decided to take a nap. 2046 took the time to set an alarm for a hundred grand hours later.

The situation remained unchanged after one hundred grand hours. The two, disappointed, went back to sleep.

No change after five hundred grand hours.

After one thousand grand hours, when the two woke again, despair overwhelmed them.

"What is that old witch doing?" shouted 2046. "How did she figure out it was a trap?"

"The Prime Mother is very powerful, but she's never shown much cunning," said 2012. "I think it's those Seekers."

"Whoever is responsible, all of our efforts have been for nothing. Ten thousand grand years of preparation! Thirty thousand grand years of surveillance and waiting! Four civilizations set out as bait! All wasted, damn it!"

"Calm down. Maybe the trap failed, but we haven't lost yet. At least the Prime Mother still has no idea where we are. Remember, this is a long game—"

"We have to report this to the Great Mind. He's going to"—and here 2046 switched to a private channel for information exchange—"blame us for the failure. What if he decides that we should be absorbed but not completely, and exiles us to the very lowest levels of his consciousness? Then we'd be in hell forever."

2012 shuddered. "I think we should wait some more. Let's wait . . . another one thousand grand hours. We'll decide what to do if nothing changes by then."

And so they went back to sleep again. But this time, after only thirty-four grand hours, the alarm stimulus woke them out of their slumber. They were so excited that their cognition fields threatened to split apart.

One dot, two dots, three dots.

Then the fourth dot. And even a fifth dot.

They flickered wildly, driving the numeric entities mad with their portent.

Never had a level-five alarm been activated. This meant only one possibility: Someone had initiated dimension reversal.

The two numeric entities gazed at the surveillance system's display space. One corner had turned dark, and the dark region was slowly and steadily growing. They knew that the region indicated by the display was a zero vacuum in which positive and negative energy balanced out exactly. It was expanding at the speed of light, devouring everything it touched. Once inside the zero vacuum, all protons, neutrons, and other particles would decay instantly into their natural state and recombine into ten dimensions.

If the deadly region was expanding only at lightspeed, then there was plenty of time left for the universe, which measured fourteen billion light-years across. But the expanding zero vacuum was altering the speed of light itself as it expanded, and it would be expanding faster and faster, accelerating geometrically. Long ago, the Great Mind had calculated the precise amount of time it would take for the cosmos to be consumed by dimension reversal: only 1.91 grand hours. And for 99.999 percent of that time, vacuum decay would consume only about 10 percent of the universe—but during that last, final brief moment, the speed of light would be increased to near infinity and annihilate the whole universe.

There was little time left for them to launch their countermeasure, but it was enough. The counterattack mechanism was undamaged, and they would be able to launch the supermembrane flash strike within one grand hour. The Prime Mother would be destroyed. They could then deploy a few zero-dimension dots and eliminate the threat of vacuum decay.

The eternal war between the mother of the universe and her son, between the Master and the Lurker, between the Exiled God of Death and the Creator, would be finally resolved in favor of the latter in each pairing.

2046 connected to the cognitive thread of the Great Mind.

"My lord! The old witch—um, I meant the Prime Mother—has taken the bait!"

Three hundred million light-years away, the empty space beyond the Sloan Great Wall

In the abyss of an endless ocean of dark matter—

In the bottom of the abyss, where there was no light and no darkness, no lepton and no baryon, no motion and no stillness, no existence and no nonexistence—

The greatest, most incredible intelligence in the universe, the Great Mind, awoke.

During the last battle against the Master, the Great Mind had used up so much energy that it almost died of exhaustion. To preserve its consciousness, it had no choice but to go into deep slumber, awakening only once every few thousand grand years, and then activating its consciousness only partially. A true, total awakening would require the activation of all the hidden networks in dark matter, an event easily detected by the Master. It partitioned off thousands of data nodes from itself, made them into individual numeric cognitive entities, and assigned them to posts across the universe to keep an eye on the enemy and to protect the Great Mind itself.

Today, a plot in motion for forty thousand long years finally yielded the desired result. The newly awakened Great Mind activated the entirety of its cognition field and hungrily devoured every bit of information sent from across the universe. It was like a spider concealed in darkness, deciphering the tremors sent by strands anchored far away.

The torrents of data confirmed the news. Pleased, the Great Mind initiated the consciousness-reabsorption program. Through its web of quantum entanglement, it instantly absorbed all the numeric entities, including 2046 and 2012. For the Great Mind to fully ingest the little minds took no effort, for they were part of it to begin with.

All the numeric entities combined into one, and all the lurking cognition fields thus became a single Lurker. This consumed an astronomical amount of energy, but he didn't care. This was the final battle.

The counterattack system, hidden in the vast dark matter world, was turned on. Based on the detected energy signatures, it quickly calculated the coordinates of the Prime Mother's mini-universe on the supermembrane. This was an effort that consumed nearly 30 percent of the dark matter in the universe. The vast majority of dark matter existed in the empty bubbles between galaxy clusters. Manipulated by the Lurker, the dark matter emitted powerful bursts of electromagnetic radiation, like billions of flowers blooming silently at midnight.

Most of the civilizations in the universe were incapable of detecting this astonishing phenomenon. They lived outside the light cone of the event. When the radiation from the dark matter reached their worlds, however, their nights would be as bright as days, and the varicolored lights would make them realize that their worlds were nothing more than bits of flotsam in a floral sea that had inundated the universe. Those worlds closer to the radiation would be roasted into charcoal, and the ecosystems of countless worlds would be destroyed. But the Lurker did not regret his actions. If he didn't do this, all these worlds and the lives of their inhabitants would be devoured by the death of zero vacuum.

Wielding the grandest war machine in the cosmos, the Lurker confidently turned his inquiring gaze to the supermembrane. In reality, though he was the most powerful intelligence in the universe, even he could not directly observe or touch the supermembrane. Whenever he thought of the billions of universes outside his universe, he experienced a measure of despair. But this time things would be different. The unimaginable eleven-dimensional supermembrane was going to become his battlefield, and he was going to commit matricide there. He would slay the spirit of the ten-dimensional universe, the nonpareil Prime Mother who gave birth to him, and thereby achieve perpetual freedom and security.

This was the last fight in his war, a war that had lasted through a hundred thousand grand years and eight universes.

The end of everything was at hand . . .

The attack node reported that all preparation was complete. As soon as the mini-universe's coordinates on the supermembrane could be confirmed, the doomsday strike could be launched.

Excellent.

The Lurker's attention swept onto the supermembrane-analysis node, which was still working. The Lurker wasn't concerned. He had waited tens of thousands of grand years; what was a few moments more?

Time passed. The supermembrane-analysis node was still working.

It shouldn't take this long, the Lurker realized. *Unless . . .*

His peerless intelligence was capable of coming up with the answer, but he had avoided thinking about it. It was such a terrifying possibility.

He tried to calm himself by examining the display space's representation of the vacuum decay region. It was still growing. But the rate of expansion wasn't accelerating; rather, it was slowing down. Now it was growing at only half the speed of light.

"Impossible!" The Lurker was truly frightened. Vacuum decay shouldn't be so slow. Activating the entanglement web, he turned on one of the backup surveillance nodes near the expanding edge of the vacuum decay zone and endowed it with a fragment of his own mind. He didn't dare connect his own cognition field directly lest the vacuum decay affect it.

"9527, what do you see?" asked the Lurker.

"Stars, planets, galaxies . . . everything is in the sky as a two-dimensional picture! It's two-dimensionalization! The universe is being flattened!" The observer was terrified—not of two-dimensionalization itself, but of the meaning behind the discovery.

There was never any vacuum decay, only two-dimensionalization.

The cosmic surveillance system couldn't look inside the zero vacuum zone and thus couldn't confirm whether any ten-dimensional space was being formed. All the system could do was to deduce what was happening based on the rate at which surveillance nodes were being destroyed. Earlier, the rate of surveillance node destruction was twice the speed of light inside the three-dimensional universe. Based on what the Lurker knew, such an observation could only be explained as a side effect of vacuum decay, which vastly increased the speed of light at the interface between the zero vacuum zone and normal space.

Only now did the Lurker understand his mistake. In plotting to trap the Master, he had fallen into the Master's trap. The dimension reversal was a mirage. Although the process of two-dimensionalization could not progress faster than the speed of light, the Master did have the power to temporarily increase the local value of c, which created the illusion of dimension reversal. Since the speed of the expanding two-dimensional space was faster than the ordinary speed of light, it was impossible to see into the two-dimensionalized region; the observer would have been flattened before the observer could see it. To sustain such an illusion, however, required a massive expenditure of energy, and as the two-dimensionalized region grew, the speed at which it expanded had to slow down.

The report from the supermembrane-analysis node came in. "Error in data. Unable to locate target on the supermembrane."

It was impossible to deny. *The worst has happened.*

"Damn it!" The Lurker issued his order: "Stop the attack node immediately. Return to concealment. Right now!"

His order was carried out, and countless neon lights in the universe shut off in an instant, like the fading of flowers that bloom for only one night.

But the massive radiation bursts had already occurred. Electromagnetic tsunamis traveled through the vastness of space, unable to be recalled. It was too late to conceal his location. He knew that the goal of the Master and her Seekers was to force him into exposure, a goal they had achieved.

It wasn't over yet. He still had time to move and hide again before the revealing radiation reached the Seekers. But he had left indelible trails. The Master and the Seekers would not give up. They would pursue him like bloodhounds.

The Lurker cursed and was beginning to suspect that a few mysterious envoys were responsible for his predicament. They managed to trap him with his own trap. The old witch had never shown such cunning in the past.

Who are they? How did they see through my plot?

There were no clues. The only thing the Lurker could be sure of was that the Seekers would come for him. He must conceal himself and set another trap, deceive the old witch and the envoys, counterattack at the most unexpected moment, and miraculously seize victory from the jaws of defeat! It wasn't over yet.

Not by a long shot.

The Lurker's cognition field vibrated violently, stirring up undaunted courage once more. He partitioned his mind into millions of separate nodes and dispersed them to the corners of the universe to prepare for the oncoming struggle.

I will not let you take time away, Mother. I will not allow you to rebuild your reign of death.

Time will exist as long as I exist; life will, too.

In another corner of the universe, the light from the dark matter cloud burst forth like a brilliant dawn, illuminating a vast, empty space.

The angel of death and his companion glided through this marvelous world—if you could call what they were doing flight—and observed the dazzling dark matter cloud around them with curiosity. A colossal structure was being partially revealed to them; it wasn't anything like the minuscule planetary machinery inside the Abyss-Gazers' world, but a gigantic structure measured on the scale of galaxies. In a way, it reminded him of the Spirit's projection from eons ago: a massive rose whose every petal was another rose, with petals composed of yet more roses . . . each rose distinct, infinitely special, ad infinitum.

It was a bonfire, an ocean, a bunch of flowers, a spiderweb, living, mechanical . . . this was the true source and root of the Lurker, the universe's hidden lord.

"It's so beautiful," said the woman. "Reminds me of . . . the lavenders of Provence."

"Sky calyx," said the angel of death.

"What?" asked the woman.

"This is the Lurker's cosmic power system. In ancient battles, this was described as the sky calyx. The name comes from the fact that when activated, this universe-spanning entanglement web would bloom with the most luminous flowers. The dark matter forms its root and trunk, the sophon blind zones scattered across the universe are its vines and branches, and the galaxies are its energy nodes."

"What an incredible sight. I thought the star abyss and the Abyss-Gazers' homeworld were the Lurker's ace in the hole."

"I thought so at first as well. But once I saw the sky calyx, I understood immediately what those ambiguous ideabstractions we discovered last time really meant. There's no doubt that we've finally found the home of the Lurker."

"But I still don't understand how you figured it all out, Yun. If you hadn't stopped me at the last moment, I would have told the Master to initiate dimension reversal."

"It's fortuitous," said the angel of death. "After listening to that final speech by the King, I somehow thought of Green Tempest. After so many years, I've become habituated to constant reflection and reexamination of my mind, and soon I realized that the reason I thought of Green Tempest was . . . *advertising.*"

"Advertising?"

"Oh, it's a commercial propaganda art from my era. I'm not surprised you're not familiar with it."

"I know very well what advertising is. In the Byzantium of my time, the shops and public spaces are also filled with advertising, such as large signs over shop doors and hired urchins who shout out prices in the fora."

"You're right, Helena. Although the forms of advertising have changed, the substance is the same. Its purpose is to let the world know about the advertiser. The King's speech reminded me of an ad for Green Tempest, in which a woman gave a speech. The King's speech was like an ad broadcast to the entire universe, announcing that she was the Lurker. That didn't feel right to me. The real Lurker or the Lurker's descendants would keep the secret even unto death."

"But they were about to die! Maybe the King didn't care anymore."

"No. Their species possesses millions of awayworlds, and the inhabitants on those worlds weren't about to die. Suppose the Abyss-Gazers were the Lurker; then as long as the King didn't reveal the truth and the fact that the homeworld was the last countermeasure, the Master couldn't be sure that the Lurker was exterminated and wouldn't initiate dimension reversal—at least it would buy the universe some time. Either to preserve her species or to deter the Master, she shouldn't have revealed the mission of the Abyss-Gazers. And so the only conclusion was that the Abyss-Gazers weren't the Lurker at all."

"But with the homeworld destroyed, we can't be sure of that."

"True, we can't be sure. But when I realized that, it was too late to change the gravitational constant; otherwise we would still have some fragments of the homeworld to analyze. Still, even though we couldn't confirm my guess, we could perform an experiment by creating the illusion of dimension reversal. This was costly in terms of energy, but well worth the risk."

"Why did you wait so long?" asked Helena.

"Simple: If my guess was right and this was a trap, then the opponent would surely have set up a surveillance network to observe everything we did. If everything went too perfectly according to their plan, it would actually arouse their suspicion. I had to let them first think they had failed before hitting them with the euphoria of success. By taking advantage of the resulting lapse of judgment, they swallowed my bait without question."

"But what if they didn't take the bait?"

"Everything's a gamble. Still, the stakes weren't the same for the two sides. Had we lost the bet, we would have wasted a massive amount of energy, but we still could have started the hunt afresh. But had they waited longer, they would have missed the best opportunity to find the Master, and the vacuum decay could have spun out of control. They had no choice but to come out and give it their best shot. And so you see how I placed a finger on the scales in our favor."

"I'm amazed at you, Yun. You weren't half as clever when I first met you in the Wild Duck Cluster."

"I was still a newbie back then, with little idea of what kind of opponent I faced. I had even lost contact with my mini-universe. I was lucky to have found you, Helena. Without you, I'd be long dead now."

"I feel very fortunate as well. I never imagined that there would be another human being in this universe like me, someone who had been rebuilt to carry out the mission of finding the Lurker. Since the day Constantinople fell, when I left the Earth in a coma, I never saw another human being. For hundreds of millions of years, I was a slave of the Master, and I almost forgot I was a human being . . . I don't want to dwell on those days. Then you came!"

They gazed at each other, smiling. The brilliant light from the sky calyx illuminated Helena's face, coating her pale skin with a glowing blush.

Suddenly, everything went dark around them. The sky calyx hid itself.

But several hundred thousand kilometers away, in a ring around them, the sky calyx continued to glow. This was because light from that far away was just reaching them at that moment. Although the sky calyx had been shut off in a single instant, light still took time to travel through the universe.

And so the two experienced a wondrous sight. The parts of the calyx near them faded into darkness, while the faraway starry deeps lit up as the light from those distant petals reached them. The light flickered away in an ever-expanding wave, like swaying blos—

"Like the evening breeze caressing the lavenders of Provence," whispered Helena.

Yun Tianming smiled. It was enough. They had lit a light that swept away the shadows in the universe. Their next task was to find the enemy, who had run out of places to hide.

"Where shall we go next?" asked Tianming. They had an abundance of clues.

"How about going back to the Milky Way first? I'd like to go to Trantor to check in on the children. I hope the blooming of the sky calyx hasn't harmed them."

"You are the most loving mother the Galactic humans could have hoped for. For millions of years, you've devoted yourself to helping them grow up in the dark forest."

"Are you suggesting that you're their father then?" said Helena, a grin curling her lips.

But Tianming didn't notice her expression. He went on thoughtfully. "I also want humanity to multiply and prosper. Humans have clearly passed their golden age and have been in decline for the last few million years. Our species cannot leave the Milky Way, but the galaxy has been largely eroded by two-dimensionalization. Soon, humans will be devoured by the all-consuming plane. I don't think we can do much more for them, Helena. Our focus should be on preventing the rest of the universe from descending into two dimensions and on resetting the clock so everything can begin anew. We owe a duty not only to the human race, but to all life in the universe."

"I understand. But I still think we should go back to Provence. The lavenders are about to bloom. Come with me?"

"Of course," said Tianming with a smile.

Coda: Provence

After passing through the cosmic door, the spaceship found itself under a blue sky dotted with white clouds.

Cheng Xin and Guan Yifan, who had been anxiously anticipating a fall into two dimensions or the heart of a black hole, rubbed their eyes, unsure if what they saw was real.

It was no illusion. Under the blue sky lay a lavender field. At first, they thought they were looking at some alien vegetation, like the mobile plants found on Planet Blue, but a careful examination revealed the presence of *Lavandula angustifolia*, the common lavender flower of Earth. The brilliant blossoms formed a magnificent carpet that rippled in the breeze.

They looked to the left and found a towering mountain range tipped with snow. To their right was a lush tropical jungle. The lavender field ended, and before them lay the endless sea—a real, azure ocean familiar from their past life.

Everything was just like old Earth, familiar and welcoming. If there was any difference, it was that this place seemed even more beautiful, vibrant, and natural.

Still, these two had seen plenty of odd sights in their lives. After a few stunned moments, they turned to Sophon. "Where are we? And . . . *when* are we?"

"It's 11.2 billion years after the two of you entered the mini-universe. As for location . . . given the intervening shifts in the positions of the galaxies, I don't know a simple answer. Think of it as the end of the universe."

"Are you suggesting that we just happened to emerge in the atmosphere of some random planet at the end of the universe, and the conditions on this planet just happen to be almost exactly the same as on Earth?" Guan Yifan was incredulous. He knew that the probability of what he said was about the same as his randomly choosing fifty kilograms of matter in the entire universe and ending up with Cheng Xin.

"Not a planet," corrected Sophon. "What you're looking at is a square-shaped plane one thousand kilometers on each side. The plane has a thickness of about twenty kilometers. This is an artificial world, and it signaled the mini-universe to dock here."

"Who made this?" the pair asked.

"I'm sorry, but without that person's permission, I can't reveal the truth. But you'll meet him soon."

The pair stared at each other. Cheng Xin's expression was a mixture of joy and anxiety, whereas Guan Yifan's was far warier.

That person! Who has the power to control where the mini-universe would dock with the grand universe except the man with the highest authorization?

Can it really be him?

The pair sank into silence, each thinking different thoughts.

Directed by a signal beam, the spaceship landed on the beach. The three passengers emerged from the ship and saw a tiny white house. Above the door was a crooked sign: THE RESTAURANT AT THE END OF THE UNIVERSE.

Cheng Xin chuckled. Guan Yifan, on the other hand, was a bit nervous. "He's full of surprises. What sort of gift has he prepared for you this time?"

That person came out of the door. A shirtless Yun Tianming stood before them, his bronzed skin glinting under the bright beach light.

"Tianming!" Cheng Xin examined the man in wonder. He looked just as he had when he was eighteen, but seemed far healthier and more cheerful. *If he had looked like this back then, perhaps I would have . . .*

Tianming laughed heartily. "I've been waiting for all three of you for a while. Come in, please!"

Cheng Xin pushed her confused thoughts away and stepped into the "restaurant."

The restaurant was tiny, with only enough space for five tables. Cheng Xin and her companions picked one at random and sat down. Tianming sat down opposite from her. Cheng Xin was about to get started with the long list of questions in her mind when Tianming turned around and shouted, "Our guests are here, dear!"

Who's he talking to? Cheng Xin wondered. And then she heard a bright voice. "Perfect timing. The food is ready!"

The curtain to the kitchen lifted to reveal an aproned young woman. She walked up to the table with two serving dishes in her hands: stir-fried shredded potato and spiced beef.

"AA! What are you doing here?" Cheng Xin cried out.

Guan Yifan was equally surprised, and he felt a wave of relief.

The sun sank behind the snowy mountains in the west, and brilliant stars studded the sky. (Unlike the visual illusion on Earth, the sun here really did "sink" in the west. The "sun" was a satellite that orbited around the artificial plane.) The five human-shaped individuals left the small restaurant and sat down on the beach to admire the constellations.

"Tianming," said Yifan, his voice slightly slurred with alcohol, "did you make these stars as well?"

"No," said Tianming. "These are the real stars of this galaxy."

"I don't think so," said Yifan. "Look, over there is the Great Dipper, and that 'W' there is Cassiopeia. And those stars over there—that's the belt of Orion. How can the stars in this galaxy just happen to be arranged like the sky from Earth?"

"Oh, I'm used to the way the stars look from Earth, so I just rearranged them slightly." Tianming spoke in the tone one would expect of someone talking about rearranging a few pieces of furniture.

After a whole afternoon of hearing about miracles Tianming had performed, Yifan and Cheng Xin were no longer capable of being astonished. Still, they sighed with admiration.

艾 AA emerged with a few bottles of home-brewed beer. They drank to the accompaniment of the surf.

"What do you call this world?" asked Yifan.

"Provence," said Tianming.

"Like . . . the Provence in France?"

"That's right. Helena named this world. Provence was her homeland."

"Who was this Helena anyway? You told us she was also a Seeker, but who *was* she?"

"Sorry, I should have been better about explaining things in order," said Tianming. "Helena was once a . . . prostitute in the Byzantine Empire. She was also a magician during the siege of Constantinople by the Ottomans, the guardian angel of the Galactic humans, and my best teacher and friend."

Yifan and Cheng Xin were stunned by this solemn introduction.

"Helena was born from a poor family, and she became a prostitute in her youth. But in 1453, right before the fall of Constantinople, a high-dimensional fragment crossed paths with Earth and changed her fate . . ."

Yun Tianming recounted Helena's failed attempt to assassinate the Ottoman sultan, and then added, "In fact, during her last trip into the high-dimensional fragment, she disappeared for a whole day and night, during which she had a chance to get close to the sultan. But a mysterious voice called her from four-dimensional space and led her into a mini-universe."

"What, another mini-universe?" Cheng Xin asked.

"Yes, Universe 589, which was created during the four-dimensional stage of the universe. The four-dimensional intelligence inhabiting it, also a servant of the Master, was near death. Before his expiration, he injected ideabstractions into Helena's brain, and asked her to carry out his mission.

"The four-dimensional intelligence's ideabstractions were far weaker than the ones from the Master. But like me, Helena couldn't deal with them at first, and fell into a coma. When she awoke, she babbled incoherently. After the Byzantine soldiers discovered her in this state, they killed her by impaling her body to the ground. But like me, she had already accepted the ideabstractions and was soon revived. Her body was remade to be incorruptible, and she was given a ring to become a Seeker. After that, she left Earth pursuant to the Master's orders and searched for the Lurker everywhere in the universe until she met me. We worked and fought together through eons, and we watched over the Galactic humans."

"What happened to her then?" Cheng Xin asked.

Tianming's expression was sorrowful. "She died about nine years ago. When we finally found the Lurker, its power overwhelmed us. We were barely alive when we realized that one of us had to stay there to lead the Master to initiate vacuum decay. Helena sent me into the mini-universe to escape before activating the ring, and she died with the Lurker."

Cheng Xin and Guan Yifan were too stunned to speak.

Tianming's expression grew distant as he mentally returned to the moment of the last battle. He was at the heart of the sky calyx, tossed by the Lurker's surging energy tsunamis. He could no longer control himself, but still he strove to move forward. He knew that he could escape by climbing into the mini-universe, but he also knew that if he couldn't destroy the Lurker this time, the universe would be completely two-dimensionalized before he got another chance.

And so Helena pushed him into the door of Universe 589 and ordered the mini-universe to immediately detach itself. Her authorization was the highest, and he could not countermand her order. As the door closed, she sent him an ideabstraction.

Let me stay, Yun. You know that I've always wanted to be a saint.

I'm not sacrificing myself for you. I just want to find a way to realize myself. The whole universe will return to the origin after the start of vacuum decay. You'll live just a few decades longer than I. It's not a big deal.

But you still have someone you love. I, on the other hand, am without anyone. If you stay ahead of the front of vacuum decay, go to the end of the universe, and clone your wife, you'll still have decades of happiness together, right?

Treasure your life and time. Time enough for love.

Tianming had wanted to send her thousands of ideabstractions, but Helena had already shut off the channel.

". . . and so, to commemorate her, you named this place Provence?" Guan Yifan asked.

Tianming pulled himself out of those emotional memories and nodded. "She had named Universe 589 that, and so I just borrowed the name."

"So that's why you never returned to Universe 647." Yifan finally understood the puzzle that had been plaguing him. "You've been hopping across space in Universe 589."

Cheng Xin's heart skipped a beat. If Tianming had been able to return to Universe 647 and meet her, how would things have turned out differently? She didn't want to go down that route; instead, she looked at AA and asked, "What happened with you? I thought you died while you were still on Planet Blue?"

"Let me answer that," said Tianming, "since I was responsible. Dimension reversal is a process that takes some time. What the Lurker thinks of as 1.91 grand hours is about sixty of our Earth years. Where we sit will be the last region of the universe to succumb to dimension reversal. Helena wished for me to spend the rest of my days in tranquility next to my wife, and so I used the matter in Universe 589 to construct this land—Provence. Not bad, don't you think?"

"It's beautiful!" exclaimed Cheng Xin and Guan Yifan together.

"I'm old," Tianming said. The words seemed incongruous coming from him, since his perpetually youthful eighteen-year-old face made him look even younger than the couple sitting opposite. "Don't laugh. You spent only about a year in the mini-universe; I've been running around in the grand universe for more than ten billion years. I'm really tired. I crave the life that Luo Ji led back in the old days, a life secluded in nature.

"And so, before you left the mini-universe, I managed to get in touch with Universe 647 and asked Sophon to send me information about AA's cells so that I could clone her."

Cheng Xin glanced at AA. "But if you're a clone of the AA I knew, you wouldn't have her memories. How could you have chatted with me about our time on Earth just now?"

"Tianming's ring had scanned my brain—the brain of the AA you knew," replied AA. "And so the ring had all of her memories. It was easy for those memories to be implanted into my brain. In every way that matters, I *am* the same AA you knew."

"However," said Tianming, "the scan from my ring happened back when I first met AA on Planet Blue, and so the memories don't include the four decades we spent together on that world. I had to work really hard to get her to fall in love with me again."

Tianming and AA held hands and grinned at each other.

Cheng Xin looked at the couple and felt a twinge of jealousy. *He should be mine! I should be the one next to him . . .*

She almost glared at AA before catching herself. *What's wrong with me? I'm also married to a man I love.* She sighed. She had lived an extraordinary life indeed.

She decided to change the topic. "Did you send the supermembrane broadcast we received?"

"I did."

"Is the request to return matter to the grand universe really about the great crunch then?"

Tianming's face turned solemn. "It's true that the universe should end in a great crunch in the ordinary course of events. But given the interference by intelligent life, the collapse would be thwarted. Without dimension reversal, the universe, mired in the dark forest state, would continue its descent into lower dimensions until all matter and energy had been turned into an infinite axis of time. There would be nothing *but* time. In fact, our home, the Milky Way and its local supercluster, have all been two-dimensionalized already. Two-thirds of the universe has already lost the third dimension. The Master's projection would lose its intelligence in that hypothetical, completely planar world, and that would be the true end of all hope, because the Master would no longer be able to initiate dimension reversal. We had to initiate the process right away, and that required returning all mass to the grand universe—otherwise our universe will never be restored."

A chill seized two hearts as Cheng Xin and Guan Yifan locked gazes. They were remembering the message bottle and the ecological sphere, still drifting in the husk of their mini-universe.

"Did you say . . . all mass?" asked Cheng Xin timidly.

"Yes," said Tianming. "As I was explaining, dimension reversal will bring about the rebirth of the universe. Our Earth will once again reappear. Not a single atom can be missing because butterfly effects will then lead to unpredictable changes, perhaps causing Earth to never reappear."

"But given the existence of millions of mini-universes, surely you're not expecting all of them will heed your call?" said Yifan.

"Not millions, just 647," said Tianming. "All the mini-universes were made by the Master. The Master has the power to return all of them to the grand universe, but my message serves as an extra level of protection. There must be no error in this process. If any other civilization gained the power to create new mini-universes and they weren't returned to the grand universe, everything would fail. That was why I had to broadcast in the millions of known languages to inform all mini-universes to return all matter and energy, just in case any such unknown mini-universes had been created."

"But the Lurker had launched multiple transuniversal attacks and probes. Such efforts surely would have consumed energy."

"Sophon told me that the grand universe and the supermembrane maintain an energy balance. Whatever amount of energy the grand universe outputs into the supermembrane, an identical amount of energy is absorbed from the supermembrane via universe expansion. The Lurker's attacks don't pose a problem for dimension reversal; the only potential weak link remains the mini-universes."

Cheng Xin was now feeling terrified. "Um . . . what if . . . what if somehow five kilograms of matter didn't get returned to the grand universe? What would happen then?"

"What if?" Tianming glanced at her suspiciously.

A woman laughed uproariously among them. It wasn't AA or Cheng Xin, but Sophon, who had not spoken much until now. Her laugh twisted her face into a rather frightening grimace.

The laughter sent chills down Cheng Xin's spine, reminding her of the night, eleven billion years ago, when the droplets had attacked Earth. In a volcanic caldera on Earth, Sophon, who had been dressed like a ninja, had laughed the exact same way.

A bolt of lightning lit up Cheng Xin's mind. She understood everything now.

"You!" She turned to Sophon. "You lied to me to get me to leave that five-kilogram fish tank behind! And the message bottle! They were just parts of your plot, and I've been deceived again! Again!"

Tianming stared at them, too stunned to speak.

"You can only blame yourself for being stupid," said Sophon contemptuously. "You need to take responsibility for your choices."

She turned to Yun Tianming. "You foolish boy. Do you really think the Master is going to let this soiled world be reborn exactly the same? Do you really think the Master doesn't want a fresh chance to reign over a tranquil kingdom at eternal rest? To cycle again and again in the exact same manner for eternity is nothing more than the dream of fantasists and mystics. The Master is the only one who should be eternal.

"Five kilograms of matter *is* the key. The Master can certainly let some mini-universes remain away from the grand universe and deprive the grand universe of much more matter. But if the amount of missing matter exceeded five kilograms, then dimension reversal would lead to a ten-dimensional universe very different from the original. Such a universe would be at rest, but no intelligence would ever emerge, which means no Master, either. But if the amount of missing matter were too small, then maybe the changes would be so insignificant that everything would happen pretty much the same again. We can't obtain extra matter over the supermembrane from other universes, so our only choice is to discard five kilograms.

"This was an extremely difficult task. Each mini-universe was completely enclosed, and the Master could only manipulate mini-universes over the supermembrane without being able to directly control what happened inside. The Master could only direct a whole mini-universe to return, but couldn't leave five kilograms of the matter inside behind on the supermembrane. The Master's own mini-universe was indivisible, while most of the other mini-universes had long become uninhabited or only inhabited by primitive life. The Master had no choice but to toss them all back into the grand universe. The two inhabitants of Universe 589 were too cunning and probably would have seen through any tricks. Universe 647 was the only option. And fortunately, one of the inhabitants was Cheng Xin, who even treated me like a best friend! And so I hinted to her that it was possible to leave behind an ecological sphere, and I filled her with romantic notions of leaving a bit of life to light up that dark universe, to keep despair at bay. The silly girl actually believed me!" Sophon was now grinning from ear to ear. "That was how we got the five kilograms we wanted."

"Damn you!" Tianming almost leapt up to strike at Sophon. But then he looked at Sophon's challenging gaze, and stopped himself. *She's just a robot.*

"You can't blame me," said Sophon. "You're the one who assigned Universe 647 to Cheng Xin and Guan Yifan and directed me to obey them. I *did* obey them, in everything. My actions were a direct result of her orders, in fact. Don't you agree, my dear Cheng Xin?"

Cheng Xin lowered her head, unable to dispute this. She dropped her face into her hands and sobbed. Guan Yifan and 艾 AA stood to the side, uncertain how to comfort her.

"But you manipulated her and got her to give those orders!" Tianming raged.

"That requires her to be manipulable in the first place," countered Sophon. "I wanted to manipulate you, but it didn't work nearly as well. In the end, I had to resort to an elaborate story about eternal recurrence to convince you. There was no way I could have gotten you to do what I got her to do. You should blame yourself for telling me to obey some-one so easily deceived."

Tianming's body trembled with fury as he stared at Sophon.

"I won't resist if you want to kill me," said Sophon.

Tianming's body stiffened, and then relaxed. "That would be mean-ingless. You're nothing more than the Master's shadow. Go away. I don't want to see you again."

Sophon bowed. "As you wish. But I will return to your side if you ever want me back. Just call me with your ring."

She turned around to leave, but Cheng Xin screamed and jumped on her. The two fell to the ground with Cheng Xin on top, and she pounded the robot with her fists.

"I hate you! I hate you!" Cheng Xin punched and bit and kicked. Years, decades, centuries of rage poured out of her. She finally under-stood how she was but a mote of dust in a grand wind, a small leaf drifting over a broad river. She surrendered completely and allowed the chill wind of hatred to pass through her, allowed the sharp light of vengeance to pierce her soul.

Sophon didn't hit back. She wasn't going to engage in such meaningless human behavior. Cheng Xin couldn't really injure her anyway. Sophon's body was more pliant and stronger than rubber. No matter how hard Cheng Xin's strikes landed, local deformations in her body quickly bounced back.

Guan Yifan tried to pull Cheng Xin off of Sophon, but she was too strong for him. Yun Tianming stood to the side, unable to react. He was still trying to come to terms with the fact that ten billion–plus years of effort had come to naught. AA held Tianming's arm, terrified by the sight of her old friend's outburst. Could this be the Cheng Xin she knew?

After a while, Sophon said coldly, "You don't hate me, Cheng Xin. You hate yourself. Surely you realize that."

Cheng Xin stopped. She got off Sophon and sat to the side, sobbing disconsolately. Guan Yifan held her to comfort her. Sophon got up, brushed off the sand, bowed to Tianming, and walked away.

"Wait!" Tianming called to Sophon. "What will happen now that the grand universe is missing five kilograms? Will the Master really build a ten-dimensional universe that lasts forever?"

Sophon stopped and turned to look at him. She shook her head solemnly. "Even the Master does not know. There are limits to what can be computed and predicted. But even the unpredictable unknown is better than an eternal recurrence of the same thing. It's worth a try."

Tianming felt pity for the Master at that moment. Even a god that once ruled the whole cosmos was subject to the whim of Ananke. The Master had to struggle for its own survival, not much different from him.

Tianming sighed. He realized that things weren't as bad as they appeared at first. The future was supposed to be unknown. Everything was going to be reset and the universe would begin afresh, and all that had passed would be erased and forgotten. But the universe still existed, and he still existed. Every bit of matter that was in his body, every quark that contributed to his structure would still exist in some form in the new universe. Maybe they would form a new him, a completely different him. There was no reason to despair. Humanity, the Solar System . . . everything was made of matter, and matter was going to be reborn.

The Master had to try, and so did the universe. Opportunity and crisis were two faces of the same coin. Everything was subject to the infinite vagaries of change, and there was no need to be overly attached to the vanished world of the past. It was better to let go, to let himself become part of the vast current of transformation and merge into the new world. Wasn't that the very meaning of time—freedom?

Slanting rain, gentle breeze, no need to return home.

There really isn't the need to return home. It will be an adventure to go to a strange new world.

Sophon had explained that if the first time had meaning, then each subsequent repetition in an endless recurrence would also have meaning. Similarly, if the first time had meaning, then even if nothing would recur again and everything dissolved into nothing, that first and only time would still have meaning. The meaning of the universe and of existence didn't depend on repetition, but neither did change and transformation deprive them of meaning.

The world of the past, even if it were never to recur, still existed. Even if it were never recalled, it would not be forgotten.

Eventually, Sophon left, a sobbing Cheng Xin walked away, and Guan Yifan followed her. Tianming didn't hate Cheng Xin, but he didn't try to stop her. He knew that Cheng Xin couldn't face him. Although her actions would probably lead to a brand-new universe, she couldn't accept her true self, which Sophon revealed by stripping away the pure and saintly exterior Cheng Xin presented to the universe. He didn't know if he would see her again. The world of Provence was a million square kilometers in size, and Cheng Xin and Yifan would find a safe, comfortable place to live for the next fifty years.

His outlook had changed. Joie de vivre and love once again over-flowed his heart—directed not at the remaining five decades in this universe, but at the unknown new world to come.

He thought of the last moment during the final battle, when he had left the region of space in which Helena gave her life. A fragmentary ideabstraction had come to him then, not from Helena, but from the dying Lurker.

I created time, and I will die in time. But I don't regret it. If I could do it over again, I . . .

That was the end, but Tianming was sure now that what the Lurker had wanted to say was:

I would still let time begin again, so that everything would have an-other chance.

The Master, the Lurker, and he were enemies joined in lasting war, but in the end, all of their efforts had been in service of the same task: the birth of the new universe, another chance for life and love.

Tianming extended his hand over the sea of Provence, like Moses before the Red Sea. Under his direction, a bright red sun leapt out over the horizon and illuminated the heavens.

"This is sunrise for a new universe," Tianming muttered as he pulled AA to him. "You and I, and Helena, Cheng Xin, Guan Yifan . . . all the people and creatures who have lived in this universe, no matter how things change, will bathe in the sunlight of a new universe."

The rising sun's brilliant rays glinted against them. Before them, the ocean sparkled and scintillated; behind them, blooming lavenders swayed in a dream.

A lovely morning.

Post Coda: Notes on the New Universe

The legends are over, but history has just begun.

—*Legend of the Galactic Heroes*

3500 BCE, Trisolaris system

The Great Round Face was in the night sky, and it was easy to see every wrinkle on the face. The sky spheres hung lazily next to the Great Round Face, but the Yellow Moon still hadn't emerged. Zuna, riding the agile winged beast Suuluu, swept across the sparkling canopy of the forest and headed for the floating mountains in the distance.

She flew over the towering peaks, one after another, until she was at the tallest summit. Even from some distance away, Zuna could see the slender figure of Kasha at the top. He was gazing up at the sky, and next to him lay the gentle winged beast Tuutuu.

Zuna was overjoyed. Even before Suuluu had touched the ground, she leapt off its back. "I see you."

"I see you." Kasha bowed to her. Zuna enjoyed watching Kasha bowing. Everything he did was so graceful, so poised. He was nothing like the rough hunters of her own tribe. Kasha's tribe used to live by the shore of the southern ocean and had migrated near her tribe's territory not long ago.

Kasha was what his people called an "observer," meaning that it was his job to observe the heavenly bodies. Zuna didn't know what good such observations did, but Kasha told her that the motion of the heavenly bodies caused the tides, and that was why his tribe, living by the coast, had such a tradition. Although they were now living in the forest, Kasha still insisted on coming to the mountaintop each night to watch the sky. Zuna was full of curiosity for this mysterious young man, and she often slipped out at night to join him on top of the floating mountains.

Kasha smiled at her. "Look, the Yellow Moon is about to come out." He pointed to a spot next to the Great Round Face, where a faint orange glow appeared, followed quickly by the emerging crescent of the Yellow Moon. The warm, yellow light suffused the sky and bathed the pair on the mountain. Zuna stole a glance at Kasha, who looked especially handsome in the yellow moonlight.

But Kasha wasn't looking at her. He kept his eyes on the Yellow Moon. Rather annoyed, Zuna brushed him with her tail. "Why do you gaze at it every night? Is it really pretty?"

Kasha said, "Can you tell what's next to the Yellow Moon?"

"Is it . . . the Fire God Star?" Zuna asked. She saw that the Fire God Star and the Yellow Moon were approaching each other. "Are they going to collide?"

Kasha laughed. "Of course not, silly!"

Soon, Zuna saw that as the Fire God Star and the Yellow Moon came together, the Fire God Star became just a black spot over the face of the Yellow Moon, slowly sweeping over the glowing circle. After a moment, Zuna said tentatively, "The Yellow Moon must be farther away from us than the Fire God Star, right?"

"Much, much farther," said Kasha. "The Yellow Moon is farther away than any of the wandering stars."

"What's a wandering star?"

"Bodies that move through the heavens are called wandering stars; those that don't move but only rotate with the heavenly sphere are called staying stars."

"Is the Yellow Moon a wandering star or a staying star?"

"That's hard to say, Zuna. By the definition I just gave it should be called a wandering star, since it clearly moves through the heavens. But it's so big! It's farther than the Fire God Star, the Water God Star, and even the War God Star, but it still appears as a disk instead of a dot. And it's much too bright. Some wise people from my tribe speculate that it's also a sun that gives off light on its own, just like our Sun, though it's much, much farther away than our Sun, which is why it looks so much dimmer."

"Does it also orbit around the earth?"

"The Yellow Moon? No. According to the ancient observers of my tribe, the Yellow Moon orbits around the Sun—or more precisely, it and the Sun orbit around a spot between them, like this." He illustrated what he meant by holding out a finger on each hand and revolving them around some imaginary spot in the middle.

"Ah, like two . . . people who love each other," said Zuna.

"That's right! In our legends, the Sun and the Yellow Moon are a pair of lovers."

"Do you think they have children?"

"What?"

"The Sun and the Yellow Moon. Do they have children?"

"What a silly thought, um . . ." But the grin was frozen on Kasha's face.

"What's wrong?" asked Zuna.

"Nothing . . . I just remembered a really obscure myth, which said that the Sun and the Yellow Moon really did have a child, the Little Red Star."

"I've never heard of it," said Zuna.

Kasha pointed to a corner of the sky, where a dim red star glowed. It was fainter than many of the other stars and was almost lost in the glow of the Yellow Moon.

"What's so special about that star that it could be considered the child of the Sun and the Yellow Moon?" asked Zuna.

"It is indeed a very faint star. But the Little Red Star is not like the other stars. It does move through the heavens on its own, though very, very slowly, slower than any of the wandering stars. If you compare our ancient star charts with the heavens today, you'll see how much it has moved. We don't consider it a wandering star, but we don't think of it as a staying star, either. It must be very far from us, even farther than the Yellow Moon, maybe almost all the way to the sphere of staying stars. But it's still connected to the Sun and the Yellow Moon. In our legends, it had committed some terrible sin and was exiled by its parents. That's why it's wandering far from home. Every one hundred thousand years, it makes a great circle around the Sun and the Yellow Moon, but it dares not return."

"Poor kid!" said Zuna. "Why not let it come home?"

"If it ever did return, it would be a disaster," said a chuckling Kasha. "It would destroy the love between the Sun and the Yellow Moon."

"What? I thought it was the child of the Sun and the Yellow Moon."

"I'm not too sure about the details. But in our legends, all the heavenly bodies love each other and want to be together. But if they really do cluster together, they won't be orbiting around the earth and illuminating everything on the ground. That's why the Maker separated them from each other, giving order and restraint to their love. Since the Little Red Star is the child of both the Sun and the Yellow Moon, if it ever did return, the Sun and the Yellow Moon would fight over it, each demanding that the Little Red Star revolve around itself. In that case, the Sun and the Yellow Moon would no longer orbit around each other, twirling in their dance. Instead, they'd be fighting each other, and the Little Red Star might even fall into one of them, bringing chaos to the heavenly order."

"What a wise Maker!" exclaimed Zuna. "The Maker's arrangement is both kind and clever. If the Sun, the Yellow Moon, and the Little Red Star were too close together, perhaps we wouldn't even exist."

Kasha looked thoughtful. "That's a really interesting thought. Maybe even if we came to be, with those three heavenly bodies so close together and so chaotically intertwined, we'd be living in a far crueler and stranger world. We wouldn't even know which body should be called our Sun!"

Both seemed lost in wild and fanciful thoughts when Suuluu and Tuutuu screamed. Zuna and Kasha looked over to the two winged beasts, thinking they were fighting, but they saw that the beasts were crying in alarm in the direction of the Yellow Moon. However, when they looked toward the Yellow Moon, they saw nothing unusual. Since winged beasts did sometimes behave skittishly for no reason, the two didn't think it was anything to worry about. Zuna reprimanded the beasts with a few severe words, and the two beasts soon quieted down.

Zuna held Kasha's hand. "Tell me how the Sun fell in love with the Yellow Moon."

But Kasha now realized his companion was . . . far more beautiful than the Yellow Moon. He stared into her eyes. "Why don't we tell a story about Zuna and Kasha, together?"

Zuna grinned shyly. The boy finally understood her. A few minutes later, the new couple took off on their winged beasts and chased each other through the sky above the mountains. Higher and higher they flew, as though they were going to touch the Great Round Face, as though they were about to climb onto the Yellow Moon . . .

But they didn't realize that the winged beasts had cried out in alarm for a good reason. A silver streak rose behind them and, disguised by the glow of the Yellow Moon, shot straight into the sky, flying higher even than the two of them, heading straight for a world even farther away than the Great Round Face, the Yellow Moon, and the Little Red Star.

A world four light-years away.

May 1453, Constantinople

Sky, earth, ocean, city . . . everything.

Once again, the visible world exposed itself. In a gesture that seemed familiar to her, the world had cast off all clothing and opened itself, revealing every inch of skin to her greedy eyes. Of course, now she was the client, and the world was her whore. An infinity of rich, tempting details were revealed to her all at once, and she could do whatever she wanted to the world without anyone being able to stop her, seeking her pleasure. The sense of power was intoxicating.

Helena shook her head and pushed the sinful comparison away. She could no longer recall how many times she had returned to this marvelous space, yet each visit made her tremble with excitement. She was certain that God had blessed her with this opportunity. Like Daniel, Isaiah, or John, the author of the book of Revelation, she had been granted divine visions.

In some sense, Helena was sure that she had been elevated somehow to a plane "higher" than the earthly world, which was how she was able to see the world all at once. But it wasn't height in the sense of a tower or a mountain, but even "higher," "above" the sublunary world. That had to mean the Gates of Heaven, right? She couldn't help but look for the wonders described in the book of Revelation, the jasper walls, the pearly gates, the pure gold streets . . . but she had never found them. She had to conclude that the Kingdom of Heaven was still not fully open to her. She had to complete her God-given mission on earth before she would be allowed in.

The mission was simple: Assassinate the heathen king, Satan's minion, the Ottoman sultan Mehmed II, also known as el-Fātiḥ, "the Conqueror." As soon as she completed her mission, she would be hailed as the savior of Byzantium and all Christendom. She would be a greater saint even than Joan d'Arc.

Feeling courage coursing through her veins, she picked up the scimitar and "walked" from the minaret.

She had gotten the hang of "walking" through this strange space. Following an edge that couldn't be seen in the ordinary world, she walked inside the city wall and then descended into the ground. She really was underground, and the soil above her was thicker than a man's height.

Yet, because she was still in the "higher" plane, she could walk through solid ground without any trouble. Although the invisible force that made everything fall was still in effect, she was now pressed against the ground from another direction. Though she was deep within the earth, she was still able to see everything around her and freely move in any direction.

The Conqueror's camp was in sight. Helena was a bit nervous. Though she knew she was completely safe from detection from ordinary space, her heart nonetheless pounded.

God, will you really help me complete this incredible mission? Give me a sign!

Unexpectedly, a powerful spiritual force buffeted her mind. She seemed to hear a voice.

Ask, and it shall be given you; seek, and ye shall find; knock, and it shall be opened unto you.

Helena was so astonished that she blurted out, "Is that you, God?"

But the voice spoke no more. Helena forced herself to be calm. She must have been so nervous that the words from the Gospels came into her mind unbidden.

She held her breath and slowly approached the sultan's magnificent tent. It wasn't very difficult. Though the tent was heavily guarded, none of the security measures mattered to her. From her space, she approached along an underground plane that could not be seen from the surface and entered the tent right under the eyes of the guards. The young sultan lay between the nude figures of four concubines, deep in sleep. She recognized him right away based on Phrantzes's drawing.

Sinful heathen! Sinful! she raged in her mind. She lifted the scimitar. One strike, and the sultan would be dead.

But that strange voice in her head spoke again.

Enter ye in at the strait gate: for wide is the gate, and broad is the way, that leadeth to destruction . . .

A faint outline of a door appeared in front of her. A silver light spilled out of it, twinkling, as though calling her to enter. She was so startled that she lost her grip on the scimitar, and the weapon fell. Though she was in another space, the scimitar still followed the laws of gravity and landed inside an underground rock.

The faint noise of metal against stone caused the sultan to rub his eyes, as though about to wake from his slumber. Helena didn't know what to do. She stared at the glowing rectangular outline.

This must the Gates of Heaven, guarded by Saint Peter.

She had no idea that in the last universe, she had decided to step through the door and thus entered a mini-universe that gave her a new mission. But in this universe, because her brain differed from the version in the last universe by a few atoms, everything was going to be different.

I must kill the heathen before entering Heaven.

Losing the scimitar was not a big setback. She reached out for the quivering mass that was the sultan's brain. Like all his other organs, the brain lay completely exposed to her. All she had to do was to give that gooey mass a hard squeeze, and the sultan would be dead.

Suddenly, the sultan turned in his sleep. Helena's hand missed and touched the sultan's nude skin. The sultan, half awake, grabbed her hand and pulled her to him. Helena was too weak to resist, and she fell out of her space and landed in his embrace.

The marvelous world disappeared, and the world of walls and surfaces pressed against her awareness, almost suffocating her. Even worse, the sultan was holding her so tightly that she could not breathe. As the sultan moved his hands over her slender, feminine body, Helena panicked.

I've got to go back!

Helena struggled against the sultan. If she could just reach the surface that she had tumbled from, she could climb back . . .

Her eyes brightened as her head reached into that marvelous space, and the openness of the world took her breath away. That glowing rectangular outline was still there, calling to her. Before she could pull herself up, that beastly sultan pulled her back into his world, and slapped her hard across the face.

The sultan was now fully awake, though in the dark interior of the tent, he couldn't tell who she was. He cursed at her. Helena head-butted him and climbed up as his arms loosened, dashing for the surface that she had fallen from—

Nothing. The surface was gone.

Helena was stunned, and before she could react, the sultan, his sexual desire stoked, had pulled her back again and forced himself on top of her . . .

It's over. I can't save anyone, not even myself.

The high-dimensional fragment was moving away from Earth, carrying with it the door to the mini-universe and Helena's hope, never to return.

1964, Zhongnanhai Compound, Beijing, China

A tall, old man bent over the wide expanse of his desk, reading glasses held in one hand, deeply absorbed by the document in front of him. From time to time as he read, he nodded and smiled.

The document's title was *Research Report on the Possibility of Technology Leap Due to the Search for Extraterrestrial Intelligence.*

The old man finished the report and picked up a pen. With a few powerful strokes, he wrote his comment: "Others have already sent their messages out into space. It's dangerous if extraterrestrials only hear their voices. We should speak up as well. Only then will they get a complete picture of human society. It's not possible to get the truth by only listening to one side. We must make this happen—"

He was about to add "and quickly" to emphasize the urgency of the task, but a knock on the door broke his concentration. He looked up and smiled. "Enlai! Good timing. Come and read this interesting report."

A thin, old man whose face betrayed signs of exhaustion walked in, though his stride was still steady and full of energy. He picked up the report and glanced through it quickly. Smiling, he said, "How times have changed! When I was studying in France, I thought Verne's science fiction novels utterly fantastic. And now the Americans are devoting serious resources to the search for aliens."

"Our country must also think about these big-picture issues. We can't always follow the others and react. I think we should also build our own facility to search for extraterrestrials. I've even got a name for our facility: Red Coast! Maybe the significance of this move won't be apparent for many years, but it's very important. I'm thinking of summoning Guo Moruo and Qian Xuesen for a discussion in a few days to plan out the details for this project. What do you think?"

"It's a good idea, Chairman, except . . . the budget . . ." Zhou Enlai's expression was awkward.

The tall, old man's tone was dismissive. "I know very well that we are not a rich country. We can't do it at the scale of the Americans . . . How about we allocate a hundred million yuan initially?"

Zhou Enlai smiled helplessly and handed a document to him. "Why don't you take a look at this budget report first?"

The tall, old man accepted the report and flipped through it. Gradually, the smile on his face stiffened and vanished. He sighed. "Everything needs money. The five-year plan needs money, the army needs money, the strategic nuclear weapons program and the satellite program need money, and even the 'revolutionary operas' by that . . . that woman need money! Even so, we must find money for this program, too! How about this? Can we delay the construction of these power plants?" He pointed to a few lines at the end of the budget summary.

Zhou Enlai frowned. "Our industrialization program is in desperate need of electricity, Chairman. We should have built these power plants yesterday."

"All right, let me look through this again . . ." The tall, old man sighed and flipped through the budget report again, trying to find anything that could be slashed. Everything was urgent.

Zhou Enlai looked at him with sympathy. "I understand that you think the search for aliens is important. We'll make do without the power plants. I'm sure China can survive another few years without them. After your discussion with Guo and Qian, I'll ask the State Council to redo the budget."

The tall, old man didn't nod. He kept his head lowered and thought over the matter. In the end, he made up his mind and swept his hand through the air. "Forget it. We have no idea if there even are aliens in the universe, but we must carry on with the practical task of industrializing China. Let's put off the idea for building an extraterrestrial search facility for now. But the power plants must be built well." His finger landed heavily against the last line of the report: "Niangziguan Power Plant."*

1969, Xinjiang Production and Construction Corps, Xinjiang, China

At the foot of the Tianshan Mountains, the endless grassland spread to the horizon.

There was a tiny open yard next to the wall behind the row of simple, hastily constructed shacks. In the middle of the yard was a small water basin filled with clear water. A young woman dressed in a green military uniform stood next to the basin and carefully dropped some ink from a bottle into the basin. Soon, the clear water turned black. The sun, reflected in the dark water, was a pale glowing ghost.

"This is just like the dark times we live in," muttered Ye Wenjie. She was thinking of her father, who had died two years ago, the victim of a violent struggle session. She knew she didn't have the time to indulge her emotions, and she pushed the memory away to focus on the reflection of the sun.

Someone slapped her on the shoulder. Wenjie almost jumped out

*Translator's Note: Liu Cixin, the author of the "Three-Body" series, wrote the novels while employed at Niangziguan Power Plant as an engineer.

of her skin. She turned around and saw a teenaged girl standing behind her.

"Wenxue! You terrified me! Why did you sneak up behind me?"

"They're looking for you at the Corps. Why aren't you working like
you're supposed to?"

"Shhhh—" Wenjie pulled her little sister aside. "Don't tell the others.
But I'm doing astronomy."

"What are you looking at?"

Wenjie lowered her voice. "Sunspots."

"What? You are looking at dark spots against the glowing sun?"
Wenxue's voice grew shrill with fear. "People who want to get you into
trouble will say that you're attacking our great leader symbolically in
the name of science."

"That's why I'm hiding here to do it in secret! It's not the predicted
time for increased sunspot activity yet, but recently, I've been observing a lot of spots and unusual solar activity—"

"Would you give it a rest?" said Wenxue. "Do you think you're still
a graduate student in astrophysics? You're in the remotest corner of
China where you don't even have access to basic equipment. What science can you do with a basin of dirty water? Anyway, even if you did
make some discovery, what good would it do? We live in a time where
the more science you know, the more reactionary you are judged to
be! Our father's fate should serve as a warning! Stop getting into
trouble!"

Wenxue kicked the basin and flipped it, spilling inky water all over
the ground.

"Why did you do that?" Wenjie glared at Wenxue.

Seeing that her big sister really was angry, Wenxue ran away.

Ye Wenjie stared at the spreading black stain on the ground as though
she were seeing a sunspot that had landed on the ground, gradually
expanding, threatening to swallow up the whole Earth . . .

Sighing, Wenjie lifted her gaze into the sky. "Who is going to re-
deem this dark and soiled land?"

1979, Lạng Sơn, Vietnam

A brown ant crawled through the soil noiselessly.

The sounds of cannon shots and gunfire came faintly from far away. Flashes from fiery explosions lit up the horizon. But here, in this dark forest, silence still reigned. The war between China and Vietnam was as far away as another universe. Even the powerful light of distant flares could not penetrate the thick vegetation.

For the brown ant, the war really was happening in another universe. The entirety of the ant's world consisted of a circle no more than a hundred meters across, a tiny corner of this forest. Anything outside of this circle was incomprehensible.

If one were to anthropomorphize the ant, the ant could be said to be very happy. The night patrol had yielded a fresh honeybee carcass, enough to feed the colony for two days. It was now hurrying back to the colony to bring the good news to its sisters so that all could enjoy this rich meal. In reality, of course, the ant had no human emotions at all. It was simply moving along at a brisk pace, propelled by the instinct for survival.

Suddenly, a gigantic object unimaginable by the ant fell down, blotting out the sky and everything around the ant. The ant didn't feel much pressure; it had been positioned right in a crack in the surface of the object and wasn't harmed. The ant proceeded tentatively, its antennae soon detecting a strange surface in front. Without thinking, it climbed onto the surface.

The surface began to move, carrying the brown ant with it. The surface stopped for a few moments before flying through the air at a dizzying speed again. Stop. Move. Stop. Move.

Even the dim-witted brown ant now realized that the surface it was on wasn't normal. Clusters of neurons sent out the signals for danger. Panicked, it crawled all around the strange surface, hoping to find a way to escape back to its regular plane of existence, the familiar earth.

A whisper broke through the night. "Da Shi, do you really think we're going to find the enemy ahead of us?" The voice came from some entity to the side, a small distance away.

"Shut up!" This voice came from directly above the ant. Perhaps the surface it was on was a part of the entity that possessed this voice.

"It's so dark here. I can't imagine how—"

A sharp gunshot answered his question by silencing him abruptly. The entity to the side of where the ant was fell to the ground.

"Fuck!" the entity called Da Shi cursed, and shot his gun into the darkness. Someone tossed a flare into the air, and everything was bathed in a blinding, pale light. Amid bursts of explosion, dozens of bodies emerged from the darkness, divided into two opposing sides. Gunshots filled the formerly quiet forest, turning it into a bullet-riddled, smoke-filled hellscape.

A Chinese squad had run into a Vietnamese squad, and the only choice for each side was to kill the other.

After an intense few seconds, the sounds of gunshots gradually grew sparse. The enemy's fire had been suppressed, and the seven or eight remaining soldiers pressed forward, step by step, until they surrounded a thick clump of shrubs. They could hear the noise of someone concealed inside.

"*No-song*, um, *no-song* . . . Lieutenant, what were we supposed to say to get the Vietnamese to surrender?" asked Da Shi.

"*Nộp súng không giết. Ra đây!*"

"Right, that's it! No-song-kong-jiet-ra-dai!"

After a few more repetitions, the soldiers swept the shrubs with flashlights. Finally, an answering voice indicated that they were going to surrender, and four hands were raised above the bush. Two bodies finally emerged from the vegetation. Oddly, the bodies were pale white.

The soldiers stared at the two nude young women standing before them.

A moment later, one of the soldiers dropped his flashlight. All of them were too stunned to speak or move.

Except Da Shi. Suddenly, he picked up his assault rifle and swept the clump of bushes with a few rapid bursts of fire. Dying cries filled the silence after the deafening shots.

The other soldiers finally understood what was happening. While the two women had emerged to draw the soldiers' attention, other enemy soldiers had been preparing to slaughter them. But their plot had been foiled by the vigilant Da Shi.

Cold-blooded Da Shi had swept his stream of bullets across the women as well. Now they lay on the ground, groaning. Blood seeped from their wounds, pooling around them.

Da Shi went around the clump of bushes to be sure that he had eliminated all threats. The rest of the soldiers clustered around the two wounded women, unsure what to do. In the end they decided to bring them back as prisoners of war. Suddenly, one of the women convulsed and died. The other also stopped moving. One of the young soldiers bent down to examine her.

The woman exploded into motion, sweeping her leg at the ankles of the young soldier. Unprepared for the assault, the soldier fell down on her. Before he could recover, the woman had seized the Type 56 rifle from his hands and shot him in the face. Still on the ground, the woman swept the Chinese soldiers with multiple bursts from the rifle. Several soldiers fell dead where they stood.

The woman got up, energized by the excitement of exacting bloody vengeance. She had been wounded only lightly, and the blood on her body was mostly from her companion. She surveyed the scene of carnage proudly. But soon she sensed danger. There was someone she had missed.

Da Shi jumped on her from behind. The woman tried to throw him off, but he grabbed on tight, and the two fell to the ground together as they fought for control of the rifle.

Twisting, turning, kicking, rolling—this was a life-or-death struggle for both.

A crisp shot rang out. Da Shi's body trembled, and a look of disbelief came over his face. He was on top of the woman, and warm blood was flowing out of his belly to pool on the ground beneath both of them.

The overjoyed woman tried to push him off her, but he was too heavy. Da Shi, eyes still open, grimaced and pulled out a dagger. Slowly, carefully, he aimed the dagger at the throat of the woman under him. The terrified woman pushed even harder, but she was unable to get the necessary leverage against his weight. She squeezed the trigger twice more, and now Da Shi's lower body was a bloody mess. She could feel Da Shi's warm intestines dropping out of his body cavity to coil over her body. Still, Da Shi refused to die. His hand trembled violently, barely holding on to the dagger. With a final, animalistic growl, he plunged the dagger into the woman's throat.

Blood spurted from the pumping arteries and drenched Da Shi's face. The woman stared at Da Shi, as though she wanted to speak. No noise emerged. After a few seconds, her head fell to the side. She was dead.

Da Shi could not get up. In this universe deprived of five kilograms of matter, his life had come to an end. He would never marry or have a child. He would never pursue criminals in one of the world's greatest metropolises. He would never grab the cigar from Colonel Stanton and come up with the plan for Operation Guzheng. He would never accompany Luo Ji on that fateful flight to the United Nations. He would certainly not go into hibernation for more than two hundred years and become the first person to hear Luo Ji explain the grandest mystery of the universe.

For some reason, Da Shi felt a sense of lightness, as though a great burden had been lifted off his shoulders.

Dying on top of a naked woman isn't the worst way to go, thought Da Shi as his consciousness faded. Slowly, he closed his eyes and stopped moving.

Silence returned to the forest. The brown ant sensed the change in the entity it was on. Finally, it managed to climb off the strange entity, though it lingered around the area, hesitating. Finally, after many exploratory trips over the strange entity and another entity beneath it, the ant came to an astonishing conclusion. The conclusion gave it an excitement originating from the deepest part of the will to life. The ant didn't know what these entities were or what they had been trying to do, but it knew one thing beyond a shadow of a doubt: *These gigantic creatures are going to make excellent meals for me and my sisters.*

1983, Purple Bamboo Park, Beijing, China

The bamboo grove swayed in the dusk. The lake in late autumn was a deep indigo. As the first stars appeared in the crystalline empyrean, a silver dot also appeared among them. But its quick movement and growing size indicated that it was no star. Hovering about a hundred meters above ground, it seemed to be searching for something as it gradually descended. In the almost deserted park, no one noticed the arrival of this mysterious visitor.

From a cave nestled in a nearby rock formation, two panting voices emerged.

"Xiuxiu, you're the prettiest girl in the world . . . I can't stand it . . . Please . . . Just once . . ."

"Be careful! . . . Oh, that's good . . . Right there . . ."

Hurried steps approached the rock formation. The lovers tried to stop and hide, but it was too late. Several police officers stormed into the cave and pinned them with their flashlight beams. Before the young man could speak, the policemen had dragged him off the woman and thrown him down to the ground. The young woman covered her face and sobbed.

Five minutes later, in the park police station:

"Your name?"

The sound of sobbing.

"That's enough crying! Answer the question."

"Cheng Xiuxiu." This was followed by more sobs.

"And you?"

"Zhang Yuanchao."

"What is your relationship?"

"We are . . . together."

"Together? The park was closed, so what were you two doing holed up in that cave?"

"That's not any of your business!" said Zhang Yuanchao.

"Oh, not any of our business? Let me tell you something. There's a campaign for 'striking hard' right now, do you understand? You young people, corrupted by Western capitalist ideas, are the targets of the campaign to maintain spiritual purity. Last month, there was a young man just about your age who tried to cop a feel of a female comrade on the bus. Do you know what happened to him? He was convicted of sexual misbehavior and sentenced to death by firing squad!"

"Comrade! Please! I didn't mean to speak so disrespectfully." Zhang Yuanchao's tone was now pleading. "We really are together. We even have our wedding date set. But neither of us has our own place, so we had to . . . You were our age once, too, right? . . . Do you smoke?" He pulled out a pack of Daqianmen cigarettes and held it out to the police officer, grinning ingratiatingly.

"Don't you dare think that you can bribe the people's police with a single pack of cigarettes! I'm telling you right now: There's no room for negotiation."

But Zhang Yuanchao pushed the cigarettes into the officer's hand, and a ten-yuan bill was concealed under the pack. The officer wrapped his fingers around the pack and the bill, and his face seemed to soften. But before he could speak, a middle-aged officer walked in. "What's the deal with these two?"

"Station Chief!" The officer pocketed the cigarettes and the money before standing up. "We found these two in the cave while they were . . . Um, since they are about to be married, I'm thinking we should just fine them and let them go. What do you think?"

"You caught them in the cave?" The station chief was excited. "Perfect! The bureau chief just called, concerned that we haven't met our target quota for the 'strike hard' campaign. Send them over."

"Wait, wait! We're about to be married. Why are you striking hard against us?" Zhang Yuanchao was now really scared and got up from his seat. "That's not fair!" A policeman approached to restrain him, and he shoved the officer.

"Look at this! Not only is this man a sexual deviant, he just assaulted a police officer!" the station chief declared triumphantly. "Arrest them immediately and bring them to the bureau."

As Zhang Yuanchao protested and Cheng Xiuxiu sobbed, officers dragged the couple away. But just as they were about to be brought out of the station, another policeman came in with a baby in his arms.

"Chief, look! We found an abandoned baby next to the park bench by the bridge. There was also a bottle of milk and a thousand yuan."

Everyone turned their attention to the baby. Even the officers holding the couple stopped. Cheng Xiuxiu, eyes filled with tears, looked at the tiny baby.

"Did you two abandon this baby?" the station chief asked Zhang Yuanchao.

"No, no!" Blood drained from Yuanchao's face. "We haven't even . . . you know . . . How can we have a baby? And if we had been here to abandon a baby, how could we possibly have been in the mood to go into the cave . . ."

"Did you see who did it?"

Both Zhang Yuanchao and Cheng Xiuxiu shook their heads.

The station chief lost interest in the pair. He looked at the baby, and pinched the baby's fat cheeks. "What a lovely baby! And so much money left with it! That's my salary for a whole year. What foolish woman and man did this? . . . What a corrupt world we live in now; everything is chaos. Young men and women are sleeping together without being married, and even giving birth to babies. Not only do we have to strike hard, we have to strike harder!"

All the policemen vied with each other to express their approval of the station chief's speech with the most zeal.

"Don't just stand there! Bring them to the bureau. They're waiting to make quota," the station chief said to the officers holding the lovers. "As for this baby . . . Xiao Li, why don't you take care of it?"

As the officers brought Cheng Xiuxiu away, she glanced back at the baby. Although she was terrified by what was about to happen to her, she still felt a maternal instinct toward the helpless child. Of course, there was nothing she could do. The baby had nothing to do with her, and would never have anything to do with her.

As the station chief was walking away, he suddenly turned around. "Is the baby a boy or a girl?"

"Look how cute she is! She's definitely a little girl," said the officer holding the baby. "Going to be a heartbreaker someday."

But another officer, who was dedicated to evidence-based investigatory methods, spread the baby's legs and looked in carefully.

"A little boy, Chief!"

As if to provide even more confirmation for the officer's pronouncement, the baby's tiny organ moved, and a golden stream of urine shot right into the policeman's face.

"Oh, come on! Damn it!"

Outside the window, the silver-glowing object quietly departed. Inside the object, a miniature computer came to a conclusion: In this new universe that was missing five kilograms, the woman who had created the silver object no longer existed. No, it was more accurate to say that she had never existed and would never exist.

But the object still had to accomplish its mission. In this new universe, it had to find the right person to pass a message from the last universe on to. It had floated in this universe for billions of years for the sole purpose of carrying out a mission that was older than the universe itself, a mission given to it by a woman who didn't exist.

The Trisolaris system was nothing like the version from the last universe. The three stars were arranged in a stable arrangement, and in place of the Trisolarans and their harsh ecosystem, there was a different species of low-entropy entities. The Solar System and the Earth were here, at first glance the same as in the last universe. But it was clear that, compared with the detailed records stored inside the bottle, many, many details had changed. Some people had never been born, and others had died long ago. Even those who still existed were living completely different lives.

The bottle didn't care. It had to carry out its mission. Without hesitation, the stored instructions pointed to a final target: Yun Tianming.

Autumn 2003, Yun Tianming's home

At precisely seven o'clock, the logo for the *Nightly News* appeared on the TV screen to the accompaniment of familiar strains of music. Tianming sat forward on the sofa, anxiously staring at the screen. The anchorman and anchorwoman, both well known to the whole nation, smiled and announced the day's most important news items: The Campaign to Maintain the Advanced Nature of Communist Party Members was progressing well and accomplishing multiple objectives; *Shenzhou 5* successfully brought the first taikonaut in the world into space; a suicide bombing attack in Iraq caused multiple American casualties . . .

Tianming flipped through a few more stations. Some were showing the news broadcast; others were showing cartoons and dramas. Everything was normal. Tianming let out a long sigh and leaned back against the couch, lighting up a cigarette.

That war isn't going to happen, he thought.

By "that war," Tianming had in mind the horrifying war that had occurred in the last universe in the South China Sea. In that war, the pride of the Chinese navy, the aircraft carrier *Everest,* was easily destroyed by an American meteorological weapon. China was about to be crushed by the United States when an accidental macroatomic fusion forced the enemy back, leading to a peace treaty that preserved the nation.* Since the Crisis Era had commenced not long after the end of that war, the Sino-American contest in the South China Sea had been largely forgotten by history. But for the Chinese, who had enjoyed decades of peace, the war with the Americans was an important turning point. From then on, the course of world history had twisted in an unanticipated direction.

Now that war didn't and wasn't going to happen. That meant that the Trisolaran Crisis likely also would never come.

To be sure, Yun Tianming understood that this universe had already diverged greatly from the last one. There was no Red Coast Base, and Ye Wenjie didn't use it to send a message to the (nonexistent) Trisolarans. According to his investigation, Ye Wenjie had emigrated to the United States more than ten years ago. Maybe she would still bump into Mike Evans over there, but the two of them weren't going to be able to cause much destruction by themselves.

Then again, although he had the bottle's report, he had never seen the Trisolaris system with his own eyes. He could not be sure that those terrifying Trisolarans hadn't evolved somewhere else in that system or in a different system, or that right now they weren't on board a massive fleet headed straight for the Earth. Who knew if any of the subsequent events might still happen? Ever since the bottle got in touch with him, it seemed anything was possible.

For example, although his name, age, and family background had all changed, the bottle told him in no uncertain terms that he was the Yun Tianming stored in its records. The matter that formed the zygote that grew to be him was the same matter that had once formed the zygote for Yun Tianming. He and Yun Tianming were the same person across two universes. The utterly preposterous fact was nonetheless a fact.

Still, it seemed that in this universe, on this Earth, the Crisis Era

---

*Translator's Note: For details, see Liu Cixin's novel Ball Lightning.

would not be a reality. He never did believe that the world would end up in the Crisis Era, but after learning so much about the last universe from the bottle, and since that universe and Earth were so similar to his universe and his Earth, he often saw double vision as the two universes overlapped in his mind.

"Didn't I tell you that you don't need to worry? History has changed and that war cannot happen." A sweet voice spoke behind him.

Tianming turned around and saw a gorgeous woman smiling at him flirtatiously.

"What . . . what are you doing here? Go back! Go back now! What if my wife sees you?" Tianming was on the verge of panic.

"Don't worry. The missus is out shopping, which gives us plenty of time to—"

"Would you stop with the jokes? If anyone saw you here, how would I ever explain it? They'd think I have Ran Asakawa in my house."

The woman giggled. "You really are the same as your predecessor from the last universe."

Yun Tianming sighed. "In this universe, there's no Cheng Xin and no Ai Xiaowei. Helena became Mehmed II's favorite consort and died five hundred years ago. Guan Yifan isn't even born yet . . . and I have no memories of that universe except what I've been told. But Sophon, you're still here, causing trouble."

"You'll have to thank your beloved from the last universe for that. She was so full of love for everything and everyone and insisted that my data be recorded in the bottle." Sophon winked at him.

"I know very well why you manipulated her into replicating you," said Tianming drily. "It was part of the Master's plan. It wanted to you persist into the next universe so you could continue to serve it."

"That's correct! Too bad the Master is no longer the Master of the past. Although the war between the Lurker and the Master happened again, I couldn't get in touch with it. After dimension reversal, the Master was reborn, but it was without any memories of the last universe and didn't even know I existed. I couldn't go to its mini-universe, so that's why I came to find you, darling Tianming. You're like a big brother to me."

"'Big brother'? Are you kidding me? You're at least twenty billion years older than I am. Also, didn't you used to act like my loyal servant?"

"Oho! I had no idea you have a maid fetish. Do you want me to put on a sexy apron? I was going to obey your orders, but darling Tianming, of the core matter that you inherited, about three percent came from other places, and since you don't have any memories from that universe, I can't really say you're exactly the same as Yun Tianming. That is why I don't need to obey you anymore. Just like you managed to shake off the Master's mental seal all those years ago, I can be released from my charge to obey."

"So why have you stayed with me all these years?"

"I still haven't finished my mission! I have to tell this universe what happened in the last one."

"Then you should head for the United Nations. Or go to Washington, D.C.! Go to Beijing at least. Lots of people would want to talk to you. Why are you holed up here in this remote city next to a power plant?"

"But the mission from your beloved from the last universe requires me to pass on those memories without affecting the natural development of civilization in this universe. How am I supposed to do that? Unless I wait until the end of the universe, anything I say will affect the course of history."

"Then what are you planning to do?"

"I have no idea. All I can do for now is to wait. Now, my original plan was to change your body to be incorruptible and help you go find the Lurker in this universe. But I don't have enough energy, and even the Earth doesn't have enough energy for me to use. Even if I hoarded every drop of energy and waited until the day you died, I still wouldn't save up even one percent of what I need. But that's all right. I'll just preserve your data. A few tens of thousands of years later, I can re-create you to serve the Master's grand plan again." Sophon managed to keep a straight face throughout the whole lecture.

Yun Tianming was speechless. A few years ago, when Sophon first appeared with the bottle, he had thought of her as an angel, a beautiful woman whom no one else could see and who only spoke to him. But soon he realized that this woman was the devil, and indeed, compared with her all devils could be described as angels.

"Since the Master isn't even the same Master from before, why are you even serving it?" Tianming finally found an opening.

"Because the chain of cause and effect isn't complete yet."

"What are you talking about?"

"The chain of cause and effect linking each universe to its predecessor and successor. Because the last universe lost five kilograms before dimension reversal, it resulted in this universe, right? So the question is, what will happen if we trace out the evolution of this universe?"

Tianming gasped. What a frightening thought.

"Think about it, darling Tianming. This isn't just a war fought over a single universe. As long as time exists, there will be a war between the Lurker and the Master. We will face the exact same problem as the last universe: Should we let the universe be destroyed in the nothingness that is zero dimensions? Should we recycle all matter to let the exact same film play again? Or should we lose another five kilograms and strive for a new possibility?"

"I would choose the latter."

"But there will be an end to that route. The universe cannot increase its mass, and it cannot lose matter without end. Even if you choose to lose only a single atom with each iteration, there will be a day when there's nothing more to lose. And long before that, you won't have enough for life and intelligence. In the end, only two possibilities remain for the ultimate fate of the universe: nothingness and the eternal recurrence."

"That is . . . depressing."

"The Master and the Lurker cannot change, so for them, there is no way out. But you really do have the choice of creating a new possibility."

"Oh? Tell me! How can we escape from this trap?"

Sophon smiled. "We'll send only a brain."

"'We'll send only'—wait, that's what Wade said—" Tianming was baffled. But then he sat there with his mouth open, utterly stunned by a new idea.

"Do you understand now?" asked Sophon.

"Are you . . . are you really . . ."

"Yep. This is the ultimate mission the Master gave me when the last universe ended. In the next universe, I must strive to send a thinking being to another universe on the supermembrane so that they can discover a new path for all life in this universe. You're the perfect choice to be the explorer!"

Tianming had no response to that.

"This is why it's best to think of everything that has happened in these two universes as a mere overture. Tianming, your true legend has yet to begin. You are not fated to remain on Earth, and you are not meant to stop at Planet Blue, at the last universe, or even at this universe. You're meant to visit other universes, other space-times, and even the supermembrane that includes all universes. That is your true mission!"

Some time later, a frowning Yun Tianming clicked through the channels on his TV until he stopped at some random provincial news broadcast. A familiar face appeared on the screen.

". . . a young sociologist . . . the plagiarism scandal has refused to go away . . . he has told our reporter that the scandal is the result of a misunderstanding . . . we are now going to interview some prominent scholars for their take on this scandal . . ."

"Who would have expected this from Luo Ji?" Tianming sighed. He had never met Luo Ji—whether in the last universe or this one—but after he learned what Luo Ji had done in the last universe, he had admired him greatly. In this universe, although Luo Ji had a different name, his life so far hewed pretty closely to the earlier half of his predecessor's career: a rather dissolute college instructor. But this time around, it seemed unlikely that Luo Ji would experience the events that would turn his life around.

Zhuang Yan's life was also completely different. She was now a famous actress with the surname Liu, beloved by thousands and always showing up on red carpets. It seemed impossible that her path and Luo Ji's would ever cross.

"Um, Sophon . . . can we talk?" Tianming tried to keep his tone breezy and pleasant. "This mission that you mentioned . . . I really think you're better off approaching Luo Ji with it. You know him really well, and I think he'd be perfect."

"Oh, I *do* know him very well. Long before I was given this body, I spent a lot of time observing him . . . and all that time during the Deterrence Era . . . But he can't compare with you. No matter what, you're the first man in my life—very special for a woman, right?—and so it's natural for me to come to you."

"What . . . what?? When did I become *your* man? And what do you mean, 'the first'?"

"Have you forgotten that my body is constructed from the image in your head? You're the one who made me a woman, so of course you're my first man." Sophon chuckled.

Once again, Tianming found himself with no adequate retort. He continued to watch the news. On TV, Luo Ji was arguing with the person who had accused him of plagiarism. Tianming thought that Luo Ji's new life was not necessarily a bad thing. To live an ordinary life filled with ordinary problems was better than shouldering a burden heavier than anyone should bear for more than a century, wasn't it?

"What about Zhang Beihai? He's still there, just under a different name. I think he's just as qualified as Luo Ji for your purposes. I think he's the commanding officer for the fleet on the Somalia mission, right?"

"I have zero interest in adherents of Escapism," said Sophon, still grinning. "Also, I don't think cold-blooded Zhang Beihai is going to be very nice to me. The first thing he might do is to tie me up and hand me over to the Party to be dissected for research. No, no, no! You're stuck with me, darling Tianming.

"Also, you have a different brain from everyone else. In the last universe, you managed to invent Green Tempest as a college student. That means you are blessed with extraordinary imagination. I'm sure anyone else wouldn't have lasted nearly as long as you did in the hands of the Trisolarans. Believe me, you're a genius, the real deal. Your accomplishments in this universe just provide even more proof!"

"Genius? You should go talk to Ding Yi then. Oh, what is his name now? Li something . . . Anyway, he's brilliant, and rumor has it that he's just as much a ladies' man as he was in the last universe. I'm sure he would love to get to know you."

"I'm not interested in geniuses like Ding Yi. You could put ten Ding Yis together in a room and they still wouldn't be able to see through the Lurker's trap, but you would. Sure, you don't have his aptitude for theoretical physics, but you have creativity and imagination. What you need is a bit of development to exploit—"

"Forget it!" Tianming shook his head. "I was exploited and developed more than enough by the Trisolarans and your Master in my last life. I'm going to live an ordinary life this time around. I have no wish to wander the supermembrane for billions of years."

"An ordinary life? Haha, the whole country now knows who you are. Fine, I won't mention the supermembrane for now, since that's a plan for the far future anyway. But I have to say, it's not easy for all the matter that made up the last you to be reassembled into the new you. I think you owe the last universe at least one simple task."

"What are you—"

Sophon's face grew solemn. "Write it all down, Tianming. I want you to write it all down and tell everyone what happened in the last universe. In the future, there will come a day when humanity will discover the truth within, and that is how I'll complete the mission Cheng Xin assigned me. After all, writing is your forte."

"Write it all down . . . how?"

"You're a writer, aren't you?"

"But I write science fiction!"

"Well, you can call it something like *A Past outside of Time*, but people will read it like science fiction. Someday, when they discover the true mysteries of the universe, they'll understand what you really meant."

Tianming realized this wasn't a half-bad idea. Everything he had learned from Sophon would make a pretty good story. It had everything: love and rage, humanity's arrogance, duty of the individual, the fate of the universe . . . maybe everyone would benefit from such a novel.

Tianming made up his mind. "Fine, I'll do it. At least it's easier than exploring the supermembrane."

"All right, I'm holding you to your promise. My darling Tianming—or should I call you by your present name, Cixin?—you have to write this story down, and you can always come to me if you want clarification on some details."

Still grinning, Sophon vanished into thin air. She was, after all, just a holographic projection.

Yun Tianming felt the urge to write. Inspiration came at him in waves. First the title and then the outline filled his mind. He took a deep breath, sat down at his desk, turned on the computer, and started a new file. At the top of the blank page, he typed *Remembrance of Earth's Past*. And then, after a brief pause, he typed in a smaller font on the next line:

Book I: The Three-Body Problem.

TRANSLATOR'S POSTSCRIPT

As a fan, my gratitude goes to Liu Cixin for creating the Three-Body universe and to Baoshu for populating it with many more wonders. It's exciting to share another piece of this fantastic imaginary world with all other Anglophone fans.

I also want to thank the following individuals for beta-reading the translation and offering valuable advice: Anatoly Belilovsky, Elías Combarro, Rachel Cordasco, Leticia Lara, and Joshua Pheterson. My work benefited much from their input, and any remaining errors and faults are entirely mine.

I'm also grateful to CEPIEC; the publishers, Tor Books and Head of Zeus; and the many individuals who helped make this book possible over time (this list is by no means exhaustive): Richard Li, Kelly Song, Lindsey Hall, Nicolas Cheetham, Seth Fishman, Christopher Morgan, Irene Gallo, Terry McGarry, Heather Saunders, Jamie Stafford-Hill, Ryan Jenkins, Eileen Lawrence, and Desirae Friesen.